The Neverglades
~ volume one ~

DAVID FARROW

illustrated by CHRIS BODILY

This is a work of fiction. Names, characters, organizations, businesses, places, and events are either the product of the author's imagination or used fictitiously. Any resemblance to actual persons, living or dead, or actual events is entirely coincidental.

Cover design by Lance Buckley

Illustrations by Chris Bodily

Copyright © 2019 David Farrow

All rights reserved.

ISBN: 978-1076535078

DEDICATION

CS, MK, BP, AH, AC, AC, VB, ST –

To the East we go.

CONTENTS

1	Lost Time	1
2	Zombie Radio	29
3	Remember Me	59
4	The Wendigo	91
5	Purple Moon	117
6	On the Mountain of Madness	135
7	Lucid Dreams	163
8	Devour	199
9	Fallen Night	223
	Acknowledgements	235

LOST TIME

Pacific Glade is a quiet town, mostly. That's one of the perks of living so far away from everyone else. It's the kind of place where you'd let your kids wander long after the sun goes down, a place where you don't mind animals coming out of the forest to nuzzle your heels and beg for scraps. We get next to zero tourism. Some people joke that we should call it the Neverglades. We're that blip on the map you'd never notice unless you were driving through. The whole town could disappear from the face of the earth one day and the rest of the world would never notice our absence.

If you've spent most of your life here, like me, you grow used to its idiosyncrasies. Take the weather. We've had hailstorms in July and hot December nights that would make you want to jump headfirst into Lake Lucid. The woods make noises too. The usual hoots and howls, of course, but sometimes when it's late, you can hear these strange scraping sounds from the trees that make the fillings in your teeth tingle. And let's not forget that summer when every single chicken in the Glade vanished overnight. They never found a trace of those critters – not even a single feather left behind.

Par for the course for the average citizen. But when you work here as a homicide detective, you notice other things. Bodies with unexplained wounds and markings. Trails that lead nowhere. Pieces that don't quite fit together, no matter how much you turn them. Eventually you have to accept that not all cases can be solved. It's a shitty feeling, but that's reality for you. Some killers never get caught. Some deaths have no satisfying explanation. You take the good cases with the bad and hope you leave the world at least a little better than you found it.

The case that changed everything for me started out no different from all the others. I was driving down the highway in my police cruiser, flipping through stations on the dash, when Olivia Marconi's voice came crackling over my comm radio. "You there, Mark?" she said. "We've got a suspicious death at the gas station on Minnow Street. This one's got your department written all over it."

I brought the radio up to my mouth. "Be there in a sec," I said. "Try and keep the body warm for me."

"Just get over here, asshole." I could usually tell when Marconi was messing with me, but there was no smirk in her voice this time. That didn't bode well. My smile fading, I stepped on the gas and rocketed down the highway toward the center of town.

No matter where you go in the Glade, drive far enough and you'll find yourself surrounded by trees. And not just any trees. I'm talking a full-blown forest, with twisted branches and canopies that make everything dark as night, even in mid-afternoon. The nearest town is a twenty-minute drive through acres of wilderness. I remember growing up and hearing stories from the other kids: that the stuff we saw on TV was all propaganda, that there was nothing more to the world except an endless forest that branched out in all directions and swallowed up the horizon. Pretty morbid for a bunch of kids. But then again, kids are pretty morbid. I would know. I've got two of my own.

It was getting late when I finally pulled up to the Minnow Street gas station, and the darkening treetops flashed with spirals of red and blue. The lot was absolutely packed with cruisers. Parking further down the street, I stepped out of my car and crossed the lot to slip underneath the police tape.

Sheriff Marconi was speaking to a boy in a red cashier vest when I walked in. He couldn't have been more than sixteen. His skin was slick with sweat and he wouldn't stop fidgeting. He kept wringing his hands together and wiping them on the sides of his pants in a constant, agitated motion. When Marconi saw me enter, she placed a hand on the boy's shoulder and said something too quiet for me to hear. She left him alone with his private trauma and came over to join me by the door.

"Poor kid's scared out of his wits," she said under her breath. "I don't blame him. This one's a doozy, Mark. They've even got a federal agent investigating the case."

"Seriously?" I asked. "That was fast." I craned my neck, but the shelves were swarming with cops. I couldn't make out any unfamiliar faces.

She shrugged. "Must have had somebody in the area already. He got here just a couple minutes after we did."

"I'll go see what he's up to," I said. "Maybe he's spotted something our guys have missed."

"Be my guest." She grimaced. "But brace yourself, Mark. It's not pretty over there."

I tipped her a quick salute and worked my way through the aisles, heading toward the scene of the crime. It wasn't hard to find. Cops were streaming in and out of the shelves, ushering curious spectators away and trying to stifle the overall panic from the other customers. I pushed through the mob and found myself staring down at a hopelessly mangled body. There was something unnatural about the way he was sprawled out on the floor – something disjointed and almost a little spidery.

I recognized the federal agent right away. He would have stood out in any crowd. Easily seven feet tall and slender as a pole, he loomed over the other cops like a statue. Everything about him was gray. Fedora, trench coat, even the pallid color of his skin. The smoldering tip of a cigar protruded from his teeth. He turned to face me as I approached. His eyes were a strange shade of purple that I'd never seen before. They seemed to spin under the overhead lights.

"Uh, hi," I said, holding out my hand. "Detective Mark Hannigan. Nice to meet you."

The tall figure stared at my outstretched hand for a few seconds, then shook it. "Same to you," he said. His voice had a gravelly quality, like his throat was coated with pebbles. Thin wisps of smoke escaped from his teeth and billowed around the end of his cigar.

"What should I call you?" I asked after a few seconds of silence.

"For now, 'Inspector' is fine," he said. "But don't mind me. What are your thoughts on our friend here?"

I leaned down and examined the body. The man's face was hanging in flaps: jagged red streaks that had already begun to fester. The stench was something awful. His nose had disintegrated into a mass of gore and bone. The limbs sprawled across the tiles bent backwards at impossible angles. In a few places, chunks of bloodstained bone jutted through the skin. I'd seen some pretty grisly stuff on the force before, but this took the cake. Bile churned in my throat and I withdrew quickly from the body.

"Do we have an ID on the vic yet?" I asked.

"His license says Edgar Guerrera, although it's hard to tell if he's the man in the picture. His face is too disfigured." The Inspector knelt down and traced the tiles around the body with one bony finger. He drew it back and rubbed his fingers together. A fine stream of shiny powder trickled to the floor.

I frowned. "Is that glass?"

"I think so," he replied. He rose to his feet, brushing the powder off of his coat. "Look at the way the body's slumped. The lacerations, the broken bones. It's almost as though he went straight through a windshield."

"But that's crazy," I said. "There's blood everywhere, sure, but no footprints or drag marks. If this was really a car accident, he either staggered in here after the fact, or somebody else lugged him in."

"Maybe," the Inspector said. "But why go through all

that effort? Whoever did this didn't even try to hide the body." He flicked some ash toward the crime scene. The body was splayed out across the tiles, limbs spread wide like a human starfish. Blood glistened in puddles under the sickly fluorescent lights. It was messy and gory and awfully conspicuous. Whoever did this wanted the body to be found.

"What is it, some kind of warning?" I asked.

The Inspector gazed down at the body. "It's possible. Of course, that's assuming this was murder, that someone left the body here intentionally. If this was just a freak accident, then we've got an entirely different situation on our hands. And that worries me."

"I'm not sure I follow you, Inspector," I said. But he didn't elaborate. He kept staring down at the body, purple eyes spinning, lost in thought.

Shrugging, I took out my phone and snapped a few photos, trying to capture the scene from every angle. Marconi and I could get a closer look once I got the pictures back to headquarters. All the while, the Inspector stood utterly still. If it weren't for the curls of steamy breath escaping from around his cigar, I might have mistaken him for a statue after all.

* * * * *

Marconi was leaning against her cruiser when I left the store. I watched as she pulled a stick of gum from her pocket and brought it up to her mouth like a cigarette. Marconi had quit smoking a month ago and had taken up chewing gum as a substitute. I almost never saw her without a wad in her mouth. She said it helped her relax, and who was I to judge?

I walked over and joined her by the cruiser. "What did the kid say?"

She snapped the gum in the back of her cheek. "He was shelving some cereal boxes when he heard this loud crumpling sound, like someone crushing a really big can of soda. He went over to the next aisle to check it out and found our friend Mr. Guerrera just lying there. Said he screamed for a few seconds before running to the bathroom to puke. His story checks out with the few customers we could get to talk about it."

"Sounds like it happened in a matter of seconds," I said. "But how is that possible? Guy looks like he's been in a car crash. No one gets that mangled, that quickly. Let alone in a fucking gas station."

Marconi turned her head and stared at the convenience store doors. The Inspector had just wandered outside, cigar tip still smoldering. He shoved his hands in his trench coat pockets and strode off down the sidewalk. His stride was strange. His body didn't rise and fall with each step – it stayed completely level, as if he were gliding along the ground. I watched the steady glow of his cigar as he turned the corner and disappeared from view.

"What did you think of *that* guy?" Marconi asked. "I only talked to him for a few seconds, but he gave me the creeps."

"He's... definitely something," I said. I craned my neck, but the Inspector was long gone. "Never seen anybody quite like him. Not a bad detective though."

Marconi gnawed on her gum for a few pensive seconds. "Well, I hope we wrap up this case quick," she said. "I'll rest easier when the feds are off our backs."

She spat the wad back into her hand and folded it into the empty wrapper. I stood back as she opened the cruiser door and hopped into the driver's seat. Before she left, she rolled down the window and gave me the dimmest of smiles. "See you back at the station," she said. Then she revved the engine and rolled backwards out of the parking lot.

* * * * *

The coroner's office confirmed what we'd already suspected: the victim's wounds were consistent with those of a car crash. It wasn't the lacerations or the broken bones that had killed him, it was blunt force trauma to the head. That explained the mangled mess of his nose. What it *didn't* explain was how a car crash victim had ended up sprawled on the floor of a convenience store. The security footage wasn't much help. It showed Edgar Guerrera entering the store and browsing the shelves, but after a few minutes the camera went on the fritz and grew riddled with static. By the time it came back into focus, Edgar was dead. Sabotage? Had someone messed with the security cameras to conceal their involvement in his death?

Nothing seemed to make any sense, and trying to find meaning in this case had me working late into the hours of the night. My wife, Ruth, called me a few times to make sure I was okay. I couldn't tell her too much about the case, for obvious reasons. But Ruth was perceptive. She'd seen a couple of my cases on the news and she knew how dark these things could get. I promised her I was fine and that I'd be home within the next few hours. She didn't quite sound convinced, but said she'd leave dinner in the fridge for whenever I got back.

My investigation into the life of Edgar Guerrera brought up zilch. He worked at a car repair workshop down in the lower Glade and doubled as the night janitor at Pacific High. He had a wife and two daughters and went to church with his family on Sundays. I couldn't figure out why anyone would want to kill this guy. He was as vanilla as they come. He had no obvious enemies, nobody who harbored enough of a grudge to murder him in such a gory and visible way. Unless the Inspector was right and this was somehow a freak accident. Which left us where? That line of reasoning made even less sense than the murder theory.

By morning I was a walking headache, and it only got worse when news of another dead body came over the police channel. The officer seemed reluctant to describe the details, which could only mean one thing: this was a gory one. I thought back to the mangled mess of Edgar Guerrera's body and wondered what kind of fresh horror they'd stumbled onto this time. There was no point in putting this off until later. Grabbing my jacket, I headed out the door and climbed into my cruiser.

The body had been found on the front porch of a house in the lower Glade, down by Spokane Falls. The few details I could get over the radio were maddeningly vague. All I gathered was that the victim was young and female. However she had died, it was too gruesome to announce over the airwaves. I stepped on the gas and urged my car to go a little faster.

The victim's house was a pretty little number: white fences, low-hanging eaves, a front yard laden with flowers of all colors. The falls crashed like pistons in the background. I drove up the driveway, talked for a bit with the officers on duty, then got out of my car to investigate the scene. I pulled on a set of latex gloves as I did so. A pair of cops were standing together and muttering to one another by the front porch. They stepped aside warily to let me through.

The porch reeked of rotten body smell and I had to hold a hand over my mouth and nose before I dared to go any closer. The victim was a blonde-haired girl in her late 20s or so. The entire left side of her body had collapsed into a splattery mess of gore that spread outward in all directions. One green eye still stared blankly into the distance. I knelt down, surveying the splintery remains of her limbs for anything out of the ordinary. It was difficult. My eyes were swimming and I had to fight back the urge to retch.

When I looked up again, the Inspector was slouched in the doorway. His fedora was pulled low and his face was framed by a halo of smoke. That damn cigar again. It was like an extension of his body – I almost couldn't imagine him without it.

"Did the feds send you down here?" I asked. "They can't possibly think there's a link between these cases. I mean, aside from their sheer weirdness."

"I go where I'm needed," he said. "Right now I'm needed here."

It didn't sound like he was going to offer anything more, so I stood up and began peeling off my latex gloves. "The officers who got here first said her name was Vivian Tracy. A couple of them actually knew her from around town. She volunteered down at the soup pantry and ran a reading group at the public library. Bright kid. Her neighbor was the one to phone us about the body. Said she was walking home from the supermarket and just saw Vivian lying there. She didn't get close enough to see the gorier details, but it sounds like she saw enough."

The Inspector nodded. "Do we know anything about the neighbor?"

"Not much. She's getting on in years, so she likes walking to the store to get some exercise. Apparently she didn't know Vivian all that well, but she said she seemed like a nice enough girl. Not the kind of person someone would want to murder."

"Just like Mr. Guerrera," the Inspector said quietly. It sounded like he'd done some research of his own.

I cast another glance at the body. "If this even was murder," I said. I'd seen suicides leap from buildings before. I'd watched medics scrape viscera off the sidewalk. There was no doubt in my mind that Vivian Tracy had fallen to her death. But how was that possible? The porch roof overhead was still intact – she obviously hadn't come crashing through it. And there was no way our would-be murderer could have dragged the body here. The splatter made it all too clear that this was the point of impact.

"What the hell is going on here?" I muttered.

The Inspector leaned down and tilted what remained of Vivian's arm with one gloved hand. Her skin was streaked with blotchy green patches. It reminded me of the grass stains my sons got on their knees after soccer practice.

"Is that significant?" I asked him.

"Everything's significant," he replied, straightening up. "You should know that by now." Smoke trailed from his cigar in slow, almost thoughtful spirals.

My head was starting to throb again, and the insistent crashing of Spokane Falls wasn't doing much to help. I rubbed my aching temple. It had been a long day and a half. Maybe things would start making sense if I went home and recharged my batteries.

* * * * *

It was around three in the morning when the cell phone on my dresser began to buzz. I've always been a light sleeper, which is lucky for a detective – you never know when you need to be on your feet in a hurry. I fumbled for the phone and brought it up to my ear. "This is Detective Hannigan," I said, keeping my voice to a whisper. Ruth was fast asleep next to me and I didn't want to wake her.

"It's me," said the voice on the other end of the line. The Inspector? The connection didn't muffle his voice, which created the unsettling illusion that he was crouching by the bedside, speaking directly into my ear. I rubbed my eyes and peered around the bedroom. Just to be on the safe side.

"How did you get this number?" I mumbled.

The Inspector either didn't hear me or chose not to answer. "I've been doing research down at the station and I may have picked up a lead on the Tracy and Guerrera deaths," he said. "Could you head to the Skokomish Bluffs area and do some recon?"

I squinted at the clock on my desk. "I'm off duty, Inspector. Are you sure you can't ask one of the other officers? I'm pretty sure Marconi's out patrolling right now."

"No, it needs to be you, Mark," he replied. "Call me when you're on the road and I'll give you the specifics."

"Hang on, Inspec – dammit." The man didn't leave much room for conversation. I stared at the glowing screen of my phone for a few seconds before sighing and placing it down again.

Ruth's eyes were open when I turned to get out of bed. They glittered a little in the light from the window. "Duty calls?" she asked. She drew back the covers a few inches and began to knead the fabric with her right hand. The moon dappled her bare skin with the shadows of leafy branches.

I leaned over and kissed her gently on the forehead. "I won't be gone long," I promised.

She surveyed me, silent, her eyes refusing to give away what she was thinking. "Just stay safe," she said at last.

I told her I would and slipped out of bed, grabbing my jacket from the bedpost and tripping hastily into a pair of work boots. I called the Inspector as I headed outside and fumbled through my jacket pockets for the keys to my Camaro. "Okay, I'm here," I said. "Tell me what you've got."

"Both victims had ties to a high school teacher named Ellory Pickett," he replied in that strangely crisp voice. I glanced around again before slipping into the driver's seat. "He's a botanist. Teaches environmental science at the school where Edgar did his janitorial work. He's also a head volunteer at the youth group Vivian Tracy attended up until her death."

I paused, waiting for more. "That's it?" I asked. "You got me out of bed for a connection this flimsy? I'm sorry, Inspector, but there's nothing to even *remotely* suggest that this is a lead. People know other people. It's not so unusual for both vics to have mutual friends in a town this size."

The Inspector let out an exasperated noise that I can only describe as a hiss. "But that's the thing," he said. "They *don't* have anyone in common. I checked as many sources as I could and as far as I can tell, Ellory is the only link between our victims. Plus, Ellory himself seems to have dropped off the radar. He hasn't shown up at school for the past week and nobody has seen him around town since then. He's holed up in his house doing God knows what. That's why I want you to do a little snooping. Scope out his home and see if he's up to anything suspicious."

I sighed. "Fine, I'll humor you on this one. But you'd better be onto something here."

The voice at the end of the line was quiet for a few moments. "I don't know if you believe in intuition, Mark. But every nerve in my body went on edge when that man's name came up in the database. One way or another, he's involved with this. And I intend to find out how."

He gave me Ellory's address and hung up before I could get another word in. A real talker, that one. I shook my head, turned the wheel, and headed down the back roads that would take me all the way to Skokomish Bluffs.

When I was a kid, the bluffs had a reputation for being haunted. Indian burial grounds and such. You know how it is. But mostly the bluffs were just quiet. We almost never had disturbances this far out of town. The few people who lived here kept to themselves, and so did the animals who poked their heads out of the forest from time to time. This was off near the edge of the Glade, where you couldn't walk ten feet without stumbling into a line of trees. The view from the top of the bluffs was stunning. During my younger years, I used to come out here with my friends and watch the setting sun sink beneath the line of treetops. It made the entire forest look like it had gone up in softly burning flames.

I drove through a couple acres of wilderness before the ground sloped upward and the trees gave way to a grassy emptiness. The road beneath my tires was more dirt than pavement. From time to time, the occasional house would rise from the landscape and flit past my side window. Most of them had seen better days. Grimy, warped wood that glistened in the moonlight and shutters hanging askew. That sort of stuff. A few lone cattle drifted through the fields, nibbling aimlessly at the grass.

It wasn't hard to find Ellory's house. The place was in much better shape than the houses I'd seen before, and there was a massive greenhouse sprouting from the back that seemed to teeter on the edge of the bluffs. Hadn't the Inspector said Ellory was a botanist? I parked my car in a nearby thicket and cut the engine, my headlights fading. Then I settled back into the driver's seat and waited.

What was I waiting for? I didn't have a clue. The likelihood that Ellory would be awake at this hour, let alone doing anything suspicious, was close to nil. But the Inspector had been insistent on me coming here, so I figured I owed him the benefit of the doubt. I kicked my feet up on the dashboard and stared at the empty windows, watching for any signs of movement.

Around quarter past four, the front door opened suddenly, and I froze where I was sitting. An elderly man with feathery white hair came limping onto the front porch. Ellory? He looked older than I'd expected. I followed him as he hobbled over to the porch swing and eased into it with a visible wheeze of breath. I sank deeper in my seat and dialed the Inspector from my cell.

"Anything?" he asked right away.

"I'm at Ellory's house, and he just walked onto the front porch," I said under my breath. "It's a little late for him to be out, don't you think? Especially someone his age."

I could practically see the Inspector wrinkling his brow. "His age? What do you mean?"

"I mean he's seriously old. Old enough to be my grandfather. I don't know, Inspector, seems like you might have made the wrong call on this one."

There was a sharp intake of breath from the other end of the line. "Don't go anywhere near him," the Inspector said. His voice, usually so collected, now bordered on frantic. "Shit. Shit, this is bad. You need to get back to the station now."

I peered through the front window again. Ellory was drifting lazily on the porch swing, hair floating about his head like wisps of white cotton candy. "He's an *old man*, Inspector. He practically had a heart attack just walking across his porch. How could he possibly be dangerous?"

"That's no old man," the Inspector insisted. "Trust me. If he – if that thing gets its hands on you, it's all over. You need to get out of there."

Ellory jerked his head up suddenly, as if he could hear the Inspector's gravelly voice from all the way across the lawn. His swing froze in place. I tried to crouch beneath the dashboard as his eyes darted back and forth. I didn't think he could see my car from here, but those eyes seemed remarkably sharp for someone his age, and I couldn't shake the sense that they could see in the darkness. They reminded me of the time I'd taken a hiking trip with my friends up in Catamount State Forest. We'd seen an actual cougar prowling the rocks on the cliff over from ours, its eyes glowing yellow in the light from the moon. If it could have leaped the gap and devoured us, I'm sure it would have. That was the look I saw in Ellory's eyes.

"I'll meet you back at the station," I whispered into the phone.

Ellory sat there for a few more minutes, peering into the night, before he pried himself from the porch swing and shuffled back into the house. I didn't waste any time getting out of there. I started the engines as quietly as I could and pulled away from the thicket, leaving trails of trampled leaves behind me. Before long I was out of the Bluffs and zooming down the streets toward the police station. The trees loomed like sentinels around me, and for the first time in a very long while, I was thankful for their cover.

* * * * *

The Inspector was waiting by my desk when I finally got back to the station. He had a stack of papers in his hands that he kept flipping through. "What's all that?" I asked. He glanced up, startled, as if he hadn't heard me come in.

"I've been looking through my research and I've found a disturbing link between the victims," he said. He handed me the papers and stabbed at the first source so hard his finger almost poked through it. "Look at this article. Edgar Guerrera was involved in a car accident eight years ago that nearly killed him. It was a four-car pile-up. The paper says he would have gone through the windshield on impact if he hadn't been wearing his seatbelt. And look at this." He shifted the papers and showed me a grayscale printout. "It's a blog post from Vivian Tracy. Apparently she was skydiving with her college roommate last summer when she had a close call with her ripcord. Her parachute almost didn't open. A few more seconds and she would have hit the ground full force."

I glanced through the Inspector's sources. The newspaper didn't say much about Edgar's car crash, but the vehicles in the picture had been crumpled like used soda cans, and I had a hard time imagining anyone walking away from this one. The post from Vivian's blog was cheery and riddled with emoticons. There was a photograph of her plummeting through the air, laughing, with a stretch of grassy ground waiting far below to meet her. The girl in this picture had no idea how close she would come to dying. I thought of her body, splattered in a puddle on the front porch, and an unpleasant tingle crawled over my skin.

"This can't be coincidental," I agreed, handing back the files. "But what do these sources have to do with Ellory Pickett?"

The Inspector reached for the desk and withdrew another sheet of printer paper. "This is a license renewal, issued to Mr. Pickett just last year." He passed it to me, his fingers taut.

The license was newly issued, just as the Inspector had said, but the figure in the photo was far too young to be Ellory. That's not to say there wasn't a resemblance. His nose had the same crooked bent to it, and his stringy black hair was already starting to thin. I could imagine it growing white and wispy in several years' time.

"This guy's only forty years old," I said, looking up from the paper. "The old man I saw on Ellory's porch must have been his father or something. There's no way a person could age that much in the course of one year."

The Inspector snapped his fingers. "But that's just it! Ellory *has* aged. Several decades in a matter of months. I knew what we were dealing with the second you described him to me. There's something inside him – something that's been eating away his years until he became that dried-up husk you saw."

I furrowed my brow. "You want to run that by me again?"

The Inspector began to pace in agitated circles. "You don't have a word for what this thing is. Let's just call it a 'time-eater.' It's messing around in the past, turning these people's near-death experiences into *real* death experiences."

"Whoa, whoa, slow down," I said. "What are you saying?"

The Inspector stopped his pacing. "This... entity doesn't perceive time the same way you do. It's not a linear progression. It's like a piece of latticework, a series of avenues that go forward and backward and sideways in all directions." He tried to gesture with his hands, but gave up. "This thing is reaching back in time and tweaking little details – an unbuckled seatbelt, a faulty parachute pull cord – so that our victims die years before they should have. The past tries to catch up to the present, and *wham*. Instant death. The time-eater takes those missing years and feeds on them. That's how it stays alive. It's like a parasite, leeching the life force out of others."

"Okay, hold up," I said. "I don't quite understand what you're talking about, but do you hear how crazy you sound? I agree that whatever's happening here is weird. But you can't just go around inventing monsters that fill in all the blanks. There's a perfectly rational answer to all this, and we'll find it. Just give us time."

"We don't have time. Didn't you hear me? This thing *feeds* on time." He rubbed his cheek hastily, clouds of dense smoke billowing from his mouth. "I know you don't believe me yet, but this is your answer, Mark. So grab your car and let's go. We need to stop Ellory before he feeds again."

He slammed the papers onto my desk and strode to the door, his trench coat whipping behind him. I glanced down at the wrinkled stack of files. Ellory's impassive face stared up at me, his dark eyes blank and unreadable.

I wasn't ready to buy into the Inspector's "time-eater"

theory just yet. But what was it Sherlock Holmes said once? *When you have eliminated the impossible, whatever remains, however improbable, must be the truth.* Ellory Pickett may not have been a time-eating monster from outer space, but he was a common link in both of our mysterious death cases, and he may have played some sort of role in the murders. It was worth a look at least.

"I must be insane," I mumbled to myself. But I followed the Inspector out of the station, making sure to turn the lights off behind me.

* * * * *

Marconi wasn't too happy to leave her patrol at this hour of the night, but I told her that we had a lead on the mysterious deaths, however tenuous, and the Inspector had requested backup just in case. I trusted Marconi. She was a hell of a shot and she excelled under pressure. I'd witnessed her handle bomb threats and lines of incessant gunfire without breaking a sweat. It wouldn't be an exaggeration to say she'd saved my life a few times over. There was no one I wanted more on the force to watch our backs.

She met us in the heart of Skokomish Bluffs, her headlights off and her engine reduced to a low thrum. It wasn't an unusual sound to hear this far into the wilderness – it could have easily been the purr of a mountain cat. Ellory's house waited for us at the top of the bluffs, tiny as an architect's model from where we were standing. The dim moonlight glimmered off his greenhouse. Marconi glanced up at it, then back at us.

"You boys want to tell me what you're doing in the ass-crack of nowhere?" she asked.

"Just stay here and keep an eye on the place," the Inspector said. "If you hear any sort of commotion, grab your gun and follow us immediately. Don't hesitate to shoot if necessary."

"Sorry to drag you into this," I said, putting one hand on the hood of her cruiser. "It should just be a simple Q&A, but the Inspector's getting kind of paranoid, you know.

Given how extreme these cases have gotten." The bluffs were quiet for a few moments. An owl hooted in some distant tree. "I seriously appreciate you coming out here, you know."

"Alright, but you owe me," she replied. The smile that flickered on her face was almost a smirk, but it settled into something softer. I gave her a weak salute and turned to join the Inspector.

We kept to the shadows as we ascended the hill toward Ellory's house. "Keep your gun ready," the Inspector said under his breath. I hesitated – this was supposed to be a peaceful investigation – but he sounded so earnest that I slipped my pistol out of its holster. I gripped it with both hands, the metal cold under my fingers. It felt heavier than usual. Maybe there was something in the air out here.

The building couldn't have been more than one story, but it loomed over us as we approached. We climbed onto the front porch with hesitant footsteps. A gust of wind picked up, causing the porch swing to drift lazily back and forth.

I reached out to ring the doorbell, but the Inspector stopped my hand. The front door was open just a crack, revealing a dark foyer with a welcome mat and a dried potted plant. He gestured for us to go inside.

"We don't have a warrant," I hissed. "Are you crazy?"

"Trust me, a warrant is the least of our worries," he replied. He ducked his head and slipped across the threshold. Swearing under my breath, I held up my gun and followed him into the dark entrance hall. I nearly stumbled over another flower pot in the process. They were strewn everywhere along the rug, roots upended, dirt spilling out in clumps.

The Inspector reached down and picked up one of the fallen leaves. It was gray and crispy, and it crumbled into dust at his touch. "The time-eater's been feeding," he said quietly. "It must have sucked all the juice out of Ellory's plants before moving on to humans. But even that's not enough. Its vessel is aging faster than it can feed."

"If you're done speaking gibberish, can we get a move on here?" I whispered. Jesus, this was so illegal in so many ways. Ellory could sue the shit out of us for entering his house without a warrant. I wasn't exactly sure what the Inspector was trying to accomplish here.

A ceramic clatter issued from the back of the house, and the Inspector froze. "The greenhouse," he said. He rose from his crouched position and darted through the doorway, his slender body disappearing in the darkness of the next room. I gritted my teeth and raced after him.

The kitchen was already empty when I stepped inside. Where the hell had he run off to? Another clatter came from deeper in the house, louder this time – it sounded like someone had thrown a flowerpot onto the ground. I dodged past the kitchen table, overflowing with empty plates and silverware, before ducking into a side hallway and heading toward the greenhouse.

The door had already been thrown open for me, so I hurried inside. Everything had an eerie silver tint in the moonlight. Plots of earth stood on raised platforms, dried ferns and withered flowers slumping in piles on the soil. Flowerpots were perched on every spare inch of shelf space. I spun in a slow circle, keeping my gun held up, eyes peeled for any sign of movement. I couldn't tell where the crash had come from. There was no ceramic littering the ground, no splatter of roots and dirt. My shoes made light tapping noises on the linoleum as I made my cautious way to the back of the greenhouse.

Then a hunched shape came lunging at me from behind one of the raised platforms, fingers bared like claws. Ellory? His head was thrown back, and his wispy hair fluttered behind him as he ran. A guttural cry rose in his throat and pierced my ears. Without thinking, I raised my gun and fired off a single shot. Ellory veered out of the way with almost inhuman agility, moving far faster than any man his age should be able to. Then he crashed into me, knocking me against a glass cabinet and latching onto my arm with one clawed fist. I cried out. My gun flew from my hand and skittered away across the greenhouse floor.

Veins popped under his grip, glowing in lines of neon red beneath my skin. The same red glow pulsed from his open mouth. At first I thought his teeth were missing, but no, it was more than that – the space between his jaws had been completely hollowed out. No gums, no tongue, no esophagus. Just a gaping maw where his mouth should be.

I kicked at his shins and tried to struggle free, but his grip was stronger than I would have expected from an old man. If he even *was* an old man anymore. His eyes had taken on an odd silver sheen, like he was wearing mirrored contact lenses. A tangled sort of snarl escaped from the void that was his throat.

His grip tightened, and suddenly my brain was flooded with images. At first they were just flashes: memories that zipped past me with a crackle and a burst of static. But eventually they took on a stuttering sense of cohesion, like a film reel spinning. I recognized this night. It must have been three years ago, when I was still new to the force. I saw myself crouched behind my police cruiser, gun clenched in one sweaty hand, listening as bullets whistled past the car and shattered somebody's windshield. Red and blue lights spun in circles around me. When the firing stopped, I lunged up and aimed my gun at the shooter, shouting orders to surrender. The bullet caught me in the chest before I could even finish speaking. It knocked the wind out of me and sent me sprawling on my back. If it hadn't been for the Kevlar vest I was wearing, I would have died that night. The bullet had stopped just inches from my heart.

Except this memory was different. As Ellory squeezed my arm, the Kevlar began to disintegrate beneath my uniform, shriveling away, as if it had never been there in the first place. Maybe it hadn't. This was my missing seatbelt, my faulty ripcord; Ellory was erasing the safety blanket from my past. As the Kevlar shrank away, I could feel the bullet resuming its suspended course, burrowing through my shirt and sinking its cold metal body into the flesh above my heart.

Then the Inspector burst out of nowhere, barreled into the old man, and sent him crashing to the floor of the greenhouse. His fingers detached from my skin with a strange wet sucking sound. The memory of my night in the crossfire jerked backward, like the sensation of an elastic snapping, and I collapsed against the glass cabinet. It came crashing down on the pots of dead flowers. I drew in a shuddering gasp of air and tried to regain my balance. The memory of the bullet still burned against my chest, but my shirt was dry, and I didn't think it had pierced the skin.

I could have been a bit woozy from Ellory messing with my mind, but as I staggered to my feet, I thought I saw the old man pick up the Inspector and hurl him through the back wall of the greenhouse. His body smashed through with enough force to make the glass explode outward in a shower of tiny shards. Ellory leaped through the gaping hole and threw himself on top of the Inspector. I got down on my knees and began scrambling through the mess of soil and broken glass, searching for my fallen gun. My vision was swimmy and I had to stop a few times to keep myself from keeling over out of dizziness. But I kept moving. I'd seen what Ellory – or the thing inside Ellory – was capable of. I had to stop him before he got his hands on the Inspector too.

At last my fingers closed around a familiar metal handle, and I got shakily to my feet, gun in hand. I stumbled through the jagged hole and back into the fray. The stretch of grass behind the greenhouse couldn't have been longer than twenty or thirty feet. Beyond that was a dizzying drop into the wilderness. The Inspector grappled with Ellory, cigar still clenched beneath his teeth. The smoke that billowed from his lips had turned a dusky shade of red. As they fought, they staggered farther and farther backwards in an effort to drive the other one over the edge.

Ellory scrabbled at the Inspector's arm, trying to sink his claws in and start the whole time-eating process all over again. But as strong as he was, the Inspector was stronger. He moved too fast for my delirious eyes to follow, his trench coat whipping behind him like the wings of some avenging angel. I aimed my pistol at the pair of struggling figures, but I couldn't get a lock on Ellory in my current condition, and I was too afraid I would take out the Inspector by mistake. Blood pumped in my ears. I'd been in plenty of scrapes during my time on the force, but never had I felt so helpless.

The Inspector managed to thrust Ellory away from him for a few seconds, so that the old man stumbled back to the lip of the cliff, his arms swinging in a pinwheel. I pointed my gun at him, trying to squeeze out a bullet before the creature could get his balance again. But it was too late, his jaw was unhinging and he was lunging at the Inspector, eyes gleaming, claws extended –

Bang! Bang!

Ellory staggered backward, two fleshy red holes appearing in his chest. Silver goo dripped from the wounds and into the knee-high grass. I turned to see Marconi advancing on the old man, her gun drawn. Ellory bellowed at her – the throaty, tortured yell of an angry animal. She fired again, and again, each shot driving him back just a little further, until finally he stepped backwards and slipped off the edge of the cliff. His scream was shrill enough to make my eardrums bleed. It lowered in volume as he plummeted toward the forest floor, then cut off suddenly in a choked cry of agony. The ground gave the slightest of trembles. Then a sigh escaped into the night, as if the earth itself had let out one loud, miserable gasp of breath.

I got unsteadily to my feet and limped across the yard toward Marconi. I'd seen her take down guys twice her size without flinching, but when she lowered her gun, her hands were visibly shaking. "What the hell was that, Hannigan?" she shouted.

"The investigation was a bust," the Inspector replied. I jumped – I'd been so focused on reaching Marconi that I hadn't heard him approach. "Mr. Pickett resisted our questioning and became violent, and was unfortunately killed when he tried to assault Detective Hannigan. It's unlikely he had anything to do with the recent deaths. We should return to the station and go back to the drawing board on this one."

Marconi frowned at him. I knew she wouldn't buy it. Marconi was a massive skeptic, but she also believed her own eyes, and she'd seen the thing Ellory had become. There was no way she could have missed that guttural scream. It still hung in the air, like the static that pricks up the hairs on your arms right before a thunderstorm.

"Okay, fine," she said at last. She glanced between the two of us, her eyes narrowed. "I'll play along for now. But someday, Hannigan, you are going to tell me exactly what the fuck happened tonight."

I lifted a hand to my ear and felt a damp spot just below the earlobe. I drew back my bloody hand and stared at it for a few moments in the moonlight. Then I looked up at the Inspector. The face hidden beneath his fog of cigar smoke was dark and unreadable.

"I'd like to know that too," I said.

* * * * *

The next evening, I was driving through a dense patch of forest on my way to patrol in the lower Glade. It had rained that night. Clouds of mist billowed up from the road and swept over my cruiser, looking for all the world like a wave of swampy spirits. I turned on my high beams and gave the windshield a few wipes to clear away the drizzle.

A particularly dense cloud washed over my car, and when it cleared, the Inspector was waiting for me on the edge of the forest. I almost drove right past him. Slamming my foot on the brakes, I yanked the wheel to the right, tires splashing through the puddles that lined the uneven stretch of street.

I climbed out of the cruiser and stood across from him, light raindrops still pattering on roof of my car. Neither of us spoke for some time. His fedora was low enough to hide his eyes, and the tip of his cigar still smoldered, even in this damp weather.

"Are you going to tell me what actually happened last night?" I asked.

The Inspector blew out a single smoke ring. "I need to show you something," he replied.

And then… the Inspector wavered. I'm not sure how else to describe it. Nothing about his outward appearance changed, but it looked as if his body had been hollowed out, like a doll or a puppet, and there was something much larger encompassing it – something unseen pulling the strings. The illusion, whatever it was, lasted no more than a few seconds. He was just the Inspector again. Tendrils of steam escaped from his cigar and mingled with the misty air.

"You're not human," I said. The words felt strange coming out of my mouth, but they also felt right. "You're like that thing we fought up in Skokomish Bluffs."

"I am not a parasite," he replied. He didn't sound offended – just a bit sad.

I could have tried to argue with him, with the rational side of me that knew he must be lying. But Sherlock Holmes was right. I'd glimpsed the improbable that night on the Bluffs, and it may have thrown askew everything I thought I knew about the world, but it was the truth. There was no point trying to deny what my own eyes had seen. Did that scare me? Of course it did. The foundations of my reality had grown shaky, and part of me was still clambering for that one sane foothold. But sometimes rationality can only take you so far.

"Why do all this?" I asked him. "We must be… I don't know, like animals to you. Or talkative bacteria. Why bother going through all this effort to help us?"

The Inspector looked away from me, his hidden eyes

staring off into the mist. The tip of Mount Palmer floated in the midst of it all, crags piercing the clouds. It could have been some eldritch beast loping through the fog.

"Reality – all the stuff you see around you, and all the stuff you don't – it's huge. There are beings out there with shapes and sizes you couldn't even begin to fathom. And those with any sort of sentience look down on you people like protozoa. You're specks in a petri dish, bits of dim light that aren't worth the effort to snuff." He looked down at his hand and flexed his slender fingers, as if he was still unused to his borrowed shape.

"But not to me," he said. "I look at humans and see honor. Love. Loyalty so strong you would take a bullet for the ones you trust. Archaic values to some of my kind, but I think they're worth protecting. Maybe that's naïve of me. But I don't think so."

He took the cigar from his mouth and tapped it against the side of his trench coat. Flecks of ash trickled from the tip and vanished in the soggy ground.

"So in some ways, you're right," he said. "You're small. But you're not insignificant. Don't ever forget that."

The sound of his voice gave way to crickets and the ever-present rustling of the trees. I stared up again at Mount Palmer, thinking of the odd weather patterns, the missing chickens, the noises in the woods, the countless unsolved cases we had buried back at the station. "It's the Neverglades, isn't it?" I said. "There's something about this place. Something that brings all the strangeness to the surface."

He pondered the question for a moment. "In most parts of the world, beings like me keep to ourselves. We stay behind the veil and don't bother getting involved with humans. But the veil is thin here. There's a rip in reality, if you will. And sometimes things like Ellory slip through – mindless, hungry things."

"And if more of them get through?" I asked, turning to him. "How do I know you've got my back?"

The Inspector smiled. He may not have been one of us, but that one gesture seemed so genuine, so human, that I half wondered if we were rubbing off on him. "I told you before: I go where I'm needed," he said. "When the time comes, you'll know exactly where to find me."

He tipped his hat to me, drops of rain rolling down the brim. Then he took a step backward into the forest. The trees shifted around him, their branches sweeping in like leafy arms to enfold his silhouette. I watched as his body shrank away and became one with the darkness. Soon there was nothing left of the Inspector but the glowing tip of his cigar. It pulsed like a tiny firefly bobbing its way through the trees. Then the mist settled in around me, cold and heavy, and I found myself alone on that barren stretch of highway.

Zombie Radio

I knew I was in trouble when Nico Sanchez appeared in the door of my office and said, "You've gotta see this body, Hannigan." Never a good way to start a conversation. I looked up from my paperwork to see the officer hovering in my doorway. Sanchez had kind of a blanched look on his face, although that didn't mean much - the guy had never had much of a stomach when it came to dead bodies. Probably not a great quality for a cop to have, but hey. Nobody's perfect.

I was the one people usually came to with weird shit, and if Sanchez wanted me to come look at a corpse, there must have been something funky about it. Joy upon joys. Still, the alternative was sitting here going through autopsy reports, so any kind of distraction was good in my book. I got up and followed him down the hall to the mortuary.

"Who's the vic?" I asked.

"Name's Harvey Jackson. Found dead in his apartment this morning. The coroner doesn't think there's any foul play involved but they're keeping him on ice in case the autopsy reveals drugs in his system or something."

"I take it you suspect differently," I said, "or we wouldn't be talking right now."

"Don't know what to think, honestly," Sanchez replied. "But I think you oughta have a look."

We reached the mortuary doors and strode inside. Harvey Jackson was laid out on the examiner's table, pale and scrawny and buck naked. His eyes were closed and I was struck, as usual, how much the dead looked like they were just sleeping. The ones who died peacefully anyway. At a certain point a body can only get so mangled before that illusion of sleep goes out the window.

Sanchez approached the cadaver with some hesitance. The pale operating lights didn't do either of them any favors. Jackson had the complexion of a stained white blanket and the officer looked positively sickly. You could tell Sanchez had been fit at some point, but the years had given him a bit of a gut, and his once-chiseled jaw was rounded by baby fat. He scratched at his stubble and stared down at the body.

"So gross," he said. "You seeing this, Hannigan?"

I stepped around the table to get a closer look. The body itself was in decent condition – for a corpse at least – but its left ear was splattered with a viscous gray substance that looked like chunky glue. As I watched, a stream of the stuff burbled out of the ear and dripped onto the table. I stepped back before any of it could splash onto my uniform.

"Is it supposed to be doing that?" Sanchez asked.

"The body's been in the cold chambers since this morning, right?" I said. "Any excess bodily fluids should have dried out by now. This... this stuff is fresh." I looked up at Sanchez. "How did our victim die again?"

"Aneurysm, supposedly. The coroner seemed kind of distracted when I was asking him about it. I guess he's never seen anything like this either."

I glanced down at the puddle of gray goo. It had stopped bubbling, but the surface was still wet and slick. Something inside this guy's skull was leaking and I was pretty sure I knew what it was. I looked over at the medical tray, picked up the bone saw, and gave the button an experimental press. It whirred to life with a soft mechanical whine.

"Get the coroner," I told Sanchez. "I think we'd better crack open this melon."

Jackson's eyes snapped open, wide and blood-red, and a hand shot out to seize my wrist. The bone saw clattered to the floor, scraping noisily against the tiles. I cried out as the vise-like grip left bruises on my skin. Sanchez stood there, too shocked to make a move, as the dead man heaved himself off the table and lifted another hand to wrap around my throat.

"Sanchez!" I managed to gasp out. "Fucking do something!"

His cop instincts finally kicked in and he grabbed the metal tray, sending medical instruments flying as he raised the plate and bashed the corpse across the head. More of that gray substance sprayed from its ear as the body let go of my throat and staggered off to the left. Its eyes were wide, but dull, and I wondered if it could feel pain. It scrabbled against the wall of drawers, struggling to maintain its balance.

I reached for the gun by my side, but a loud *bang* suddenly echoed in the tiny space, and I figured Sanchez had beaten me to the punch. It was a damn good shot – the corpse's head exploded on impact, strewing chunks of gray across the wall and all over my uniform. I clenched my eyes shut and prayed that none of it got in my mouth. When I opened them again, the headless body was jerking on the ground, goo gushing from the hole in its neck. A few seconds later and the dead body went back to being dead again.

"Nice shot, Sanchez," I said. But when I looked over at my fellow officer, he was still standing, dumbstruck, clutching the medical tray in his stiff hands. The shot had come from somewhere behind him. Light footsteps clacked on the tiles, and a slender figure stepped out of the darkness, gun still raised and smoking. Or maybe that was the eternal cloud of smoke billowing around his thick cigar.

"Inspector," I said, massaging my throat. "You've got impeccable timing."

* * * * *

Sanchez ran off to get the coroner, for all the good he could do at this point, while the Inspector knelt by the corpse and examined the gooey splatters. I half expected him to stick one of those abnormally thin fingers into the puddle and taste the gunk, but he just stared down at it. In complete defiance of the laws of physics, tendrils of smoke drifted down from his cigar and hovered above the body, as if to get a closer look.

"I was wondering if this might be your kind of thing," I said. "I mean, before headless wonder there tried to kill me. His brain —"

"It's been liquefied," the Inspector said. He rose from the body, all seven feet of him, and stared thoughtfully at the wall of drawers. "Something got into his ear canal and turned his cerebral cortex to mush."

A week ago I would have called the man insane, but brain-melting ear slugs were far from the weirdest thing I'd seen in the Neverglades. "Do you know anything that could do this?" I asked.

"That's the problem," he said. "This could be any number of entities. You saw with Ellory that human vessels don't endure possession well. In his case he was sucked dry by the time-eater. For our poor friend here…" He gestured toward the grisly puddles. "Whatever was squatting in his skull was too much for his brain to handle."

"Is it gone?" I asked. "Did you kill it?" We both eyed the corpse warily, as if it could get up again at any second. I imagined the stump of its neck gushing all over the place as it heaved itself off the ground and tried to pick up where it had left off. But the body remained slumped, cold and pale, any dregs of life drained and gone.

"This one won't bother us anymore," the Inspector said at last. "But these are almost never isolated incidents. If there's some kind of hive out there infesting people's brains, we need to track down the source and destroy it. So keep your ear to the ground. I'll scour the town and see what I can find."

Just then Sanchez returned with the coroner, who saw the mess and promptly lost his lunch. I helped the man get to a trash can before he could empty the contents of his stomach onto the already goo-stained floor. When I looked up again, the Inspector was gone. There was only a little wisp of smoke hanging in the air where his cigar had been.

* * * * *

I was in the process of searching the death records in our databases for similar cases when my cell phone buzzed on my desk. I grabbed it before it could vibrate too long and stared down at the screen. Olivia Marconi was calling.

"Shit," I mumbled. I leaned back in my chair, answered the call, and braced myself.

The first words out of her mouth: "Do we need to have a talk, Hannigan?"

"About what?" I asked. I minimized the file I was reading.

"Sanchez has been blubbering to me all morning about the walking dead, which ordinarily I wouldn't give two shits about, but he says a corpse woke up in the morgue and tried to strangle you. You want to verify that account with me?"

"Come on Marconi, you know Sanchez. Have you ever heard of that guy being a reliable witness?"

"Answer the question, Hannigan." Marconi's voice grew low, and for the first time I thought I heard a trace of concern. "You have a habit of getting involved with some weird shit. No offense. I'm not saying the dead are rising but if something strange happened in that morgue, I want to know." A pause, and then: "Is this another Inspector thing?"

"Who?" I asked, too casually.

"Don't pull that shit with me," she said, back to being all business. "You know exactly who I'm talking about. The federal agent who showed up on the Pickett case."

"Oh yeah. Him." I brought up the file I'd been reading and rocked back slightly in my chair. "He may have shown up."

"Jesus, Mark." Marconi was practically shouting. "You couldn't have opened with that?"

"I didn't want to bother you if it turns out to be nothing," I said. "Okay, sure, we had a dead body that wasn't quite as dead as we thought. But this isn't another Skokomish Bluffs situation. The Inspector and I can handle this one."

"Like hell you can." Marconi was silent for ten solid seconds, and then: "As soon as you learn anything, you call me. Understand? You boys aren't walking into another situation like *last* time without my backup."

She hung up without saying goodbye. Not that I expected her to.

* * * * *

It was late in the afternoon when my cell phone buzzed again. "Inspector," I said, bringing the phone to my ear. "Tell me you've got good news."

"I've got a lead, at least," he replied. "Jackson's last known location was the Mountain Ridge Country Club. He and several other men gathered there last night to watch the Seahawks game. Apparently Jackson made it back home before morning, but none of the rest did. I've checked with all of their families and we've got ten missing people on our hands."

"You think their brains turned to mush too?" I asked.

"I think we should check the country club, at any rate," the Inspector replied. "I'm on my way there as we speak."

"Likewise," I said, grabbing my jacket. "I'll be there in ten."

I'd never been to the country club before, but I had a rough idea of where it was located; it was one of those fixtures I always drove past during my patrols in the outer reaches of the Glade. As I wound my way through the streets of town, orange sunlight glared off my windshield and turned the forest backdrop into a silhouette. The Inspector, too, was barely more than a shadow when I met him in the club's parking lot. Only the speck of his cigar glowed in the darkness.

"You feel it, don't you?" he said by way of greeting. "There's something wrong here."

I looked up at the squat one-story building. It was unassuming enough - a yellow structure with a chipped paint job, front porch, and pair of bronzed rifles hanging above the door - but I knew what the Inspector meant. It was too quiet here. The blinds were down and I couldn't hear a single sound, not even a bird chirping in the eaves. It felt like the two of us had stepped into a circle where nothing moved, nothing breathed. My hand drifted toward the pistol at my waist and hovered there.

"Well, no point in waiting around," I said. "Let's case the joint."

The lights were off when we entered the country club, and only the barest of dying sunlight poked through slats in the window blinds. I tried the light switch and only met with a dull popping sound. There was power somewhere in the building, though; I could hear the staticky voice of a radio host from the other room. It sounded like your standard sports broadcast.

The Inspector lifted a thin finger to his lips, and I nodded. We crept through the darkness toward the sound of the radio. The floorboards creaked under our shoes, so any element of surprise we'd started with was gone. I could only hope the worst thing we'd find was a bunch of guys gathered around a handheld radio, waiting to hear who'd scored the latest run.

Dozens of animal heads sprouted from the walls, and in the dark they had an uncanny look of liveliness about them; they might have just been sticking their necks through narrow windows. The wall space between the animal busts was filled with countless photographs and certificates, none of which I could make out clearly. There was a pile of construction materials strewn across the floor near us. I nearly tripped over a stack of planks as I followed the Inspector toward the soft drone of the radio.

The subsequent clatter was louder than I would have hoped, and seconds later I heard another creak of the floorboards, this time from across the room. I grabbed the Inspector's shoulder and forced him to stop. We grew quiet, listening, waiting for the sound to come again. Nothing but the radio. I began to wonder if it was just the building shifting, old as it was.

Then something moved in the shadows, and suddenly a figure in spattered overalls was rushing at us, eyes vacant. My hand shot to the gun at my hip, but the Inspector was faster. He grabbed a shovel from the construction heap and swung it at the man's chest. It collided like a dusty sack of bricks. The man kept coming, arms extended, and the Inspector wound back for another strike. This time he aimed for the forehead. The entire head detached from the body and rolled into the corner, joining the collection of hunting trophies hanging from the wall.

"Shit!" I said, pistol in hand. "Whatever got to Jackson got to him too."

Another man leapt out of the rafters, this one wearing a plaid shirt and grime-encrusted cargo pants. He fell on top of the Inspector and nearly knocked him to the ground. The two of them grappled for a few seconds before the Inspector swung the body around and into the wooden paneling, headfirst. I couldn't tell if the Inspector was just strong or if the man's head really was that brittle; it popped on impact like a water balloon, spewing gray gunk across the wall.

"Mark, behind you!" the Inspector shouted.

I whipped around and fired three shots at the approaching figure. The first two went wild, but the third clipped him in the temple, sending a spray of hair and brain particles flying. The body continued to stagger toward me, so I placed another shot right between the eyes. *Bang*. This time the body fell forward and slumped onto the floor, its head disintegrated.

More were coming now, emerging from the darkness where they'd been crouching. They moved quickly, but clumsily, like toddlers learning how to walk for the first time. I picked them off from a distance. Headshot after headshot, they went down, their neck stumps bleeding gray goo onto the wood. Soon there was a pile of headless bodies lying strewn across the floor. I waited for more to come, breathing heavily, but it seemed we'd gotten the last of them. The Inspector stood in the corner, brushing the sticky substance off his hands.

"Did we just slaughter the entire country club?" I asked him. My pulse was racing a little too fast for comfort and I felt unable to lower my gun.

"Those things we just killed – they weren't men," the Inspector said. "Not anymore. Whatever parasite wriggled into their brains made sure of that." He stopped wiping his hands and looked at me. "You're not a murderer, Mark. You were just cleaning up an infestation."

I knew he was right, but still, I'd blown the heads off a dozen men today and it was going to take some time to get that image out of my head. I looked away from the stack of bodies and turned toward the other room. The door was hanging wide open, and the sportscaster droned on behind it, oblivious to the massacre that had just taken place.

"There may be more of them back there," I said, lowering my voice. I clenched my gun and nodded toward the open door. The Inspector said nothing in reply, but he glided past me to peer into the shadowed space. I noticed for the first time that his footsteps were silent. He could have been hovering a few inches in the air for all I knew.

"I don't hear any movement," he said. "But keep your weapon drawn, just in case."

He slipped inside, and I followed him, letting my eyes adjust to the darkness. The windows on the far side of the room were boarded shut so even less light could get through here. I could tell at least that an open bar stretched across one of the walls, and there was a pool table in the corner, a single cue stick leaning up against it. There were plenty of round tables strewn throughout the room, although most of the chairs were lying on their sides. It looked like there had been some sort of scuffle. The place was deserted now, though, near as I could tell.

The radio we'd heard since we walked in was sitting on the closest table. It was an old thing, probably manufactured in the 90s, judging by the pair of tape cassettes. The antenna poked up at a haphazard angle. I listened vaguely as the announcer went on about who was at bat and which teams were expected in the playoffs this year. Part of me wondered why this device was still running when everything else about the place seemed to be so dead.

"I think we got them all," I said, holstering my gun. "They must have —"

"Hush." The Inspector lifted a hand and pointed at the radio. The sound grew louder at once, although the static was worse than before; it sounded like the scrabbling of a thousand rats across pavement. In the midst of the noise I heard what the announcer was actually saying, and the flesh crawled on my neck.

"The Angels have given up three runs trying to get home again, but don't worry, listeners — there'll always be a place in Hell for our feathered friends." It was a man, or at least it sounded like a man; he had the same drawl as those old-timey announcers you always heard in vintage movies. "In other news, Santiago is off of the pitcher's mound with a broken wrist, and Williams is a dirty fucking cunt who'll be the first to die when the cleansing comes."

"What the hell?" I muttered.

The voice cut out, replaced by an ululating sound that reminded me of a garbled war cry. It was so loud I could actually see the speakers trembling. Then it died as quickly as it had arisen, replaced by a gentle hum and the sound of women laughing in the background.

"You've been listening to *SPORTS*," a new voice said, clearly female. "Stay tuned for your daily horoscope."

"Inspector —" I tried to say, but he gestured for me to shut up. A third voice had joined the chorus, this one a low, sultry baritone, like a man trying to talk up some pretty young thing in the back room of a bar. A theremin played lazily in the background.

"I want you to imagine a man, listeners," the voice on the radio purred. "A man who loves you very much. A man who wants nothing more than to enfold you in his scaly wings and squeeze you with the force of his love. I want you to breathe in his scent until you have no reason to breathe at all. I want you to crane your neck until it breaks and howl at that blood red moon. Can you do that for me, listeners? Can you howl at that moon with me?" Then the radio erupted in a screech that couldn't possibly have come from a human throat. I could feel my eardrums throbbing and I clapped my hands over them to block out the awful sound.

"It's the radio!" I shouted to the Inspector, my voice muffled. "That's what's melting people's brains!"

The Inspector wasted no time darting over the fallen chairs and picking up the radio. He turned the machine off, but that inhuman screech still issued from the speakers, so he tore the thing in half with his bare hands and flung both pieces against the wall. I lowered my hands, numb, as the inner mess of machinery sparked a few times and went dark. The nightmare shriek faded out with a diseased sort of *blip*.

"Someone's been eating their Wheaties," I commented, but the Inspector wasn't listening to me. He leaned down and picked through the wires, frowning. The smoke billowing from his cigar had taken on a peculiar shade of orange.

"It's in the radio waves," he said at last. "That much is obvious. But where's the source?"

"Unless it's a private broadcast, it's got to be down at the community radio station," I said. "Pacific Glade isn't that big. If you get your news via radio, it's not like you've got many options."

"Then we need to get there as soon as possible and stop this broadcast," he said. "Or we could be dealing with a whole town of brainless corpses before long."

"You don't have to tell me twice," I replied.

* * * * *

The Inspector rode with me to the radio station - whatever vehicle he'd used to get to the country club seemed to have vanished into thin air - and we spent most of the trip in silence. Being some kind of otherworldly, interdimensional being, he probably didn't have much use for small talk. He didn't say a word until we arrived at the station and got out of the cruiser, slamming the doors behind us.

"We don't know what we'll find in there," he warned. "Whatever you do, Mark, don't let go of your gun."

I nodded and patted my holster. The doors opened for us automatically, and we strode into a cool, spacious lobby, with a receptionist's deck and a few cushioned chairs. Photos of smiling radio execs lined the walls, along with a few pieces of Pacific Glade memorabilia: news clippings about local heroes, pictures of Lake Lucid at sunrise, even an old ham radio perched on a little shelf by the window. The floor was carpeted in a blue-and-white checkered pattern. As we approached the desk, the receptionist looked up from her computer and smiled at us.

"Can I help you, gentlemen?" she asked.

In response, the Inspector lifted a badge – no idea where he'd gotten that from – and shoved it in the woman's face. "FBI. We have a reason to believe one of your stations is broadcasting terrorist propaganda and we want it shut down. *Now.*"

The woman looked up at him, raising a quizzical eyebrow. I fully expected her to protest or make a fuss. Instead, she asked, "What frequency is it?"

I shared a look with the Inspector. In the confusion back at the country club I don't think either of us had taken a closer look at the radio's call letters; we were too focused on shutting the damn thing up. Thankfully the Inspector spoke up before I could think up some half-assed explanation.

"The signal's been bouncing from station to station, near as we can tell. It took us a long time to track it back to the source." He stowed the badge back in his pocket and said, "Ma'am, this broadcast is a domestic threat. Several people have already been killed because of it. We need to shut it down before it can hurt anyone else."

Damn, he was good. The woman still had a puzzled expression on her face, but she seemed to believe us, at any rate. She rose from the desk and led us over to a side door. We followed her into a dimly lit hallway with a few dark doorways and a single window at the end of the hall. A neon red ON AIR sign hovered above the first two doors. The receptionist brought us to the door at the far end, this one devoid of any sign, and rapped a few times on the frame. "Marcy!" she called softly. "There's a couple of men here to see you."

Light spilled into the hall as the door opened and a woman's face peered out at us. It looked like we'd caught her in the middle of filling out paperwork. A decorative lamp on the desk lit up her dark skin and vivid blue business dress. She eyed me and the Inspector with some unease.

"Yes?" she said. "I'm wrapping up for the night. Is there something I can do for you?"

The Inspector flashed his badge again and recited the same bullshit story he'd told the receptionist. I expected her to get indignant and demand that we leave at once, but Marcy surprised me. "Terrorist propaganda," she said, with a snort of laughter. "That's a new one. Do you boys want to hear what we actually broadcast here?"

"Of course," the Inspector answered, glancing warily at me. Marcy brought us to one of the ON AIR rooms and pushed the door open quietly. The space inside was divided by a large pane of soundproof glass. Behind it, two men in flannel shirts and headphones were having a conversation into a set of mics. Their voices issued from a mess of buttons and speakers on our side of the glass. Neither voice matched the sports announcer or the sultry baritone we'd heard at the country club.

"So, Alan, I heard you met a pretty young thing down at the Hanging Rock. Care to elaborate for our eager listeners?"

"Let me tell you, Joe, I haven't been this disappointed since Barbra Streisand didn't swallow."

"You always were a nasty old dog, Alan."

The older of the two men, Alan, made a jerking off gesture with his hand - presumably for the benefit of his costar, since of course the audience couldn't see it. Joe burst into a fit of laughter and said something about freaky women, but at that point my cheeks were red and I was trying not to listen.

"It may be garbage, but it's harmless garbage," Marcy said. She closed the door on the two men. "I don't know where you got your information, officers, but we're not broadcasting propaganda here. Just good old-fashioned bathroom humor."

She went on, but I wasn't listening. I'd just seen something through the window that had made my blood run cold. The Inspector hadn't spotted it yet. He was staring at the closed door as if he was trying to burn holes in it with his eyes. Hell, maybe he was. I had no idea what he was capable of. His cigar smoke had taken on a shade of deep, cherry red.

"Did you used to have another station?" I cut in.

Marcy paused. "Ages ago, yes," she said. "There's a radio tower about a mile away. But it hasn't been operational for almost ten years now. There was something wrong with the building - asbestos, I think."

"I don't know about asbestos," I said, pointing to the window, "but I think you might be wrong about that tower."

Everyone turned to look. In the distance, just close enough to see, a steady red light was blinking in the darkness. Beside me, I felt the Inspector tense up, his fingers growing tight around his fake badge.

Marcy frowned. "That can't be possible," she said. "We moved all the equipment to this station when we switched locations. There's nothing left to broadcast over there."

"It's very possible," the Inspector muttered. "And I think it's safe to say we've found the source of the signal." He stowed the badge in his coat pocket and strode off down the hallway, leaving me to hurry after him. I took a second to glance back at Marcy. A strange sheen had come over her eyes, and her face had grown solemn.

"Be careful over there," she said.

Her concern caught me off guard. Even though she couldn't know the truth, she could at least sense at the shape of it. Like anyone who grew up in the Glade, she understood that there was something fundamentally different about this place. Something… off. And she knew that whatever was behind that signal was bad news.

"We'll be okay," I replied. "Just doing our job."

* * * * *

Normally I wouldn't let another soul touch the wheel of my police cruiser, but the Inspector was already in the driver's seat when I joined him outside, and I figured, what the hell. I wasn't going to pick a fight with Detective Lovecraft. There was a lot more at stake tonight.

The Inspector pulled out of the parking lot, tires skidding, and sent us rocketing down the road toward the distant blinking tower. My seatbelt dug harshly into my shoulder blades. I pulled my phone out of my pocket, fully prepared to call Marconi, but found my fingers typing out another number instead. My wife answered on the third ring.

"Hello?"

"Hi honey, it's me." Tires rumbled in the background, and I asked, "Are you driving?"

"Um, yes," she said. "I took the kids out for ice cream. I hope you don't mind – you've been out so late, you know, and they were getting antsy."

I could hear Rory arguing with Stephen in the backseat: the soundtrack of my life these days. But that wasn't the only thing I heard. There was another voice in the car. A smooth, male baritone announcing tomorrow's weather.

"Do you trust me, babe?" I asked.

A pause. "You know I do." Another pause, longer this time, and then: "Are you about to do something dangerous?"

"Don't worry about me." I glanced up at the radio tower, now looming closer than before, growing steadily in size as the car shot through the forest. "Just listen – turn off the radio and drive the boys straight home. Lock the doors and grab the baseball bat we keep under the bed. And whatever you do, *don't turn on the radio.* I can't stress that enough."

My wife said nothing for a few seconds, and I wondered if she thought I was crazy. Then the announcer's voice went dead. Rory and Stephen kept up their banter, oblivious to what was going on in the front seat.

"We're almost home," Ruth said. "I'll make sure the boys stay inside. And Mark? Stay safe."

"I always do," I replied. It was a lie I'd uttered many times before, and would no doubt utter again. But that was just part of the job. We'd accepted a long time ago that tomorrow was never guaranteed.

"I love you," she said, and the phone went silent in my ear. I lowered it to my lap and stared through the windshield. The tower jutted out from the trees before us like a great skeletal finger, stabbing at the clouds. The red light at its tip pulsed brightly in the growing darkness.

"We're here," the Inspector announced, and the old wooden structure appeared suddenly among the trees. Its windows were boarded up and most of the paint on the paneling had peeled away. By all rights the place should have been dead, but there was still that glowing light up top. It flashed in and out as it broadcasted its deadly signal across the Neverglades.

The Inspector brought the car to a stop, and I stepped out, slipping my cell phone into my pocket. Ruth and the kids would be all right. I was the one who needed to watch his back.

The front door was boarded up with a set of planks, but the Inspector tore them off with his bare hands, the rusty nails squealing as they came loose. He tossed the boards casually aside. I watched them as they flew through the air, struck a tree, and tumbled to the forest floor in a heap.

"You know, you're awfully strong for such a scrawny guy," I said. Even as the words left my mouth, I saw the Inspector's body ripple, his true form flashing into view for a second. It was like getting blinded by a thousand-kilowatt camera flash. I had to blink a few times to clear up the afterimage.

"Let's go," he said, ignoring me. "We can't afford to waste any time." He forced open the door with his shoulder and hurried inside. Pistol raised, I followed him into the gloom.

So far, so good – except for one big fuckup. In my concern for my family, I'd forgotten to call Marconi.

* * * * *

If I had any doubts that we were in the right place, they evaporated the second the Inspector and I stepped inside. The supposedly abandoned station was teeming with machinery. Cracked, rusty consoles sat on every spare surface, vines poking through the holes in their screens. Or at least they looked like vines. A closer look revealed that they were actually thick, tangled wires. The wires sprouted from the walls, too, stretching across the ground in spiral patterns, each cable heavy with purple moss.

"I wouldn't touch anything," the Inspector said, ducking underneath a hanging wire. "That kind of moss doesn't usually grow this side of the rift. I have no idea what it'll do to human skin."

I inched forward cautiously, being careful to tiptoe around the fuzzy purple wires. They gave off a slight metallic stench with a tinge of ozone. There was a faint humming in the air, almost imperceptible, and I realized the wires were vibrating. The closer we drew to the next room, the stronger the vibrations grew. I could feel the sound jostling around my skull.

"It's an organism," the Inspector muttered. "Not just a radio wave. And its heart is close by. You can hear it."

I hissed out a warning as he placed a hand on the door, but the Inspector pushed it open anyway, revealing a flickering space the size of a small studio. The wires grew dense and more tangled than ever as they retreated into the dark space. The Inspector brushed them aside and entered the room. I followed him, gun raised, keeping a wary eye on the dangling cables.

The space behind the door was another recording studio, bigger than the one at the community station, but utterly devoid of people. Tiny portable radios lay in piles on the floor, all tuned in to the same staticky channel. Every so often I heard the occasional blip of a voice but couldn't make out what it was saying. A single outdated TV set sat on a table behind the soundproof glass. The pane itself was shattered, wires stabbing through the holes, but the curved screen of the TV was intact. A dark shape lurked behind the static. I could barely make out the outline of a human face and neck.

"Show yourself," the Inspector said suddenly, scaring the shit out of me. His cigar smoke had turned a pungent yellow. He crossed the room and placed a slender hand on the glass.

"You've proven you're capable of human speech," he said. "So let's have a conversation."

The vibrating hum grew louder, and the image on the screen became less shaky, took on sharp lines and curves. At first I thought I was looking at a silhouette - a person's face cast in shadow. But the image grew crisper, and I realized, the hairs on my arms prickling, that the figure had no face at all. Just a pure black dome for a head, like a chunk of carefully sculpted obsidian.

The stony face that wasn't a face cracked at the bottom, stretching into an unnaturally wide smile. The teeth that grinned out at us were pristine white and razor sharp. It was like staring into the maw of a shark.

"Inspector, Inspector, the noble defector," it jeered. "Come to play with the paramecium, have you?"

It was all the voices we'd heard at the country club mashed into one: man, woman, animal, howling static, an abrasive mix of all the worst sounds you could imagine. Each syllable made my head throb. I wanted to clap my hands over my ears, but that would mean letting go of my gun, and I sure as hell wasn't doing that. So I stood there and endured the voices with gritted teeth.

The Inspector seemed unaffected by the grating sound. "Why I'm here is none of your concern," he said to the figure behind the screen. "What I want to know is *how* you got here, and why you're killing these people."

The shark-like smile curved upwards in an arc that would have stretched the limits of any human face. "Because they have hands," the voice said. "Because they have feet, and tongues, and *brains*, and I am not so gifted." Static rushed in, and the voice dropped an octave. "But you wouldn't know, would you? Mr. Too-Good-to-Walk-Around-in-a-Flesh-Suit?"

"You didn't answer my first question," the Inspector said. "How did you get through the rift?"

The figure opened its mouth, but instead of speaking, a chorus of game show bells came ringing out. "*Oooh!* That is the *wrong* question!" said a tinny announcer's voice. "Please step inside the box to await your punishment." Then canned laughter from an invisible audience.

"Box? What's it talking about?" I asked.

The laughter cut out. The figure on the screen whipped its head around so fast the image blurred for a moment, and even though it had no eyes, I knew it was looking at me.

The mouth opened again and a long, orange tongue licked the tips of those razor-sharp teeth.

"The brave detective," said a new voice, and I nearly dropped the gun, because it was *Ruth*. The thing inside the TV had captured her voice to a T. I felt my hands grow numb around the pistol, but I kept it aimed at the screen.

"You're not my wife," I said. "You can cut the shit now, because I'm not falling for it."

"Of course I'm not your wife," said the familiar voice. "I'm better than her. You love each other but your flesh suits keep you separate. I can be in you - *with* you - in ways she never could. I can bring you unity. Intimacy like you've never known. I can be every rush of euphoria, every surge of happiness. You want that. Don't you?"

Of course not, I wanted to say, but my lips wouldn't move, and neither would the rest of my body, for that matter; every muscle had gone rigid. The voice continued to murmur sweet nothings in my ear, and then I felt it - something cool, airy, and *sticky* crawling into my ear canal, digging invisible claws into the flesh.

"No!" the Inspector bellowed, and the glass pane shattered inward, sprinkling jagged shards across the floor. The TV set flew backwards and crashed against the wall. As the screen cracked, I felt the invisible presence vanish from my ear, and all at once my muscles turned to Jello. My weakened body slumped against the nearest pile of wires. A patch of moss brushed my hand and pain instantly shot down my arm. As I yanked it away, I saw that my skin had become red and inflamed, as if I'd touched it to a burner on the stove.

The overhead lights began to flicker, and a sudden whirring filled the room: the sound of an automatic door sliding open. At the far end of the studio, in a darkened corner we hadn't noticed, a pair of men lurched out of the shadows. They moved with the same clumsy gait as the corpses from the country club. The Inspector almost didn't see them in time, but he reacted quickly when he did, throwing the first body against the wall and kicking the second square in the chest. As the man staggered back, I lifted my gun and shot him between the eyes. Gray goo splattered across the wall of wires as the headless body slumped to the ground.

The shadows stirred, and I shouted, "There's more of them!" I got to my feet and fired another couple of shots into the darkness. None of them hit home, but in the flash of gunfire, I saw about five or six other figures hobbling toward us. The Inspector pulled out his own gun and fired at lightning speed, taking out three of the corpses in less than a second. But they were coming still, even the ones missing chunks from their skull, and our ammo wouldn't last forever.

"This way!" the Inspector yelled suddenly, grabbing me by the arm and dragging me down a side hall. The wires here were thick as boa constrictors and there were more TV sets strewn across the ground, each displaying the same dark, grinning face. Staticky voices drifted up from them as we passed.

"Barbasol is the number one way to soothe your existential dread of the fleshy prison you call your body!"

"And it's one! Two! Three strikes you're dead at the old - ball - game!"

"It's raining blood and guts out there, folks, chunks of viscera dropping from the sky! Bring an umbrella and a vomit bucket to work."

"Inspector, Inspector, the monster detector. Does your friend know who you really are? Does he know the things you've done?"

The Inspector responded to this last taunt by smashing in the closest TV screen with the toe of his boot. The canned laughter that followed had something dark and heaving in the background, like the sound of a grizzly bear throwing up. I could feel my ears burning again but there was nothing I could do except run, run, run.

Finally the two of us burst out of the hall and into the fresh air of the night. I wanted to book it to the cruiser and get the hell out of there, but the Inspector held me back. "Look!" he said. We were standing underneath the radio tower. Up close, I saw that every beam was teeming with purple moss. Dangling from the center in a sticky blue cocoon was a shape I can only describe as an enormous human heart.

Scraping footsteps echoed from the hallway behind us. I pivoted and fired a few shots back into the darkness, but they went wild, the demonic voice laughing as the bullets ricocheted off the walls. The walking corpses were almost on top of us and I couldn't understand why the Inspector was holding me still.

"When I say run," he said suddenly, "I want you to head straight for the cruiser. Do you understand?"

"What about you?" I asked, firing another bullet. This time it sunk into a meaty shoulder, but otherwise did little to slow the body down.

The Inspector spun me around so that we were staring eye to eye. His purple irises flashed an alarming shade of red that I'd never seen before, matching the cloud of crimson smoke billowing from his cigar.

"DO YOU UNDERSTAND?" he barked.

I nodded. What else could I do?

As the walking bodies grew closer, the Inspector stepped away from me and tore the cigar from his mouth. I say "tore" because the thing came free with a great ripping sound, like someone pulling off a band-aid; the noise was so harsh it made me wince. The tip of the cigar ignited like the head of a massive match. Then, as I watched, the Inspector drew back his arm and launched the cigar through the air at the dangling blue heart.

It flew like a torpedo, changing its shape in a subtle way I still can't describe; one second I was looking at a cigar, and the next I simply wasn't. The glowing object struck the center of the cocoon and exploded on impact. Hot white fire spread along the tendrils of moss, turning the tower into a fiery beacon against the sky. Bits of hot debris rained around me, singeing my skin, and I realized the Inspector was shouting for me to run.

I raised an arm to shield my face as I rushed through the blaze. The fire was spreading fast, unnaturally fast, and for a scary moment I thought it had surrounded me on all sides. Then a hole opened in the flames and I darted toward it. The sleeves of my uniform were still alight after I staggered through, so I flung myself onto the ground and rolled back and forth in the wet grass, trying to stifle the flames.

A guttural shriek made me look up from where I was rolling. The radio tower had turned into a blazing white pillar, with the writhing heart caught in the center. There was no sign of the bodies that had been chasing us - or of the Inspector, for that matter. I lay still in the grass as the shriek rose a few octaves, becoming less and less human, before reaching its highest pitch and dissolving into a final mess of static.

That was the moment the radio tower sank in on itself like a drooping wet sandcastle. The flashing beacon at the top collapsed into the center with an almighty crash, bringing the entire structure down, causing great embers to leap outward and spark against the grass. I rose to my knees and felt for my gun. Nothing should have been able to survive that collapse. But if a set of charred, flaming bodies came staggering out of the wreckage... well, god forbid I be caught with my guard down.

I waited for three minutes for something - anything - to emerge from the ruins, but when a shape finally appeared among the flames, I held my fire. It was the Inspector. His seven-foot silhouette melted out of the fire as easily as someone might slip through a light waterfall. Before I could ask him if he was okay, he knelt down and picked something small off the ground. The flames came rushing inward as if sucked by a great vacuum, billowing over themselves until they spiraled down, down into the thin shape the Inspector held in his hand. When he brought the cigar to his mouth again, it was glowing bright - but the blaze behind him had vanished. There wasn't even a single spark left behind.

"Jesus," I breathed. "Did you kill it?"

The Inspector nodded. Behind him, the crispy patches of purple moss were decaying into puddles of goop, much like the stuff inside the radio victims' skulls. The bodies that had been chasing us were barely more than charcoal. My own skin was red and inflamed - between the moss and the flaming debris, I wouldn't have been surprised if I had a few third-degree burns - but at least I'd made it out. At least I was alive. In a job like this, you're grateful for whatever miracles you can get.

"That fire must have been seen for miles," I said. "We should get the hell out of here before somebody comes to investigate."

"Agreed." The Inspector stuffed his hands into his coat pockets and glided away from the wreckage, leaving me to follow in his wake. This time I was the one to slip into the driver's seat. I kept the headlights low and stuck to the side roads, and when the trees lit up with the flashing strobe of another police car, I slipped off the curb and waited in the shadows. The cruiser zipped past us unaware, its sirens blaring.

"The broadcast is dead," I said. "So does that mean this is over? No more brain-melting zombie waves?"

The Inspector frowned. "Yes and no. I don't think our friend in the TV set will be bothering us anymore. But there's still the question of how it got here in the first place, which is my biggest worry right now."

"What do you mean?"

"I mean that old station was supposed to be abandoned - no wires, no speakers, no functioning equipment. But somebody restocked the place since Marcy and the others relocated. Somebody unknowingly - or knowingly - gave that thing a home. A base of operations." He turned to look at me in the darkness. "If there's someone out there letting beings through the rift *on purpose*, and giving them the tools to survive on this side of the veil... we should all be worried. This could be so much bigger than a single rogue time eater or a brain-hungry hive mind."

The thought had crossed my own mind already, and it only made me more uneasy to hear the Inspector vocalize it. The trees around us burst into flashes of color as a wailing fire truck zoomed past. I wondered what the officers would make of the collapsed tower, the charred bodies, the heaps of old radios and TVs. It must have been like walking into an episode of the *Twilight Zone*.

"What did that thing mean?" I asked. "The thing in the TV set. It asked if I knew who you really were. If I knew the things you've done."

The Inspector didn't speak for a moment, but his cigar smoke took on a thin, wispy quality. His eyes had faded back to that unusual shade of purple. He still didn't look quite human, but something of the monster in him had melted away, and he seemed strangely vulnerable sitting there in the passenger seat.

"I've lived a long life, Mark," he said. "And when you've lived as long as I have, you look back on your early days with something less than pride - maybe even disgust at what you were, before you became what you are. You'll have to forgive me for not wanting to dwell too long on those old days." He breathed out a single smoke ring. "Not yet, at least."

"Fair enough," I said. "But one day you and I are going to have a chat."

If this prospect worried the Inspector, he didn't show it. He simply reached into the pocket of his coat and withdrew a rectangular slip of plastic. "Here," he said, passing it to me. I turned it over in my hands. The surface was reflective, so I could see my own face, but nothing else; the card itself was blank.

"That's my calling card," the Inspector said. "I try to keep my eyes open for any sort of disturbance in the Glade, but sometimes I miss things. So if you're tracking something dangerous - something more than just a human criminal - and you need my help, ignite that card."

"Ignite?" I said, raising an eyebrow.

"Trust me," he replied. "I'll come as soon as I can."

I shrugged and tucked the card into my pocket. "Hopefully we get a breather first," I said. "This was a messy one. I don't know how I'm going to explain this in my reports."

"You'll think of something," the Inspector said distantly. "If you don't mind, Mark, I think I'd like to walk back on my own. Just to clear my head. You understand."

"Are you sure?" I asked. "It's a long walk back to the station."

The Inspector smiled. "I think I'll be okay." He opened the door and stepped out into the night. Before leaving, he placed a hand on the frame and said, "We did well tonight."

"Are you kidding?" I said. "*You* did well. That thing with the exploding cigar was insane. Maybe one of these days I'll save your bacon instead of the other way around."

His smile grew a fraction. Then he closed the door, gentler than I expected, and strolled off toward the moonlit horizon.

Before I revved the engines and began the journey back to the station, I watched the Inspector wander down that stretch of road. Part of me expected his body to just vanish as soon as he got too far, dissolving into mist; but he didn't. He remained a lonely figure with his hands tucked into his pockets and his fedora bowed. And I realized, then, that something the monster had said had struck home with him. It was hard to imagine someone like the Inspector being hurt by such a trivial taunt. But he *was* hurting. I could see that now.

I wished I knew why, wished I could talk to him, but this wasn't the time to push it. He'd tell me when he was good and ready. In the meantime, there was nothing else to do but get back to my desk and try to bury this whole case in mounds upon mounds of paperwork.

* * * * *

That was the plan, anyway. When I got back to my office, Marconi was waiting for me by my desk. She was chewing her customary wad of gum so furiously I thought she might crack a tooth.

"Marconi," I said, wrinkling my brow. "What are you -?"

She slapped me across the face, hard enough to make my jaw sting. I raised a hand to my cheek and half-expected to draw away blood. I'd seen Marconi pissed before, but never to this extent; her eyes burned with anger and her lips were drawn in a definite scowl.

"Hannigan," she seethed. "I told you to call me the *second* you got a tip on this case. Now you stumble back in here reeking of smoke with burns all over your skin. You want to tell me what kind of shit you've been up to behind my back?"

"Jesus, Marconi, I'm sorry," I said. Talking was painful; every syllable made my jaw throb. "Things escalated quickly. The Inspector and I were forced to act on a sudden lead and I forgot to call you in the confusion. It's nothing personal."

"You think I was born yesterday?" she said. "Much as it pains me to admit, you've got a good head on your shoulders, Hannigan. You don't just *forget* things. For some reason you're keeping me out of these investigations and I want to know why."

I remained silent. My jaw hurt too much to talk and I wasn't sure I had an answer for her anyway.

"I'm a big girl. I can protect myself," she said. "So don't feed me any bullshit about 'keeping me safe.' If anything, *you* need *me*. You boys would have been toast if I hadn't stepped in up in the Bluffs." She took a step closer to me, and I thought I saw some of the anger dwindle in her eyes. "I just want to help, Mark. Why won't you let me help?"

I met her gaze. It was surprisingly hard; maintaining eye contact with Marconi was like staring into a bright light for too long. "Look, I know I haven't exactly been open with you," I said. "It's just, these cases, with the Inspector - they're different. Weirder than anything I've ever seen. If you really want in, I guess I can't stop you. But if you open this door, there's no closing it. And you may not like what you find on the other side."

She snapped her gum and smirked. "You always had a melodramatic streak, you know that?" she said. "But don't patronize me, Hannigan. I know we're up against some dangerous shit. I saw that thing up on the Bluffs, and if there's anything even half as crazy still running around out there, it's my duty to stop it. It's *our* duty. So promise me. Promise you'll call me the second this Inspector of yours comes on the scene."

What could I say? Marconi was one hell of a cop, and truth be told, it was better to have her around. Aside from some archaic sense of chivalry, there was really no reason to keep her out of this.

"I promise," I said. "But Jesus, Marconi, lay off the physical violence next time. My jaw's still stinging."

She smiled and slapped me again - this time on the shoulder. "I'm just glad your sorry ass is still alive," she said. "Now go home and wash up. You've got plenty of reports to file tomorrow."

"Yes ma'am," I replied.

Marconi left, leaving behind the faintest whiff of bubblegum, and I decided to call it a night. My body was burnt all over and I was in desperate need of a shower. Plus Ruth and the boys would be waiting for me back home.

I don't get nights off too often, but when I do, it's usually a quiet affair. A beer with dinner, TV with the boys, and maybe a little fun with Ruth if we're both not exhausted from work. Tonight, though, would be different. The thought of doing anything physical made my entire body ache, and after what had happened at the station I wanted to steer clear of television for a while. So maybe this would be a quiet one. Just a peaceful night in with the people I loved.

After such a long, chaotic day, I think I deserved that much.

REMEMBER ME

  There's something funny about dusk in the Neverglades. Ever since I was a kid, I remember staring out my bedroom window and watching the sun dip lower and lower in the sky, until at last it came to rest just behind Mount Palmer. And then it would stick there. For a solid half hour, the sun would refuse to set any further, as if it had hit some unbreakable barrier on the horizon. Sometimes we wondered if it would just stop one day and leave us under an eternal sunset. But no matter how late it dawdled, there would always come a time when that sliver of light would slip below the mountain peaks, and night would finally sweep in around us like it was supposed to.
  I'm in my forties now, and even though the setting sun doesn't amaze me like it used to, I still find myself staring at it sometimes. Take tonight for example. I strolled out into my backyard and found myself blinded by the little halo above the peaks of the distant mountains. Call me a poet, but it looked an awful lot like the yolk of a huge, molten egg.
  As the sun hovered in its usual spot, I got to work building a fire. I'd retained a thing or two from my years in the Boy Scouts and it wasn't long before I had a little bed of flames burning in the fire pit. I blinked a few times - the sun had seared flashes of color into my eyes - and pulled the Inspector's card from my pocket. The light shimmered off its mirrored surface and threw rainbows across the lawn.
  Dubious, I flicked the card into the flames below. It caught right away, spitting purple sparks into the air and letting out a faint *hiss* as it did so. When I looked up, the

Inspector was standing by our toolshed. A couple of months ago his sudden appearance would have scared the shit out of me, but I'd seen a lot since the Inspector had come to town, and these little magic tricks had long since ceased to faze me.

"Inspector," I said. "How goes it?"

The tall man who wasn't really a man squinted at me through his cigar smoke. His trench coat and gray fedora looked muted in the orange sunlight.

"Mark," he said. "You burned the card. Is there an emergency? Another body, or a strange disappearance, maybe? I didn't pick anything up on my usual networks."

"Well," I said, "you could say there's an emergency. Of sorts. My wife cooked a dinner for five people and we only have four people to share it with."

The Inspector said nothing for what felt like a solid minute. His cigar smoke, a barometer for his ever-changing mood, had taken on a kind of acidic green.

"I don't understand," he said. "There's no emergency? No trail of bodies to follow?"

"Jesus, you're morbid," I said. "Everything isn't always death and darkness, you know. It wouldn't hurt for you to lighten up every once in a while."

"I still don't understand why you called me," the Inspector said, frowning. His look of confusion was so convincingly human that I almost forgot he was an eldritch monstrosity from the world next door.

I leaned down and picked his card out of the dying embers. The surface was streaked with a little ash, but otherwise it looked clean and whole again.

"Just come inside, okay?" I said. "I'd like you to meet my family."

* * * * *

"So this is the famous federal agent," Ruth said, pulling a tray out of the oven. She eyed the seven-foot-something gray skinned Inspector with the usual amount of incredulity, but her smile was warm, and I knew things would be okay here. Being a good host was in Ruth's DNA.

"I'm still waiting on the pot roast, but please, make yourself at home," she said. "There's a closet in the front hall if you want to drop off your jacket."

"Thank you, but I'm quite alright," the Inspector said in his gravelly voice. I noticed that his cigar had stopped spewing smoke, and in fact the cigar itself seemed to have flickered out of existence when I wasn't looking. I knew it was still there, though. The Inspector wasn't the Inspector without it. I could just barely make the thing out if I concentrated hard enough.

"Thanks hon," I said, giving her a kiss on the cheek. Then I gestured for the Inspector to follow me into the dining room. Ruth and I had already laid out the plates and silverware, and I could hear Rory and Stephen arguing with each other through the ceiling, probably angry over some video game. The Inspector took a graceful seat and stared down at the tablecloth as if he'd never seen anything like it before.

"Thanks for doing this," I said.

"It's highly unusual," the Inspector replied. "But I appreciate you thinking of me."

I nodded. The two of us fell into an awkward silence, broken only by the clatter of Ruth working in the kitchen.

"I'm glad you're here," I said at last. "Fighting this fight with us. Because you know we wouldn't stand a fucking chance without you, right? We'd be like ants waging war on a boot. This is the least I can do."

The Inspector nodded dimly, but didn't say anything; the boys had smelled the pot roast and were now wandering into the dining room, still bickering about quick scopes and hit points and other things that were surely outside the understanding of an old fart like me. They glanced at the Inspector but somehow seemed to find him less interesting than video games. They joined us at the table as Ruth walked in with a steaming platter of pot roast and green beans and mashed potatoes.

And so we ate. Or at least the puny mortals at the table ate; the Inspector would bring bits of food to his mouth, and the food would disappear, but I never saw him actually chewing. Probably shoving it all into a pocket dimension or something. Thank god no one else seemed to notice. I think most rational minds censor that sort of stuff to avoid the risk of going bonkers.

Ruth, bless her heart, spent most of the meal trying to engage the Inspector in conversation and learn more about his supposed job with the government. And even though he mumbled that most of it was classified, he spun some surprisingly detailed anecdotes about life in the "agency" and his many grueling years in Washington. I mean, don't get me wrong; I knew the Inspector was good. But I hadn't expected him to be such a fantastic bullshitter.

It wasn't the greatest of get-togethers, but it wasn't bad either, and eventually the Inspector settled into the closest thing he was going to get to comfortable. Even Rory and Stephen did their part to make him feel included, complimenting his fedora and passing him seconds on the pot roast. They tried to play it cool, but I knew they liked it when I brought coworkers over for dinner. The detective life isn't exactly glamorous, but to twelve- and sixteen-year old boys, it's the coolest thing on wheels.

I was halfway into my green beans when the police radio on the counter crackled to life. "*Pursuit on Bear Street,*" said the voice of the chief. "*Suspect is tall, white, mid-30s, name of John Whedon. Last spotted leaving the Hanging Rock bar around 5:30. All officers in the area converge on Bear Street immediately.*"

"Oh shit!" Rory said through a mouthful of mashed potatoes.

"Rory," Ruth said in her warning voice. Rory's cheeks flushed and he hastily swallowed his food.

"Sorry Mom," he said. "It's just, they're finally going to catch that son of a... that jerk."

The Inspector looked around the table, his brow

furrowed. I noticed he'd given up the pretense of eating his meal. The cigar was back in his mouth, and he was chewing thoughtfully on the tip.

"Turn on the TV," Stephen said. "Maybe they've got it on the news."

Under other circumstances I would never have left dinner half-eaten, but this was a big case, one of the biggest in years, and I could feel the buzz permeating the room. I got up and headed into the den. The rest of my family trailed behind me as I picked up the remote and flicked over to the local news. I was dimly aware of the Inspector joining us, his eyes hidden below his fedora.

"Look!" Rory exclaimed.

Lena Dashner, head anchor of Glade News 5, was in the process of outlining the Whedon chase. "The suspect was on trial last year for the murder of his longtime girlfriend, Pacific Glade sweetheart Marcy McKenna. Although he was acquitted, new evidence has come to light that has brought his guilt into question." Two images flashed onto the screen: Whedon, a flat-faced man with blank eyes, and the poor dead Marcy. The picture they'd used showed her laughing at some celebrity gala, her teeth a gleaming white and her dark hair falling in a cascade over her shoulders.

"Police warn all citizens that Whedon is suspected to be armed and very dangerous," Lena went on. "If you see him, *do not approach him* and call the police immediately." The image shifted from Marcy's face to an aerial view of Bear Street, where no less than seven cop cars were gathered around the Hanging Rock. They looked like a group of flashing mechanical lions surrounding their prey.

"They're finally going to get that bastard," Rory blurted.

"Rory!" Ruth said again.

"What?" he said. "We all know he did it. It's about time he gets what's coming to him."

I glanced at my oldest son. Stephen wasn't nearly as outspoken as Rory, but there was a hardness in his eyes, and

I knew he agreed. We had all loved Marcy. No one had rested easily this past year knowing her killer had escaped justice. Honestly, it was about goddamn time for this asshole to get his just desserts.

"Mark?" the Inspector said quietly. "Can I speak with you in the kitchen?"

I tore my eyes away from the screen, where the squadron of cars had left the Hanging Rock and were now wailing down the length of Bear Street. "Sure," I said. We met up by the kitchen counter, where the police radio still spat out details of the Whedon chase. The Inspector glared at the device and it instantly went quiet.

"This doesn't seem… off to you?" he asked.

"I'm not sure what you mean," I replied.

The Inspector frowned. "That report said John Whedon was accused of murdering Marcy McKenna sometime last year. But Marcy is still alive. Or at least, she was two weeks ago. We spoke to her, don't you remember? At the radio station. When we were working our last case."

"You must be thinking of someone else," I said. "You weren't here when it happened, Inspector, but the McKenna case was big news last year. It was, like, JFK big for us. I think we all remember where we were when we heard what happened." I lowered my voice and looked warily toward the den. "He stabbed her thirty-seven times, Inspector. With a pair of scissors. They almost couldn't recognize her when they found the body."

"I'm not mistaken," the Inspector said, with a touch of irritation. "It was the same name, the same face. Do you really not remember?"

I tried to think back to that earlier case, to picture the woman we'd talked to at the radio station, but I only got as far as the hallway full of doors - everything past that made my head ache, like the throbbing of a potential migraine. I shook my head.

"I'm sorry, but my memory's fuzzy," I said. "I think I would remember talking to a dead person though."

"Something strange is going on here," the Inspector murmured, mostly to himself. "A thought specter? A doppelganger? But that doesn't explain your memory lapse... hmm." He began to pace the kitchen. "This is going to require some further investigation, I think."

Lena Dashner was still talking about the Whedon case in the other room, and a dim part of me registered that as being weird; this was a big story, sure, but wouldn't she have moved on by now? And yet another, stronger part of me wanted her to keep on going. I wanted to hear every detail of the chase, to watch as the police drew closer and closer to the fugitive, their lights flashing, their sirens blaring a warning across the Neverglades. Hell, I even wanted to be on the scene when they caught him. My fingers twitched, and I was struck by a sudden urge to jump in the car and join the hunt - an urge I did my best to suppress.

"For the record, I think this a wild goose chase," I told the Inspector. "But if you think something fishy's going on, I'll help you look into it. For Marcy's sake."

The Inspector nodded, but he still looked perturbed. "I'll wait outside," he said. Then he was gone, out the door in a cloud of yellow smoke.

A real social butterfly, that one.

* * * * *

Instead of heading to the police station, the Inspector had me pull over next to the Pacific Glade community library. Getting there proved surprisingly difficult, because I kept having to stop to let streams of marching pedestrians past. They were swarming into the streets, most of them clutching blunt objects of some kind. I saw a lot of baseball bats and golf clubs and the occasional weed whacker. At one point I waited at an intersection for five minutes for the wave of walkers to let up.

"What on earth are they doing?" the Inspector asked.

"It's Whedon," I said. "Gotta be. He made a lot of people really angry and now that he's being chased by police I think their tempers finally boiled over. They want to find him first."

I paused as a burly man wandered past the windshield, clutching what was very clearly a rusty axe. The Inspector and I watched as he lumbered down the street and disappeared around the corner.

"This is insane," the Inspector said. "I can understand people being angry, but this... this is a witch hunt. I think they truly intend to kill him."

I said nothing. Murder wasn't at the top of my list, of course, but I wanted Whedon punished as much as the next guy. And even though I was hardly going to take to the streets about it, I understood the impulse. People could only take so much injustice before they snapped.

The library parking lot was almost empty when we finally got there. I unbuckled and made a move to open the driver's door, but the Inspector held me back.

"I have a feeling we may need to leave quickly, so keep the car running," he said. "I won't be long."

"Okay," I said warily, but he was already gone. I watched as he swept up the front steps and slipped through the front entrance. I'll be honest - I wasn't totally sold on this plan. The place would only be open for another hour or so and I wasn't sure what he was expecting to find in there anyway. Plus the longer we idled here, the more time we were giving Whedon to get away.

I turned my eyes to the street and stared at the line of protesters as they passed. They marched with such purpose, such conviction, and I was struck by a sudden powerful impulse to leave the Inspector here and join the chase. My foot hovered above the gas pedal. It would be so easy to let it fall, to go tearing down the streets after the most hated man in the Glade.

But my thoughts were interrupted by the sudden reappearance of the Inspector in the passenger's seat. His brow was furrowed darkly and the smoke issuing from his cigar curled around his ears in purple spirals.

"You said the Marcy McKenna case was the big news story of the past year?" the Inspector asked.

I nodded.

"Then explain to me why I can't find a single newspaper article about the murder or the subsequent trial," he said.

"That can't be possible," I said, frowning. "I remember waking up to the headline: LOCAL CELEBRITY BRUTALLY MURDERED. The newspapers had a field day with that one. Everywhere you went people were reading about the case. I don't know how, but you must have missed something, Inspector."

He visibly bristled. "I promise you, I haven't," he said. "And another thing. You say Marcy was a local celebrity. Can you tell me what she was famous for?"

"God, I forgot how culturally illiterate you must be," I said. "Marcy did everything. She was Pacific Glade's big breakout; she had a major role in *Twin Peaks* back in the 90s and she did a lot of stuff on Broadway when her career really took off. She did charities and benefit shows and even shook hands with the President. She'd just come back to the Glade for a movie tour when she was murdered."

"Hmm," the Inspector said. "Interesting. Because when I ran a search for Marcy McKenna online, I didn't find anybody matching that description. There are a few people who share her name, of course - some of whom are moderately successful by human standards. But not Marcy herself. You'd think such a household name would be easy to find."

"What?" None of this made any sense. "I *clearly* remember watching her in *Twin Peaks*. She was one of Laura Palmer's friends from school - had a season long character arc and everything. There was a huge backlash when the network killed her off. Not that this means anything to you, of course."

"There is no Marcy McKenna credited in *Twin Peaks*," the Inspector said. "There is no Marcy McKenna on Broadway, either. And there is no record that Marcy

McKenna was ever murdered in Pacific Glade."

"What are you saying?"

"I'm *saying*, everyone in this town remembers a murder that never happened. They remember a celebrity who never was. There's no evidence that any crime ever occurred except your own memories of the event. And memories are malleable things."

"This is fucking absurd," I blurted, feeling suddenly angry. "You're telling me that the *entire Glade* has it wrong? That this whole thing is just a figment of our imaginations? I find it really fucking hard to believe that we're all sharing some hallucination."

"Two weeks ago the dead were rising," the Inspector said. "Compared to what we've seen so far, this is hardly an unusual case."

"I don't believe you," I said. It was hotheaded of me, granted, but I was seething inside for reasons I couldn't quite define. "I'm not going to let you shit all over Marcy's memory."

The Inspector moved faster than my eye could track, and suddenly his hand was on my forehead, his ashen skin cold against mine. The rage I'd been feeling melted away like an icicle in the hot sun. As the Inspector withdrew his hand, I felt stirrings of the anger come back, but they were faint, subdued; in some ways they didn't quite feel real. The emotion was artificial. It hadn't come from inside me.

"What the hell is going on here?" I asked quietly.

"I don't know," the Inspector said. "But I intend to find out. Does Marcy have a house here in town?"

"She shared a place with Whedon, as far as I remember. A ritzy place overlooking Catamount State Forest. But," I added, "as you've so helpfully pointed out, my memory's not what it used to be."

"You and half the town," the Inspector muttered. "Let's get going then. Whedon is running from a crime he didn't commit, and we have to break this collective delusion before the police catch up with him."

"Assuming the angry mob doesn't get there first," I said. The Inspector looked grim. "Yes," he said. "That too."

* * * * *

Said angry mob didn't make the trip easy for us, but once we got on the backroads things cleared up a bit more and we were able to drive down the street without any pedestrians getting in our way. The sun still stubbornly refused to set, so our way was lit from behind by a swath of brilliant orange light. My cruiser cast an elongated shadow onto the road in front of us.

The sunlight grew scarce as we entered Catamount State Forest, and the shadows of a thousand scraggly trees brushed against our own, creating a patchwork pattern. We rocketed through the woods, climbing higher and higher, the trees giving way to clearings with picnic tables and fire pits, until at last we rounded a corner and found ourselves face to face with Marcy McKenna's old house.

I had described the place as "ritzy," but it was a lot simpler than I remembered - just a one-story cottage with a ring of rose bushes and blue painted shutters. Not quite sure where the memory of opulence had come from. I parked the car and the Inspector and I got out. The shutters were all closed, and it felt like nobody was home; there was no car in the driveway and no sound from inside. The Inspector strode to the front door and rapped sharply on the wood.

"John," he said. "John Whedon. Are you in there?"

No response from inside. Unperturbed, the Inspector stepped down and circled around the house, sticking close to the line of rose bushes. I kept a hand on my holster and followed him. Halfway around the building we found a shutter that was hanging half open. The Inspector gingerly pried it all the way. The window behind it was blocked by a set of dark blinds that fluttered slightly, probably due to some inner ventilation system.

"Now what?" I whispered.

The Inspector gestured with one finger and the blinds

slid upward. Purple light spilled through the opening, so bright I couldn't look at it directly. I could make out the vague shape of it though. The light was streaming through a jagged gash in the air, a lightning bolt-shaped tear that floated impossibly in the middle of the living room. There were bookshelves and chairs and a solitary lamp, too, but the purple light gave them all a faded pallor, like it had sucked the color straight out.

The glow was so overwhelming I almost didn't see the person standing directly behind it. She was a dark-skinned woman, a little younger than me, wearing a flowing white blouse. Wind from the rift whipped back her hair and brought goosebumps to her outstretched arms. Her eyes were wide, but vacant, and the light flickered in them like dots of purple fire.

I recognized her at once. It was Marcy McKenna.

"She's *alive*?" I croaked.

The Inspector shot me a withering look and dropped the blinds again. "I'm not the type to say 'I told you so,' Mark, but honestly. What did you expect?"

"Not that!" I said, pointing at the window. "Jesus, I saw the crime photos after her murder and I still have nightmares about her hacked up face. I remember attending the funeral and watching her father break down sobbing in the middle of his speech. These things are *real*, don't you get it? I don't care if that really is Marcy in there. My memory tells me she's dead, and if I can't trust my own brain, what else do I have?"

"You have me," he said.

He strode to the front door, reared back, and smashed through the frame with one mighty kick. I watched numbly as the door teetered on its broken hinges and went crashing into the foyer. I was still too in shock to move, but the Inspector strode inside on those silent footsteps of his. His trench coat billowed out behind him.

The Inspector clearly didn't care about trivial human things like laws and property lines, but I did, and goddamn it - I couldn't just keep breaking into people's houses. Not even if the occupants of said houses were supposed to be dead. It took some serious effort to get my feet moving, but move them I did, and before long I was climbing over the busted door and into the front hall of Marcy's house.

I caught a whiff of the Inspector's cigar - it had a pungent, earthy smell - and traced the man himself to the room with all the light. He stood in the threshold and stared at the anomaly. It was even brighter in here than it was outside, and I could hear faint whispers for the first time: guttural words in some unknown language floating out of the rift. Marcy's shadow stood between us and the light, although "stood" isn't quite the right word; her bare feet hovered a solid three inches above the carpet.

"Marcy," the Inspector said, softly, the way you might speak to a dog that's been known to bite. "Marcy McKenna. Can you hear me?"

If Marcy heard, she gave no sign. The rift continued to whisper and the light continued to spill out of it, rippling like water.

"Don't!" I hissed, but the Inspector had already reached out and grabbed her arm. His grip was light, but her reaction was immediate and violent. She arched her back and let out a shriek that shook the glass in the windows. The waves of light took on a sharp, jagged quality and began to fire out of the rift like bullets. I ducked behind the closest bookshelf and winced as the light slammed solidly against the wood.

The Inspector was caught in the middle of the maelstrom, but he refused to let go of Marcy's arm. The light bullets ripped through his gray skin and left little puckered scars that drew no blood. Now Marcy was flailing, swinging her limbs in an effort to break free, but the Inspector's grip had tightened like a vise. He dragged her struggling, floating body away from the rift and into the front hallway.

"The door, Mark!" he shouted. "Get the door!"

I darted out from my cover and ducked as a bolt of light whizzed across my scalp. If those things could cut holes in the Inspector, I didn't want to think of how badly they could hurt a fragile little human like me. I ran into the hallway, gripped the door frame, and slammed it shut behind me. The light continued to pound against the other side but didn't break through.

Marcy had stopped flailing, and she wasn't floating anymore, either; cutting her off from the light seemed to have calmed her down. The Inspector loosened his hold but continued to keep her at arm's length.

"Can you hear me, Marcy?" he asked in that same soft voice. "Do you know where you are?"

She raised her eyes to him, and I saw a glimmer of that purple light still embedded there, like a tiny jewel in each of her irises. She looked between the two of us like a sleeper coming out of a deep dream. Groaning, she lifted a hand and rubbed it against her temple.

"I'm… in my house," she mumbled. "What… what are you doing here? Did you break in?"

"We only wanted to save you," the Inspector said. "We saw you were in danger and came inside to help."

I couldn't say a word; my tongue had glued itself to the roof of my mouth. Talking with her was like talking to a ghost. She was *here*, she was right in front of me, but a part of my brain that seemed just as sane and rational insisted that she was buried two miles away in Locklear Cemetery. I lifted a hand, as if to touch her, but couldn't bring myself to do it. The paradox was already straining my mind and I was afraid something critical would snap if I made physical contact with her.

"The whole town thinks you're dead, Marcy," the Inspector went on. "They're marching in the streets to find your killer. Why are they doing that? Don't they know you're here, that you're alive and safe?"

Awareness was coming back into Marcy's eyes, a cold soberness falling over her entire body. Her arm went limp in the Inspector's grip. She looked at him, then at me, the purple light flashing in her corneas. She didn't smile. And suddenly I was struck with a memory: swimming in the lake as a young boy, sinking deep, far too deep, kicking my legs in every direction as I tried to rise back to the surface, but even the sun was dark down here and I couldn't see which way was up, couldn't hold my breath, and blackness swept over me as pressure squeezed my lungs…

It was my memory. But it wasn't at the same time. Even though I could distinctly remember that afternoon in the lake, I was aware, somehow, that Marcy had implanted it in my head. It was like the surge of anger I'd felt at the Inspector earlier. It was inside me, but it had come from outside me.

"The real question," Marcy said quietly, "is if the whole town thinks I'm dead, then what the hell are you two doing here?"

The Inspector stiffened. Something dark had come into Marcy's voice, a bitterness that I didn't like one bit. She looked at the Inspector's hand like it was some sort of alien tentacle, but didn't try breaking free again.

"Is it you?" the Inspector asked. "Are you the one giving people these false memories?"

Marcy glared at him. The jewels of light spun in her eyes, and I got the sense that she was trying to broadcast some sort of nightmare into the Inspector's brain; but if it worked, he didn't show it. He chewed the end of his cigar and blew a pink smoke ring down the hall.

"So you effectively faked your own death," he said. "You turned yourself into a star and John into a pariah. But why? Why go to such extremes?"

In response, Marcy grabbed her arm and yanked back the sleeve of her blouse. The skin of her forearm was lined with thin horizontal scars. Some of them looked sore and fresh. I was struck with another memory that wasn't my own - dragging a razor blade across my skin, cutting ribbons into the flesh. The memory of the pain made my arm throb.

"Because John is an abusive fuck who deserves every second of this," she hissed. "Because he brought me so low that I mutilated myself for him. Because I can't hit back, but this town can hit for me. I made them love me. I can make them kill for me too. All it takes is one person to throw the first stone."

I felt chills run down my arms. The Inspector stared at her for a few long seconds, then pulled me aside so we could speak privately. He kept one eye on Marcy as he did so. She remained in her crouched position, in no apparent hurry to go anywhere.

"I'm the only one who stands any chance of closing that rift," he said. "You need to head back into town and contain the mob before they kill John."

"How?" I asked. "Christ, Inspector, there's so many of them and I'm just one guy. And how can I change their minds? I can't exactly tell them Marcy's alive. I'm looking at her right now and I *still* don't quite believe it."

"Listen to me," the Inspector said. "She may be controlling their thoughts and memories but she can't control their actions. Every choice they make is still a choice. If you appeal to their better nature, convince them that they're above such pointless violence, you might stall them long enough for me to do what needs to be done here. No one has to throw any stones today."

"What needs to be done?" I repeated. I looked past him at Marcy's slouching form, her eyes dark and wary.

"If we play our cards right, everybody survives the night," he said. "But that doesn't happen unless we act quickly. I can handle things here. You need to go - now."

My mind was on edge and I was pretty sure it had nothing to do with Marcy's mojo; this anxiety was one hundred percent home-brewed Hannigan. But I didn't let it keep me from moving. I left the Inspector in the hallway, ran back to my cruiser, and revved the engine. The house's front door was still knocked absurdly back on its hinges, and in the opening, I saw the Inspector's shadow lean over Marcy and pass a hand over her forehead. He looked like a priest issuing last rites to a dying patient. Marcy shuddered and went limp.

I backed out of the driveway and spun the cruiser around, but the route back through the forest was suddenly a lot more treacherous than it had been ten minutes ago, because the mob had spread. People roamed across the street in large clusters, everyone clutching a makeshift weapon, everyone looking ahead with cold, grim resolve in their eyes. I could barely go ten feet without another swarm of them stepping out in front of my car. My headlights washed over them, but no one looked back at me. It was clear there was only one thing on their minds: *Whedon*.

As I watched their procession move steadily down the street, I pictured a cliff in my mind, and the crowd pushing forward to the lip of that precipice. They could see it coming. There was plenty of time to stop, to turn around and return to safety. But they wouldn't stop. They would fling themselves gladly over the side, smiling as they plummeted to the bottom.

How could I talk that many people back from the edge?

* * * * *

I got maybe ten miles in before the crowd became so dense my cruiser had to stop in the middle of the road. I gave the siren a blare, lights flashing, but nobody spared me so much as a passing glance. I was dead in the water. Unless I was going to plow through this swarm of pedestrians, my car wasn't going anywhere.

"Fuck," I said. I killed the engine and squeezed my way out of the cruiser. The crowd was packed so tight I could barely get the door open. Instinct told me to take out my gun, so I slipped it out of the holster and edged my way through the sea of people.

"Move aside!" I barked, as loudly and forcefully as I could. "Police coming through!"

Now people were looking at me, and there was an

identical expression on all of their faces: anger, with a little bit of loathing. And I was struck by a sudden absurd thought: *I don't want the cops to get him. I want to get him myself.* Which made no sense, of course, since I *was* the cop here.

Marcy. It had to be. For a moment I had forgotten that she was alive in the first place, that Whedon hadn't killed her and she was broadcasting this anger into the town's collective brain. I shook my head and tried to focus on what I had seen at Marcy's, what I had to do now.

Stop the crowd before they kill Whedon. Stop them from throwing that first stone.

I had a feeling the crowd's anger would have devolved into violence if not for the gun in my hand. Still, they weren't going to make it easy for me. When I tried to push through the bodies closed in around me, blocking my way forward, leaving me just as stuck as the cruiser a few yards behind me. I swore again and craned my neck to stare over the crowd. Nothing but a thousand bobbing heads as far as the eye could see. With this kind of resistance there was no chance in hell of me making it to Whedon on time.

"Fuck this," I muttered. I reared back and elbowed the person next to me in the ribs. He was a small guy who clutched a garden rake like it was some kind of pole arm. He let out a cry and fell into the woman beside him, and boom, just like that - domino effect. The crowd's anger dissolved into sudden confusion. I took advantage of the opening and shoved my way through. The tree line was only a few yards away. If I could disappear into the forest, maybe I could bypass the worst of this mob.

The confusion lasted long enough for me to break through the edge of the crowd and plunge into the cover of the trees. To my dismay, dozens of other people had apparently gotten the same idea, because the woods were swarming with marchers. It wasn't nearly as packed as the road but getting through unseen was going to be impossible. And if Marcy was still broadcasting her hatred for all things police, any of these people could turn on me at any time.

None of them had brought guns, as far as I could see, but everyone had brought a weapon. Shovels, fireplace pokers, rolling pins. All sorts of household pain. If these people snapped, I'd be one messy corpse. And I wasn't sure I could shoot my own neighbors. Even if it was to save my own life.

I ducked behind a tree, stripped off my holster, and chucked it into a nearby bush. Thank god I was still dressed in civilian clothes - if I'd gone barging ahead in full police mode these people might have torn me apart. They didn't know I was a cop out here. Maybe, if I was careful, I could pass as one of them.

I kept my gun close to my side and moved quickly through the trees - not quite running, but close. Time was short and I was straddling a fine line between speed and secrecy. According to the radio in my cruiser Whedon's current location was still unknown, but things could change at the drop of a dime, and the second someone spotted him this whole gig would go up in flames.

My phone buzzed suddenly in my pocket, making me jump. I pulled it out and found a text from an unknown number. I skimmed it over, my fingers growing tight around the phone.

Catamount Campgrounds. Sequoia Lodge. They'll know any second now. GO.

The Inspector. It had to be. He must have gotten Whedon's location out of Marcy somehow. But if she knew where he was… then so did everyone else.

The crowd's attention shifted to the left, into the deeper reaches of the forest. And I knew too, all of a sudden, and it was so *obvious*, because Marcy had always called Catamount her second home, it was where she had met Whedon and it was undoubtedly where he'd go to feel safe and alone.

The campgrounds were less than a mile away. If I booked it I could be the first one to find that son of a bitch.

I fought the incoming waves of anger, but it was hard. I knew Whedon was no killer. I knew Marcy was alive and safe in her home with the Inspector. But the narrative she'd woven was insistent, and now that I was so far away, it was creeping back in. How could I have thought I'd seen a dead woman? How could so many people be so wrong about something so obviously true? We'd all seen the crime scene photos. We'd all been numbed by her loss. And we all knew who had done it. We knew Whedon was a murdering scum who had escaped justice because of a fluke in the system.

Maybe I had seen Marcy today. Or maybe I hadn't. The Neverglades were a hotbed of strange activity, and was it really so hard to believe that some supernatural force was responsible for my memories of Marcy's house? Hell, Whedon could have done it himself. I wouldn't put it past the motherfucker. He was no better than the things that lurked in the dark, no better than the monsters the Inspector and I had taken down.

I began to run. The people around me did the same, but they weren't chasing me; they were joining me. We moved with one mind, one purpose. I was suddenly leading the charge. Whedon was close by and we would be the ones to find him first. We would be the ones to bring justice to that piece of shit.

We ran for several minutes before the trees thinned out and gave way to log cabins and abandoned campsites. Catamount didn't get too many campers this time of year, so it would be perfect cover for a fugitive like Whedon. I'd taken Ruth and the boys here a few times over the last few summers, so I was roughly familiar with the layout. The grounds were deserted. Not a soul in sight.

The Sequoia Lodge was smack in the center of camp, and it would be closed right now. But I knew Whedon was somewhere inside. It was obvious, wasn't it? The place where he and Marcy had met, where they'd shared their first dance as a couple. Everyone knew the story. It only made sense that now, driven to desperation, he'd chosen here to make his final stand.

The Lodge was a sturdy building, with a mottled green roof and walls made of polished wood. The door was shut and presumably bolted from the inside, so I didn't bother trying to knock it down. Instead, I circled the building and looked for another way inside. I could feel the crowd behind me more than I could hear them: a buzzing energy, a surge of excitement threatening to spill over into bloodshed.

It didn't take long to find my in. There was a window on the side of the Lodge, maybe seven feet up, and small, but big enough to squeeze my body through if I tried. I looked around and found a large, smooth rock half buried in the dirt. I yanked it free, hefted it in my hand, and measured the arc from here to the window. I had played baseball a lifetime and a half ago, but I felt certain that if I let that stone fly, it would go soaring through that window in a spectacular shatter of glass.

All it takes is for one person to throw the first stone.

The words of a ghost.

I drew back my arm and flung the stone at the window. It broke through with a crash that echoed through the empty campgrounds. The crowd surged forward, and I found myself being hoisted up by hands I didn't know, until I was staring through the shattered pane at the dark interior of the Sequoia. I reached over the broken glass and unlocked the frame, then pushed it inward. Then I crawled through the opening and landed - less than gracefully - on the floorboards of the inner Lodge.

The room had once been filled with long wooden tables and folding chairs, but they'd all been pushed to the side for the season, and now the place was bare. A thin layer of dust covered most of the ground. Except - hang on. The coating wasn't quite even. There were patches where something had disturbed the dust, and not too long ago either. Patches that looked an awful lot like footprints. They stretched across the open floor and vanished up a flight of stairs into the upper Lodge.

"Whedon," I breathed.

Others were trying to clamber in after me, but I didn't wait for them to squeeze through. I lifted my gun and followed the trail of footsteps. The stairwell was dark, and I couldn't hear anything from upstairs except the thumping of my own heart - blood rushing like a river through my body. But I knew Whedon was up there. I had never been more certain of anything in my life.

The upstairs was a game room, a wide space with a scratched pool table and a few outdated arcade machines. Aside from the stairs there was a single exit: a door leading out onto a balcony that overlooked the flagpole and basketball courts behind the Lodge. I'd never been up here in my life but I knew these facts clearly, with a certainty so strong I could feel it in my bones. There were no steps leading from the balcony to the ground, and it was a three-story drop. Whedon had no route of escape that didn't go through me.

I clicked my tongue like I was scolding a bad dog and took a few cautious steps into the room. "Whedon," I whispered. "Come out, come out, you sick fuck."

The words didn't feel like my own, but they felt right coming out of my mouth; they suited the rage that was building in every corner of my body, like gathering storm clouds. Below me I could hear the crowd struggling to get inside, but I registered them distantly. Up here it was only me and Whedon. A cop and a killer. And I knew, one way or another, that justice would be served tonight.

The floorboards creaked; a body shifted. I turned my gun toward the old Pac-Man machine. My eyes had started to adjust to the darkness, and now I saw a shape curled up behind the game: a pair of legs drawn up against a broad chest. Anger churned in my gut, but I approached the machine quietly, cautiously. When I looked around the side,

I saw Whedon sitting there in the fetal position, a baseball bat in one limp hand and an expression of abject misery on his face.

I had no words left in me to express my hatred, so I lifted my gun instead, my finger drawing back the safety. The ensuing click made Whedon look up. He didn't look surprised to see me there, or scared, or angry; just defeated.

"Well?" he said. "If you're gonna do it, do it. It's better than what I deserve. After what I did to her."

Tears leaked from his eyes, and I hesitated, but only for a fraction of a second. There were other footsteps coming up the stairs now. Soon the crowd would be on top of us, and if I didn't do this now, they would do it for me. And I couldn't have that. I didn't care about glory, or fame, but I knew had to be the one to set things right.

The gun was cold in my hands, but my aim had never been surer. One bullet and this would all be over. It would be easy. Hell, Whedon himself was begging for it. He'd put down the baseball bat and was staring up at me with despair in his watering eyes.

"Do it!" he yelled, his voice trembling. "END ME!"

My finger tightened around the trigger, I could feel the pressure as the bullet prepared to exit the chamber, and then it would be his brains against the wall, and the mob behind me could do what they pleased with his miserable corpse -

But something lifted my hand at the last second, and even though I pulled the trigger, the shot missed Whedon by miles. A tiny hole appeared in the wall, letting in a pinprick of the setting sunlight. I looked at the hole, then my gun, then the figure cowering, bewildered, underneath the Pac-Man machine. And I felt horror shoot through me, stronger than any surge of anger, and entirely my own.

I dropped the gun, my hands shaking. Whedon stared up at me like a coma patient waking up for the first time in decades. He wasn't the only one. There was a crowd of people standing behind me, but they looked confused, as if unsure of how they'd gotten here or why they had come in the first place.

As for me? The only word that came close to how I felt was "violated." I felt like I'd just come out of a nightmare, but instead of fading, as dreams do, the details grew sharper with each passing second.

Every choice they make is still a choice.

Marcy had amplified the crowd's aggression - she'd removed inhibitions, made people more susceptible to mood swings and bitterness and fits of rage. But she couldn't force anyone to do anything. Which meant that my neighbors were capable of mob violence. It meant that I could put a bullet through a man's head in an act of vigilante justice and not bat an eye. I'd never seen that aspect of myself until tonight, and it scared the hell out of me.

What else was I capable of?

The mob had ceased to be a mob, and a few people had already drifted toward the stairs, breaking the group into several directionless blobs. I picked up my gun and tried to slide it into a holster that wasn't there anymore. Whedon got to his feet, wandered into the dissipating crowd, and vanished from my view. No one seemed to notice or care that he was there. Any animosity they'd felt toward him had evaporated like a puddle on a hot day.

I followed the stragglers outside and emerged into a forest cloaked in darkness. The sun had finally set while we were inside and Catamount had turned into a ghost camp. I thought of my abandoned cruiser, parked in the middle of the road, and the long, dark walk back to civilization that lay ahead. It made me want to cringe. Mostly, though, I just felt empty.

It had been a long sunset. But I had a feeling it was going to be an even longer night.

* * * * *

My entire body was aching by the time I got back to the station, but I felt the tiniest twinge of relief when the Inspector greeted me in my office. It was strange - the last case we'd covered had left me with a scorched uniform and third-degree burns, and yet today I felt like I'd been through the worst wringer of my life, even though I hadn't sustained a single injury this entire mission. I hadn't even cut my hands on the broken glass in the Lodge.

"How did you call her off?" I asked. "You didn't…"

"I didn't kill her," he said. "I talked her down."

I blinked. I'm not sure what I had expected to come out of the Inspector's mouth, but it certainly wasn't that.

"We had a conversation," he said. "About John. About what he'd done to her. I sympathized with her plight and told her that John would certainly be punished for what he'd done, but this wasn't the way to do it. Humans have their own special brand of justice but they are not gods. They can't just smite the people who oppress them, or they lose what makes them human in the first place."

There was a long silence. "It's funny, isn't it?" I said. "That out of the two of us, you're the one who understands humanity the most."

The Inspector's cigar puffed out a cloud of warning red. "Cruelty and abuse are not unique to your kind," he said. "Neither is vengeance. Neither is hatred. These are not foreign concepts to someone like me. I may understand them better than you do, even with all your years on the force, even with all the things you've seen. I know humanity because on some baser level, we aren't so different."

He looked away and blew a single red ring toward the door. "But love. Devotion. Togetherness. These are things I only understand because I have observed them for so long, the same way your scientists understand atoms and molecules, and the subtler workings of the universe. But like them, I will never know everything. Some things will always be a mystery to me."

I clapped him on the shoulder, surprising - I think - both of us. "And you'll always be a mystery to me too, buddy," I said. "But we work well together. Don't you think?"

He actually smiled at that. "Yes," he said. "I would have

to agree."

"I know I ask this a lot, but is it really over? I'm not going to wake up in the middle of the night and go on a sociopathic rampage?"

"If you do, it won't be Marcy's fault," he said. "I managed to close the rift that was feeding her. Her powers have already started to dwindle, and by this time tomorrow I suspect they'll be gone completely."

"Finally, good news for once." I took a seat at my desk and stretched back in my chair. The tips of my fingers were trembling, but I laced them together and placed them behind my head, hoping the Inspector wouldn't notice.

By all accounts tonight had been a victory. Everyone had survived the night, as the Inspector had promised. But it still felt like we'd lost the battle. If Marcy had held on a second longer, I had no doubt that I'd have placed a bullet between Whedon's eyes. It didn't matter that I hadn't done it in the end. Something real, something dark and dangerous inside of me, had reared its head tonight. And you couldn't shove a thing like that back into the darkness.

"I know you must be exhausted," the Inspector said, eyeing me suspiciously, "but I think you should write all this down. What happened tonight. If you wait too long, some of the important details might slip away."

I eyed the stack of paperwork on my desk with some distaste. The idea of putting this night into words brought an unpleasant taste to my throat, like rancid bile - but maybe this was just what I needed. A chance to confront this ugly part of me, to get it down on the page where I could dissect it and define it and keep its hideous face from surfacing again. At least for now.

So that's what I'm doing. It's ten o'clock in the evening and I'm still here with my pen and this cheap pad of yellow paper. Ruth knows I'm safe at the station, so that's one less thing to worry about, and the Inspector has gone off to do whatever eldritch detectives do when there's no mystery to solve. It's just me. Me and this thing inside of me.

I haven't felt it stir since the game room at Sequoia Lodge, but I know it can't have gone far. These things never do. I thought writing about it would make this easier but it's only made me more paranoid. It reminds me of what I'd said to the Inspector back at Marcy's: if I can't trust my own brain, what else do I have?

You have me, the Inspector had said.

And you know…. maybe that's good enough.

* * * * *

I would have stopped writing there, but somewhere around four in the morning, after I'd headed home and kissed Ruth goodnight and slipped under the covers, I realized I couldn't sleep. So I snuck downstairs to get myself a glass of milk or something, and lo and behold, the Inspector was standing in my kitchen. It's a good thing I hadn't gotten the glass out yet or I probably would have dropped it right on my toe.

"Inspector," I said, in a voice that was a little more than a whisper. "What the hell. Did somebody kill the pope or something? Why are you here?"

"I can't just drop by and visit?" he said, with a contorted half-smile. "Everything isn't always death and darkness, you know."

I got the sense he was telling a joke - the Inspector? Surely not - but for the love of me I couldn't figure out the punchline. I shook my head and walked past him to the row of cabinets.

"Not that I don't appreciate your lovely mug and the cloud of pollution that comes with it, but you should really go," I said. "If Ruth or one of the boys comes downstairs they're gonna flip."

The Inspector gave up all pretense of smiling and grew solemn. "I'm sorry to intrude in your home, Mark," he said. "But I need you to tell me what happened tonight."

"Tonight?" I asked. "I mean, tonight was tonight. Nothing fancy. Dinner with Ruth and the kids and an evening of garbage television. The usual stuff."

The Inspector shook his head. "No. I want you to tell me about Marcy, and what happened when you caught up with John. I need to hear it from your own lips."

"Marcy who?" I asked. "Honestly, Inspector, I have no idea what you're talking about."

He sighed. "In your bag, Mark," he said. "There's a pad of paper. I want you to read it."

"There's nothing in there except a moldy banana," I said, but I humored him, grabbing the bag from its perch on the counter. "Are you sure you haven't lost your marbles, Inspec…?"

But I trailed off. There was something else in the bag, all right. When I drew out my hand, I was holding a yellow notepad. The sheets were crammed with a tight scrawl that was unmistakably my handwriting. The only problem? I didn't remember writing it.

"What the hell?" I frowned.

"Read it," the Inspector said, a smoky snake curling from his cigar. "Then we can talk."

So I did. I read until the lip of the sun was poking its face above the mountain peaks on the horizon and my kitchen was lit up a garish pink. When I finally looked up, the Inspector was staring at me, his eyes focused and unclouded by smoke.

"This happened?" I asked. "All of this? But I don't remember any of it. I don't even remember writing this down."

"It happened," the Inspector said. "I suppose if you looked hard enough you could find proof. Clippings from the evening news. Video footage from a child on their cell phone. But no one will be looking for proof, because no one has a reason to. As far as Pacific Glade is concerned, the last twenty-four hours never happened."

"But you remember, don't you?" I said. "You're not like the rest of us."

He didn't answer me - at least not directly. He walked over to the patio window and placed a slender hand on the glass. "I went back to Marcy's house early this morning," he said. "Something felt off and I suspected it was because of her. But the place was empty. She'd packed her bags and left town within hours of the incident. But not before carefully using the last of her power to excise all memories of her from your heads."

"But that's crazy," I said. "A person can't just... erase themselves. Surely someone's gotta remember her."

"On our last case," he said suddenly, "with the being in the radio. Who helped us down at the station?"

"It was just the receptionist," I said. "Hell, Inspector, I don't even know her name. She had glasses? Brown hair? She showed us the broadcast rooms and told us about the old station. Why are you asking?"

"Because your memory is wrong," he said. "There was a receptionist, yes, but *Marcy* was the one who helped us. *Marcy* told us about the old station. You don't remember her because she doesn't want you to remember. She found the thread connecting you two and snipped it - along with all the other threads in town."

I was starting to feel dizzy, so I took a seat. "There's no way a human being could do all that," I said. "Even if she was juiced up on alien mojo."

"She was very powerful," the Inspector said lightly. "More powerful, I think, than she knew. But it's irrelevant now. The world has forgotten Marcy McKenna. I'd say she's dead, but even the dead are remembered."

I looked out the patio window, blinded by the sunrise. "Why do you think she did it?" I asked. "She could have just made us forget this whole thing happened. Why did she completely erase herself?"

"I think," the Inspector said, "she was looking for a fresh start. That's where our conversation veered last night. And what better way to start over than a clean break from everything or everyone you ever knew?"

I picked up the notepad and flicked through it absently. It disturbed me, honestly, how I couldn't remember a single shred of this - how detached I felt from the Mark Hannigan who wrote these words. The guy in these pages didn't feel like me at all. Never in a million years could I imagine myself in some act of vigilante justice. Hunting down monsters was one thing. Hunting down a disliked citizen and riddling him with bullets was another beast entirely.

"I ought to be going," the Inspector said. "Your family will be awake any minute. But please, don't hesitate to call me again. Even if it is just for dinner."

I managed a smile somehow. "Will do," I said.

The Inspector tipped his fedora to me, ever so slightly. Then he strode to the patio door and disappeared back into the glaring sunlight. I watched his silhouette for as long as I could before the sheer brightness forced me to look away.

Sunrises in the Neverglades aren't weird like our sunsets; the sun follows a perfectly sensible path upward until it's hovering in the sky like it's supposed to. But that morning the sunrise seemed to stretch into one elastic moment, leaving the kitchen in shades of vivid pink and orange. I watched the light creep slowly up the wall, thumbing through the papers in my hand. Then I rose from my seat and dumped the entire notepad into the trash.

I didn't remember Marcy, and I probably never would, but I figured it was best to give her what she wanted in the end. Fresh starts weren't such a bad thing, really.

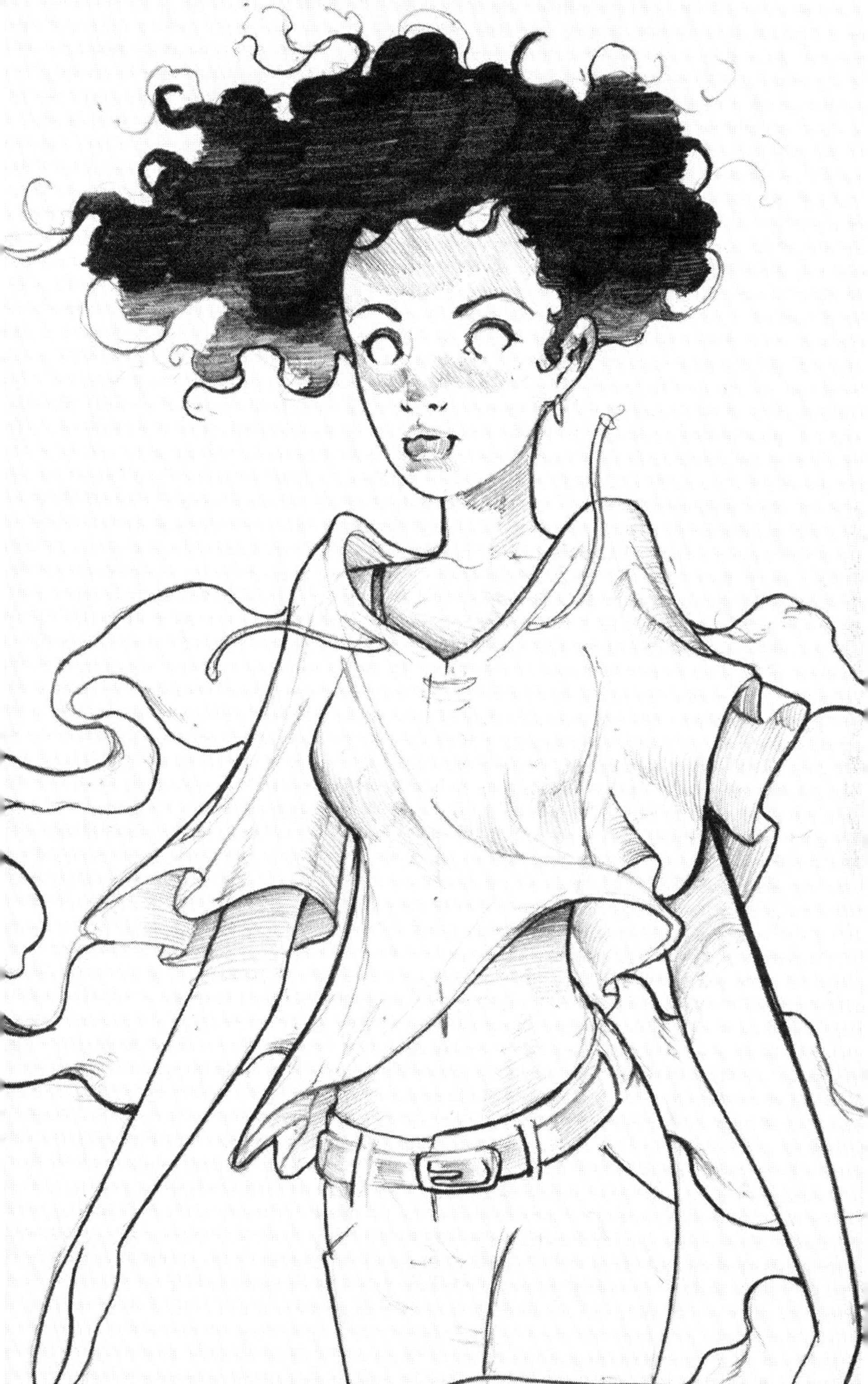

The Wendigo

Everyone in the force knew Marconi had a girlfriend, and it wasn't a big deal. We sometimes saw her hanging around the station when Marconi was getting off her shift. She was a kind-faced woman: frizzy brown hair, thin where Marconi was stocky, always wearing something bright and flowery. Marconi didn't say much about her personal life so we knew very little about this mystery visitor. I don't think we even knew her name. She was just another fixture around the station, like Larry the Drunk Wonder, who we brought in to the holding cells every Friday like clockwork.

But when she came to the front desk one misty morning, we almost didn't recognize her at first. She'd traded her floral blouse for a subdued gray shirt and jeans, and her frizzy hair was tied back in a tight bun. It didn't look like she was wearing any makeup. Abigail Shannon - our newest recruit - was working the desk that day, and she gave the visitor a dim smile.

"Name?" she asked.

"Janine," the woman answered. "Janine Zimmerman." She swallowed nervously. "I'd like to report a missing person."

I was busy grabbing my third coffee of the morning, but when I heard the tremor in her voice, I turned to look at her. She didn't seem to know what to do with her hands. They played at her hair, then fell to the counter, then drummed a rhythm on her thigh. Eventually she settled for wringing them the way one might squeeze a wet dishcloth.

Abigail pulled out the necessary forms and grabbed a pen from the top drawer. "Can you give me the name of the missing person?" she asked.

A sense of dread crept over me, and I knew, even before she opened her mouth, what name she was about to say. I placed the coffee pot back on the counter before it could slip from my sweaty hands.

Her voice faint, Janine said, "Olivia Marconi."

* * * * *

I ducked into the men's room, lit up the Inspector's card with my pocket lighter, and dropped the flaming piece of plastic into the sink. By the time the fire had died down and I'd returned to the main office, the Inspector was already there. He and Nico Sanchez were ushering Janine into one of the interrogation rooms down the hall.

I slipped in behind them before the door could close. Sanchez offered the flustered woman a chair and sat down across from her. The Inspector and I remained standing. I noticed that his cigar was smaller than usual, closer to a cigarette, really, and the smoke issuing from it was thin and wispy. I wondered what had caused the change.

"Why don't you walk us through what happened," Sanchez said in his best good-cop voice. "When did you notice the Sheriff was missing?"

Janine tugged at the sleeves of her shirt. "Um," she said. "Well, she didn't come home this weekend. We had dinner plans on Saturday but she didn't show up and she didn't call to cancel. I thought she might have been on extended patrol or something but I couldn't reach her cell phone to check in."

I had noticed Marconi's absence but had assumed the same thing as Janine: some patrol or stakeout had kept her away from the station for a while. Even so, the fact that she hadn't gone home at any point was enough to set off warning bells. It wasn't like Marconi to go so long without keeping in touch. Hell, I could barely get through most mornings without her grilling my ass for one thing or another.

"Do you know what case she was working on?" the

Inspector asked quietly.

Janine looked unsure, so I answered for her. "Marconi was looking into the whole thing with those missing campers. Some local teenagers went hiking in the Catamount Forest three weeks ago and haven't been seen since. She's been combing the area looking for any trace of those kids."

Both Sanchez and the Inspector turned to look at me. I probably shouldn't have spoken, but Janine's anxiety was getting to me, and Marconi's safety seemed a lot more important than sticking to procedure. Janine bit her lip and nodded.

"Yes, that sounds right," she said. "I think I remember something about that."

The next step seemed obvious to me: book it the hell out to Catamount Forest and scour the trees for Marconi and those missing campers. I was just about to grab Sanchez and organize the rescue mission when Janine spoke up again, and hoo boy, was that the kicker that changed everything.

"I know where Olivia went," she said faintly. "She was taken. By the wendigo."

You could see the precise moment when Sanchez slipped over from sympathetic to skeptical; his brow curled up a bit, his mouth tucking into a frown. The guy had never had the greatest poker face. I looked to the Inspector for help, but if the word "wendigo" meant anything to him, he didn't show it. He only stood there and ground the tip of his cigar between his teeth.

"It lives in the forest," Janine went on, oblivious to the room's sudden shift in mood. "It used to be human, but not anymore. It preys on lost travelers and brings them back to its lair to feed. I saw it once," she added, as if that settled the matter.

Sanchez rose from his chair and gestured for us to talk outside. The officer shifted his belt and led us out into the hall. Through the two-way mirror, we could see Janine stare numbly into space, her hands still trembling.

"The lady's nuts," Sanchez concluded. "Marconi's probably got no reception in those woods, that's why we haven't heard from her. 'Wendigo' my ass."

"So Janine is upset and making up stories to cope," I said. "That doesn't change the fact that no one's seen the Sheriff for days now. Sanchez, if there's even the slightest *shred* of a chance Marconi is missing, we've gotta act on that. You know how important the first forty-eight hours are."

The officer looked disgruntled. "I hear you, Hannigan," he said. "But we can't just drop everything and go stomping through the woods looking for her. We don't have the men to spare for an operation that huge."

"Then I'll go with the Inspector," I said. "We'll canvas as much of the forest as we can. If things get gnarly we'll get the hell out of there and call for backup." I glanced at my otherworldly partner, who hadn't said a word since we'd stepped outside. He nodded simply.

Sanchez shrugged. "Your choice, detective. Just keep an eye out for Bigfoot while you're out there."

Then he was gone, and it was just me and the Inspector standing outside the interrogation room. The tall figure looked paler than I'd even seen him. His grayish skin had taken on the complexion of ash.

"This... wendigo," I said under my breath. "Is it real?"

The Inspector pondered the question for a few seconds. "No," he said. "Not as Janine describes it, anyway. Something in those woods may be hunting down campers, but I doubt it was ever human."

I ran a hand through my hair and sighed. "More monsters. Great."

"This could be quite dangerous, Mark," the Inspector said. "We have no idea what kind of entities are out there. Are you sure you want to do this?"

"Marconi needs me," I replied. "And so does she." I gestured to the woman sitting alone behind the glass.

Janine had stopped shaking, but she was still staring out at nothing, her hand lying limp on the table. As we watched, her fingers closed slightly, then relaxed - as if gripping an invisible hand, for however brief a moment.

*****

The Inspector rode with me to the Catamount Visitor's Center, which seemed as good a place to begin as any; plenty of dirt trails wound away from the center, and the lost campers, as well as Marconi, would surely have started their hike from here. I pulled my cruiser into the sandy lot and killed the engine. The place was nearly deserted - only a few other vehicles sat beneath the shadows of the treetops. The Inspector and I headed for the center and pushed open the stained wooden door.

A young couple huddled in the corner over the wall of travel brochures - tourists in the Glade, always a rare sight - and a grizzled man in the back was thumping the side of a vending machine, which seemed to have swallowed his dollar. The Inspector and I headed to the information desk, where a gray-haired woman in enormous green-rimmed glasses sat reading a home improvement magazine.

I cleared my throat. "Excuse me," I said. "I'm Detective Mark Hannigan, and this is Inspector… Smith, from the FBI. We were wondering if you happened to see a woman in a sheriff's uniform come through this area in the last couple of days."

The gray-haired woman - presumably Sheila, given her name tag - set aside her magazine and squinted up at us. "You mean Olivia?" she said. "Nice lady. I see her down at the grocer's sometimes." Her voice was high and sweet, like she'd ingested something syrupy.

"That's her," I said, glancing at the Inspector. "You're saying she was here recently?"

"Oh yah," she said. "Looking for those campers, you know. Poor things." She began to leaf through her magazine again, as if that settled the conversation.

"Did she say where she was going?" I asked.

Sheila waved a hand toward the door. "Said something about checking out Timberwolf Trail. I told her, that's the one the campers took, you know." She flipped the page and peered up at us. "You boys looking for them too?"

"Something like that," I muttered. "Thank you for your time."

I gestured to the Inspector that we were done here, and together we headed for the exit. But just as I was reaching for the doorknob, it twisted on its own, and the door flew open from the other side. Standing at the threshold was Janine. She had a camo backpack slung over her shoulder and a water bottle dangling on a strap from her wrist, but otherwise she could have come right from the police station.

"Oh," she said.

I grabbed her arm and ushered her down the stairs, the Inspector trailing behind us. The door to the visitor's center swung shut with a low creak. When we were safely out of anyone's earshot, I let go of Janine's arm. I hadn't switched to bad cop mode in God knows how long but I could feel that old side of me starting to resurface.

"What the hell were you thinking?" I hissed. "Half a dozen people have gone missing in these woods and you were just going to wander in all by yourself? Did you even bring *any* sort of protection?"

Janine's eyes grew hard, and all of a sudden I saw the same steel in there that I'd seen so often in Marconi. "For your information," she growled, "I have a compass and a map of the area and the sharpest pocket knife I bet you've ever seen." Then she drew up her baggy shirt, and I saw a pistol tucked into a holster at her waist.

"And I've got this bad boy," she said. "Is that enough protection for you?"

I looked to the Inspector, but he had a wry smile on his face, and I knew I was on my own here. I rubbed my temple and began to pace under the porch light.

"We can't let you go in there alone," I said at last. "Even with a gun, it's just too dangerous. You don't know what's out there."

"Of course I do," she said. "It's a wendigo. I told you back at the station."

I wasn't sure why I was suddenly being so skeptical - between the two of us, I'd probably seen more weird shit than she would in her entire lifetime - but I just couldn't bring myself to believe in Janine's mystery monster. "And that's going to take it down, is it?" I said, gesturing to her gun. "Your wendigo?"

"No," she said. "Of course not. This is for bears or mountain lions. The wendigo has its own weakness." She swung the backpack around and unzipped the top pouch. Inside was the largest pile of flares I'd ever seen.

"It's like Frankenstein's monster," she explained. "Can't stand the sight of fire. If it gets too close, I'll light it up."

"Or burn the forest down, more like it," I muttered.

Janine zipped up the bag and gave me a long, pensive look. "I have to do this," she said. "Olivia's counting on me. If someone you loved was in danger, Detective, what would *you* do?"

The sympathy card. Damn. Because Janine very well knew that I'd go to the ends of the Earth - and further - for my wife and my children. I'd be a dirty rotten hypocrite if I stopped her from doing the same.

"Fine," I said. I shook my head and sighed. "So you're going wendigo hunting. Doesn't mean you're going in there alone. The Inspector and I are coming too."

Janine looked between us, then shrugged. "Couldn't hurt, I suppose. But you're going to need some supplies first. Sheila can stock you guys up before we go."

"How long are you expecting to be out here?" the Inspector asked. In the shade of the trees I couldn't see his face at all, just a blank stretch of shadow with a speck of embers at the bottom.

Janine shifted her backpack over her shoulder and looked somberly at him.

"As long as it takes," she replied.

* * * * *

Ten minutes and a backpack full of hiking essentials later, the three of us finally started down Timberwolf Trail. It was a simple dirt path, littered with bumpy rocks and crunchy fallen leaves. Every so often we passed a streak of yellow paint on a rock or a nearby tree. Even without the trail markers, I had a real hard time imagining the campers losing their way. Unless they were complete idiots and had wandered off to explore the woods on their own.

A low, thin mist hovered over the landscape, and Janine's form looked a bit fuzzy as she stomped her way along the trail. She had taken the lead without a word, mainly because her long impatient strides kept leaving me in the dust. I shifted the straps of my new backpack and tried to catch up with her.

"So… this wendigo," I said. "You told us you saw it before. Where was that?"

Janine ducked under a stray branch. "I was on a camping trip with my aunt and uncle," she said. "I was young - maybe twelve or so. We were gathered around the campfire when we heard these enormous crunching footsteps and saw a shadow the size of a house moving through the trees. My uncle grabbed a log from the fire and waved it at the shadow, warning it to get back. It stopped for a few seconds - like it was deciding what to do. Then it turned around and disappeared back into the trees. I didn't know what I had seen, but then my uncle told me the legend of the wendigo, and how it's stalked these woods for centuries." She looked at me earnestly. "I believed him. After what I'd seen, how could I not?"

I glanced at the Inspector, unconvinced, but he didn't seem to be listening. His head was turned to the trees and his eyes were hidden. He didn't duck under the low branches, but they avoided him all the same, somehow sliding past him without moving an inch. Looking at him for too long made me mildly dizzy, so I turned my eyes back to the trail.

Eventually the path tapered off and turned into a leafy clearing, with a warped picnic table and the charred remains of a makeshift fire pit. Janine led us to the table and took a seat, rummaging through her backpack. She pulled out a plastic baggie packed with trail mix and offered it to me. I took a tiny handful of nuts and raisins, popped them in my mouth, and handed the bag back to her. The Inspector politely declined when I offered some to him. He seemed distracted. The thin smoke from his cigar drifted into the nearby trees, as if searching for something.

"We should keep moving," Janine said after a minute or two. She stowed the bag away amid her stack of flares and rose from the table. I wasn't nearly as spry as I used to be and a few more minutes of rest would have done me good, but Janine was antsy, and she had every right to be.

"The campers must have spent the night in this clearing," I said, looking around. "But they had time to pack up their stuff and keep moving. Whatever happened to them didn't happen here."

Janine nodded. "We have to go deeper."

I turned to call the Inspector and nearly jumped out of my skin - he'd somehow approached us without crinkling the leaves under his feet. Maybe it was my imagination, but even his clothes seemed more battered than usual. There were scuffs on his fedora and smudges of something dirty on his trench coat. He said nothing, only tilted his head at the disappearing Janine.

I hastily followed her back onto the trail. The mist had thickened while we were resting and the branches ahead poked like crooked arms out of the gray. Janine's outline, only a few yards away, was barely more than a smudge. I scrambled across the leafy, muddy rocks until I caught up with her. The Inspector glided along behind us, his shadow as thin as the trees.

"How did you meet Marconi anyway?" I asked Janine, brushing aside a low-hanging branch.

"My nephew's a Boy Scout," she replied. "He'd gotten

his Eagle rank and the troop was hosting a court of honor to celebrate. Olivia had helped with his project so she came to the ceremony to give a short speech about him. We met at the dinner party afterward. She was… she was the first woman who'd ever shown interest in me." She looked down at the ground and smiled. "I liked her. She can be blunt - you must know what she's like, working with her and all - but she's kind, and honest, and she has a good heart. We went on a few coffee and dinner dates before making things official."

I tried to imagine Marconi cozying up in a coffeeshop or getting dressed up for dinner on the town. It was surprisingly hard. I knew she must have a life outside the precinct, that she didn't always wear uniform blue or tie her hair back in the tightest of ponytails. She had people who loved her, who saw more than just the badge. But I'd known her for so long that my image of her had just stuck. To me, she'd always be my pain-in-the-ass sheriff.

"You're married, right?" Janine said. "How did you two meet?"

I shrugged. "High school sweethearts. I know, I know, it's straight out of a sitcom, but that's how it happened. We had a lot of the same classes together and eventually we just got talking. It always felt easy with Ruth - I never felt like I was posturing, trying to make myself look good for her. I was just me. And she appreciated that."

My shoes squelched in the mud. "We went to separate colleges, but eventually we found our way back to the Glade. Everyone does - you know how it is. And we just picked up where we left off. Two years later we were married."

Janine's hand drifted away from the strap of her backpack. Her fingers curled inward, like they had at the station, as if clutching for a hand that was no longer there. Then she lowered her arm.

"I was going to propose," she said quietly. "At dinner this weekend. And when she didn't show up, I thought… I thought she knew somehow, and I'd scared her away. I couldn't sleep at all that night. And then she wasn't there the next morning, and she never called to say why, and I knew that something else had happened. Something had gone horribly wrong." Her voice hitched. "I don't even care about the proposal anymore. I just want to know she's safe."

I reached out and placed a hand on her shoulder. She looked over at me, her green eyes sad and empty.

"We'll find her," I said. "You have my word."

Janine tried to smile. Her cheeks creased, then slackened. She looked down at the ground again. Then she quickened her pace, trodding through the muck, until she was back to being a vague shadow on the trail ahead.

* * * * *

It took another twenty minutes for us to find the first real sign of a disturbance. I had just rounded a particularly tight corner on the mountain trail when the mists parted and I saw Janine standing in front of a charred, blackened tree. The trunk had been cleaved straight down the middle, causing both halves to droop to either side and leaving a small opening in the center. Sap bled from a series of long, deep gashes in the bark - what was left of it, anyway.

"Was it struck by lightning?" I asked, catching my breath.

"I don't understand," Janine said. "The wendigo hates fire. Why would it burn a tree like this?"

"Because it's not a wendigo," the Inspector said from behind us. He strode forward and ran a thin finger along the trail of drying sap. I thought for sure he was going to taste the stuff, but he simply rubbed his fingers together, leaving sticky strands between them.

"I've seen this before," he muttered. "A long, long time ago. Long enough that I thought they'd gone extinct."

"They?" I asked, not sure I wanted an answer.

"A tribe of empathic giants," the Inspector said. "Brutes, most of them, but they figured out how to tear open the rift long before any of us. Their way is messy, destructive; they leave scars whenever they cross between worlds. Scorch marks, poisoned rivers, acid rain. That made it easier for me to track them down."

Janine was staring at the Inspector in baffled silence, and hell, I didn't blame her; we'd officially taken a left turn into crazytown. Wendigos were one thing. This... this was something else. I backpedaled a bit and tried to parse through what the Inspector had just said.

"Empathic giants?" I repeated. "What does that mean, exactly? What are we going up against?"

The Inspector knelt by the tree and ran a hand along the blackened wood. "They feed on emotions," he said. "The time eater we faced swallowed up years, but these creatures, they swallow happiness. Fear. Depression. Hope. Each has a particular taste, and it feeds slowly, keeping its victims in stasis until it can suck them dry. Then it excretes this sap" – he held up his sticky fingers – "and moves on to the next world, the next food source."

Something else about the Inspector's story had unsettled me, but before I could pin down what it was, Janine found her voice. "This thing feeds slowly?" she asked. "So there's still a chance that... that Olivia might be alive?"

I stared at her. The first time I'd heard the Inspector spout his alien gibberish, I'd resisted it – and who wouldn't? There just wasn't room in my worldview for beings from outside time and space. It had taken cold, hard evidence for me to erase that doubt. But there was no doubt in Janine's eyes. And I knew, just as she had believed in the wendigo, that Janine believed the Inspector too. She'd believe any narrative that got Marconi home again.

"There's always a chance," the Inspector said cautiously. He rose back to his full seven feet. "Keep in mind, though, that by all rights this beast should be dead. It's been lurking here longer than you can possibly fathom. Which means it must be hungry. And hungry beasts aren't known to play with their food."

Janine yanked the pistol out of her holster and pointed the gun past the charred tree, into the heart of the mist. "A chance is a chance," she said quietly. "That's enough for me." Then she leaped nimbly over the crack in the wood and hurried into the fog.

I shared a glance with the Inspector. "'Longer than you can possibly fathom'?" I whispered. "How fucking old *are* you, man?"

The Inspector's eyes were hidden, but the face beneath his fedora looked grim. "Old enough to know what kind of danger we're walking into," he said. "But let's hurry. We can't let Janine get too far ahead."

There was so much more I wanted to ask him, but he had a point. We'd have time to talk later. Hopefully. I drew my own pistol, and together we climbed over the splintered remains of the tree and into the underbrush.

* * * * *

The Inspector was right: whatever we were following had left a whole mess in its wake, which at least left us a clear path to follow. Trees had been torn from their roots and blasted backwards off the trail. Some of the trunks were still smoking. The dirt had a radioactive tint of green, and the leaves under our feet grew crisper and blacker with every step. There was even a hint of ozone in the air. I had felt that same crackle at the abandoned radio station a few cases ago, and my fingers tightened around my pistol at the memory.

Janine stayed ahead of us, but never disappeared totally from view; I could always see her shadow climbing over rocks and brushing aside half-visible branches. The fog was getting even worse. The Inspector, in all his grayness, seemed to melt into it. I couldn't tell if his cigar had stopped smoking for once or if the mist was so dense I couldn't make out the difference.

"Guys?" Janine called back to us. She had stopped several feet away and was staring at something I couldn't see from this distance. I clambered forward and peered into the fog. At first I wasn't sure what I was looking at. Then a twinkle of red flashed in front of me, and I took a startled step back. The air shimmered like waves rippling outward on a body of water. As I continued to stare, I made out vague shapes in the ripples: a single gnarled tree, a pool of brackish water, distant red mesas on a flat horizon.

"It's a rip," the Inspector said. "A doorway to another dimension. The entity's been here, which means - *Janine, no!*"

Without warning, she had run forward and plunged head-on into the shimmering wall of air. There was an enormous sucking sound, like water slurping down a drain, and then Janine's figure was running through that otherworldly red desert. She had made a beeline for the grimy oasis, and suddenly I saw why: there was a body slumped on the ground by the water.

"Marconi?" I whispered.

I started to follow her, but the Inspector grabbed my arm. "Stop!" he hissed. "You have no idea what's behind that rip. The air could be toxic, the sun could burn you alive, there could be worse monsters than a wendigo slumbering there, waiting for prey to wander by -"

"Doesn't matter," I said. "If there's even a *chance* Marconi's alive in there, I have to take it. You get that, don't you?"

The Inspector looked dubious, but after a few tense seconds, he let go of my arm. I didn't wait for him to follow - I raised my gun and hurried after Janine, leaping into the world beyond the rip.

For a second the mist was replaced by a brain-splitting white void, and I felt like my body was being stretched, like a piece of human taffy. Then the world snapped back into place and I was running across a sea of gritty red sand. A surprising chill tickled the skin on my neck, despite the enormous sun that hovered precariously in the orange sky. The air seemed breathable, at least, but there was a distinct aftertaste of copper on my tongue that I didn't like one bit.

Janine had stopped running and was now staring down at the slumped body on the sand. Fearing the worst, I approached her - but it wasn't Marconi. The corpse in question was a teenage boy wearing tattered khakis and a large beige backpack. His eyes bulged out of his head like peeled grapes and his hair had turned entirely white. Sinewy green vines sprouted from his skin and dug into the ground like a tangle of thick wires. As I watched, the vines pulsed, sending bulbs of faint green light from the body into the sand below.

"I guess we found one of the missing campers," I muttered, covering my mouth and nose. The coppery stench was ten times worse over here.

The Inspector approached from behind me and knelt down over the camper's corpse. His fingers traced the pulsating vines, his brow furrowed. The smoke from his cigar was a thin, weak shade of gray.

"Fear," he said. "This particular entity likes to feed on fear. I suppose our poor friend here was afraid of starvation, or isolation, or maybe just wide-open spaces. In any case, he's been bled dry. There's nothing we can do for him now."

I looked up from the body, feeling mildly sick, and stared off at the horizon. There was something funny about it. I took a few steps past the oasis, and I realized - there *was* no horizon. The ground literally ended after a hundred feet or so. The mesas weren't distant, they were just incredibly small.

I turned in circles. For a second I forgot about the dead body. The oasis was smack dab in the center of this desert, and the desert itself was barely more than an island, floating impossibly in that orange sky. If I walked for a minute in any direction, I'd reach the end of the world.

"Inspector?" I asked. "What is this place?"

The Inspector straightened up and looked off at the fake horizon. His skin looked sicklier than usual under the light of the massive sun.

"Hmm," he said. "I've heard the empathic giants could

create pocket universes to store their food, but I've never actually seen one before. Supposedly they slow the flow of time to keep the victim alive longer, giving the entities a food source for years. Centuries, even."

I looked back at the rippling air that led to the misty forest. Through the rip, I could see leaves swirling in a sluggish tornado on the ground, inching along like footage from a stop motion film.

"Olivia's not here," Janine said. She left the camper's body and strode past the gnarled tree. There was another rip not too far away, I noticed; this one spilled over with a green light the color of unripened fruit. Janine approached the tear, set down her backpack, and pulled out a flare from her stockpile. She lit the fuse with a battered lighter and let the flare fall to the sand. Bright red lights spat from the tube and cast shadows across the ground.

"Bread crumbs," she said. "If time is slow here, this'll last a while. All we have to do is follow it home again."

Then she shouldered her backpack and stepped into the rift. There was a familiar slurping sound, and she was gone.

I looked at the Inspector. He wasn't smiling, exactly, but I could see the faintest glint of admiration in his eyes.

"Come on," he said. "Before the flare burns down. We have to follow her."

Together, we hurried forward - my body stretched like the world's largest elastic - and then the world snapped back into place. This time we were standing in a sparsely furnished room, its roof open to a roiling green sky. The wood in the walls stretched up until the planks came loose and floated, disjointed, in the void. Janine was already examining the next body. This one was a young woman in jeans and a denim vest, her hair a gleaming white and her dead fingers clutching at a shattered flashlight. The same pulsing vines draped over her corpse and vanished into the woodwork.

"Dammit," I muttered. "We're too late."

There was no point in poring over the poor girl's body,

and besides, Janine had already moved on. There were no doors out of this room, but another rip floated in the air by the far wall. This one emitted a purple glow the color of decaying violets. Janine lit another flare, dropped it on the floorboards, and stepped into the portal. The Inspector and I were right on her heels.

And so it went. Rip after rip, world after world, we trekked through increasingly bizarre pocket dimensions. One looked like the skeleton of some vast creature with three spines and a jawbone the size of a small house; the portal was buried at the base of its tail. Another was turned completely upside down, so that we had to find our footing on a narrow strip of land or fall up into a starless void. Everywhere we went we found more bodies. None of which were Marconi's, thank God, but it still made my stomach turn to see those poor dead campers with their pale skin and bulging eyes.

At every stop, without fail, Janine lit another flare to mark our progress. I wondered if she would ever run out of those things. At one point I looked back and saw a dizzying tunnel of flares, a string of lights flashing in scattered, slow-moving patterns. I just hoped they wouldn't go out before we found Marconi.

There was no sign of the wendigo, or the giant, or whatever the hell we were chasing here, and for a while I thought we might make it to the end of this cosmic maze without running into the damn thing at all. But then the last portal dumped us into a huge cave covered with glowing specks of lichen, and there it was: a hulking, humanoid shape slumped in the corner, so quiet and so still it might have been a statue. But I knew it was the wendigo. The crackle of ozone in the air was so strong I could feel my nose starting to bleed.

"Olivia!" Janine hissed. And there she was. Marconi was propped up against the wall of the cave, still wearing her sheriff's uniform, vines slithering from her exposed arms into the rock. From this distance I couldn't tell if she was breathing. The images of the camper corpses wouldn't leave my head, and when Janine broke into a run, I was only a few steps behind her.

Our footsteps were muffled by the blanket of lichen on the cave floor, but I had no idea if the wendigo was asleep or resting or just faking it, and I wasn't going to make a ruckus in order to find out. At one point Janine and I had to stop due to a deep chasm that opened up suddenly in front of us, leaving us only with a narrow footbridge. The bottom of the pit was too far down to make out but I could see the glint of sharp stalagmites jutting out of the darkness. The two of us crossed the bridge as quickly as we dared, the Inspector gliding along behind us on his usual silent footsteps.

Once we were safely on the other side, Janine rushed to Marconi and cupped the sheriff's cheeks in her hands. There were definitely strands of gray in her hair, but her eyes were closed, and the rise and fall of her chest was unmistakable. Marconi was alive.

I almost sank to my knees in the lichen, I was so relieved. But Janine was tugging at Marconi's shoulders now, and the sheriff refused to budge; the vines were wrapped so tightly around her she was bound to the cave wall. Every few seconds, pulses of bright green light traveled down the vines, sliding from her arm into the wall of stone. Janine tried yanking at the vines but they were embedded deep in Marconi's skin. The pulses grew brighter, as if sensing Janine's resistance, and Marconi shifted slightly inside her tangled prison.

The Inspector appeared suddenly by my side. "I don't mean to rush you," he said, his voice low and oddly calm, "but we have company."

I whirled around. The hulking shape in the corner had risen from its crouched position, and now a behemoth of a shadow blocked out the light from the glowing lichen. Before I'd thought of it as humanoid but there was something… wrong about it, something about the curve of its limbs and the blocky, misshapen head slumped on its broad shoulders. It was too dark to make out its facial features, if it had any at all. I couldn't tell if it had skin or scales or fur or feathers. It was just darkness, darkness made solid, and I could only stand and stare as the beast took a rumbling step toward us.

I lifted my gun, for all the good it would do, but the Inspector moved before I could. One second a man was standing in front of me, and the next - well, it's hard to say. Outwardly the Inspector looked the same, but I had the strange sense that he'd grown to enormous proportions, like a giant squeezed into a tiny body. It reminded me of that night he'd shown me his true form on the highway. The figure I knew was just a vessel, a puppet, its strings being yanked by something large and invisible. Looking at him made my head throb.

The Inspector reared back and punched the shadowy beast. His fist struck like a meteor, leaving a fiery imprint on the creature's hide, causing it to bellow and stumble back. The floor of the cave trembled with each footstep. For half a second I hoped it would fall backwards into the chasm, but the wendigo only took a second or two to regain its footing. It lumbered forward and batted at the Inspector with a clawed, misshapen hand.

I fired a single shot at the incoming limb, but the bullet sank into its hide with a sound like a muffled *thwump*. Then the Inspector was flying across the cave. His whole body went limp, as if the invisible puppeteer had left it, and when he struck the far wall he slumped into a curled position on the ground. The cigar dropped from his lips and rolled away. Its tip smoldered for a second or two, then went out.

"NO!" I shouted, feeling something snap inside me. I fired another three shots at the wendigo but the bullets only seemed to irritate it. It turned its monstrous head to look at me, and I saw a bulbous globe of eyeballs peering out of its skull, each one bloodshot and vaguely human. It took a threatening step forward. A tremor swept across the ground and knocked me off my feet, whacking my hand against the stone and causing the gun to skitter out of my grip into the darkness.

I didn't bother looking for it; what was the point? This thing had already proven itself immune to bullets and if the Inspector couldn't leave a dent on it, what fucking chance did I have? I looked to Janine, as if to apologize - but she wasn't staring at me, or even the wendigo. She had managed to pry a few of the vines off of Marconi's face and was kissing her on the lips, tears streaming down her cheeks.

Another step, another tremor. Rocks came loose from the walls and tumbled around our feet. If one of those came down on our heads we'd be done for, wendigo or not.

The creature was leaning down now, blinking its mismatched eyes. I scrambled back against the wall, but there was no time to stand, no time to run - just to cower. The wendigo swung its massive hand downward, the air whooshing as it did so, and I found myself thinking suddenly of Ruth's face - Ruth and the kids - and I closed my eyes so I could see them one last time -

Then the wendigo faltered. I opened my eyes. Its hand had halted, hovering, just a few feet above our heads. For a second I thought, absurdly, that my memory of Ruth had somehow stopped the creature in its tracks. Then I saw that Marconi was standing. She had her hand on Janine's shoulder, and even though a web of vines still trailed from her skin into the wall, her eyes were awake and clear.

And she was *pissed.*

"Hey, shit-for-brains!" she yelled. "Why don't you back the fuck up?"

The vines pulsed, but instead of the usual green, a hot red light traveled down Marconi's arms and into the stone. The wendigo yowled like a wounded mountain lion and lifted its hands to its ears, as if Marconi's voice had ruptured whatever passed for its eardrums. Marconi took a step forward, and the vines moved with her, snaking across the ground.

"You don't scare me!" she shouted. "You fucking Bigfoot wannabe!"

The wendigo made a series of dissonant yaps and staggered backwards. The cave trembled again, and I leaped aside as a boulder the size of a minivan came crashing down where I'd been standing. Marconi and Janine didn't seem bothered by the potential cave-in. They stood together, framed in the light of the lichen, two small figures in all that trembling vastness.

"And one more thing," Marconi said. She'd lowered her voice, but it still carried through the cavern as if she'd spoken through a megaphone. "Stay the *fuck* away from my friends."

The wendigo took another step back, but its foot slipped on the lip of the chasm, and suddenly it was plummeting like a felled sequoia. The enormous dark shape slipped out of view. I was afraid to move - what if it came crawling out of the pit, more pissed off than ever? Then something black and gooey spurted upward, followed by the loudest and most agonizing howl of pain I'd ever heard. The walls gave one final tremble. Then the cave fell silent.

Janine let out a choked laugh and flung her arms around Marconi. The vines had slipped from her skin like desiccated IV tubes, shriveling into nothing on the cave floor. Marconi wrapped Janine in a tight squeeze and spun her in a circle, her hiking boots barely brushing the ground.

"Goddamn," I breathed. "How the hell did you do that, Marconi?"

The sheriff noticed me for the first time. Her hair was streaked with gray and her cheeks were gaunter than I remembered, but the smirk on her face was one hundred percent Marconi. I hadn't realized how much I'd missed that smirk.

"Should've known you'd be involved in this shit, Hannigan," she said. "And *you*. Of course *you're* here."

I turned to see the Inspector approaching us, and relief flooded through me so strong I felt a little dizzy. His body didn't seem to have taken much of a beating, but his trench coat was torn and dirty, and his fedora had been knocked askew. The cigar was back in his mouth. It was still thin though, barely more than a cigarette, and it didn't smoke at all. The tip simply glowed a low orange.

"You son of a bitch," I said. "I thought you were done for."

The Inspector's smile was faint. "Yes, well, I've been through worse," he said. "But I'm afraid we don't have time to stand around celebrating. Now that the giant is dead, this universe, and all the ones it created, will come undone. We have to go."

I peered through the gloom, trying to make out the flash of Janine's flares amid all the lichen. And there it was - bright orange sparks spitting in slow motion. We had to cross the footbridge to reach it. Even as the thought crossed my mind, a rock fell from the ceiling and smashed through one of the wooden planks. That familiar trembling picked up again, and this time, I was afraid there'd be no stopping it. A loud keening sound filled the air and made my eardrums rattle.

"Can you walk?" Janine asked Marconi. The sheriff took a few shaky steps and nodded. Supporting one another, the two of them moved toward the footbridge as quickly as they dared. Rocks continued to fall around them - pebbles mostly, although there were some large chunks in there too, and one glance across the skull would cut our journey short in a second.

"We need to go, Mark," the Inspector said in his warning voice.

There was no time to search for my gun, so I hurried after the couple, arms shielded against the plummeting debris. The bridge groaned and creaked under us - it was almost as if the wood was decaying before our eyes - but we made it across in one piece, and together we lunged for the exit. The portal slurped around us, stretching us like an agonizing rubber band, before snapping us back and dumping us in an apocalyptic wasteland. Ten feet away, Janine's flare sputtered and went out.

"I see the next one!" she shouted. A hot wind had picked up, bellowing in our ears. The tremors of the cave had followed us here, and cracks were zigzagging across the dried soil. Janine held on to Marconi as we staggered through the wasteland toward the source of sparkling light.

Portal after portal, we emerged in worlds that were falling apart. The upside-down universe had been knocked askew, so we had to cling to the ground or fall sideways into space. The rickety old house had developed a sinkhole in the floor that we had to creep around. The ribcage of the massive creature had splintered and our way forward was almost buried under piles of jutting bones. In that case, and in a couple others, the Inspector had to lift the debris out of our way so we could climb through and move on.

The desert world had split into several distinct chunks, and I was worried that Marconi wouldn't be able to cross it in her condition. But she clutched Janine's hand and leapt over gap after gap, the Inspector and I trailing after them, until at last we reached the window out and stumbled back into Catamount State Forest. The Inspector turned back to do something to the portal - there was a loud wrenching sound, like someone tearing a branch off a tree - and when I glanced behind me, I didn't see anything except misty forest. The pocket universe was gone.

I was beyond fatigued, and I'm sure the others were too, but we didn't stop to rest. We were deep in mountain lion territory here and it wouldn't do to get too complacent. So we followed the trail as fast as Marconi could manage, clambering over fallen trees and squelching through the mud. We didn't stop until we reached the empty clearing where the poor lost campers had set up their fire pit. Janine and Marconi took a seat at the picnic table, but the Inspector stood off at the edge of the clearing, staring out into the forest. I went over to join him.

"You haven't been you lately," I said. "Ever since we

started this case. You look tired, your skin is sickly - hell, even your cigar looks different. What happened to you?"

The Inspector's lips tightened around the aforementioned cigar. He let out a heavy breath, but only a few wisps of steam curled around the tip, and they were gone in no time. He sighed, took the cigar out of his mouth, and tapped some ash onto the leaves.

"I don't belong here," he said quietly. "I never did. Sometimes I forget that. Being in your world, helping you fight these entities - it gives me purpose, but it drains me. I can only stay here for so long, only exert so much of my energy, before I need to return home. To recharge, if you will."

"Is that where you went in the cave?" I asked. "After the wendigo attacked you?" I remembered the way his body had slumped against the stone, how his whole form looked hollowed out. "It was like the lights went out in your eyes."

"I retreated, yes." The Inspector reached up and adjusted his fedora. "For a minute or so. I didn't want to leave you, but the giant had wounded me badly, and survival is an instinct we all share. I thought a quick dip behind the rift would give me enough strength to fight the creature again. But when I returned, Sheriff Marconi had the situation under control."

He was twirling a small object between his fingers, I saw now: a thin gray capsule with bulbed ends and a large crack running through the middle. Across the center, a peeling label in faded red letters read CAPRA.

"What's that?" I asked.

The Inspector glanced at me, then pocketed the capsule. "Something I need to look into further," he said. "But nothing you need to concern yourself with. Not yet." He let out another reedy wisp of smoke and said, "Perhaps you should check on Sheriff Marconi."

I could take a hint. Leaving the Inspector to himself, I walked over to Janine and Marconi at the picnic table. The sheriff seemed to have regained some strength. The hand clutching Janine's was firm and pink, and there was a rosy glow to her cheeks that had been absent in the wendigo's cave. The two women looked up at me when I approached.

"You never answered my question back there," I said. "How did you beat that thing?"

Marconi turned to look at Janine. Her hand clenched, and I saw Janine return the gesture: that same squeeze of closeness, this time with a hand to grip back.

"Janine told me it fed on fear," she said. "So I gave it the opposite."

Of course.

I took a seat next to the two women and stared out into the forest. The mist was starting to clear, even as the sky was darkening, and the tree branches stretching out in front of us seemed to float in a dusky cloud. A mountain lion yowled somewhere in the distance. Fireflies drifted through the twilight. The forest was alive, and we were alive, and even though we hadn't been able to save everyone today, I felt good.

"You realize I'm in this now, right Hannigan?" Marconi said. "One hundred percent. If anything else comes after the people I love in this town, I want to help. And I want to know *everything* that's going on with you and that tall drink of water over there."

I looked back at the Inspector. In the darkening light he looked more like a statue than ever; the tip of his cigar could have been one of the floating fireflies. I thought of him tearing that cigar from his mouth and igniting the old radio tower. I thought of him wrestling with the time eater at the lip of Skokomish Bluffs. He was a dynamo, a source of incredible power, and it was strange to see him so dimmed. We'd been through so much, the Inspector and I, but I wondered if I would ever really know the guy.

"You got a couple of hours?" I said. "This could take a while."

And as the forest turned to night around us, I told them everything.

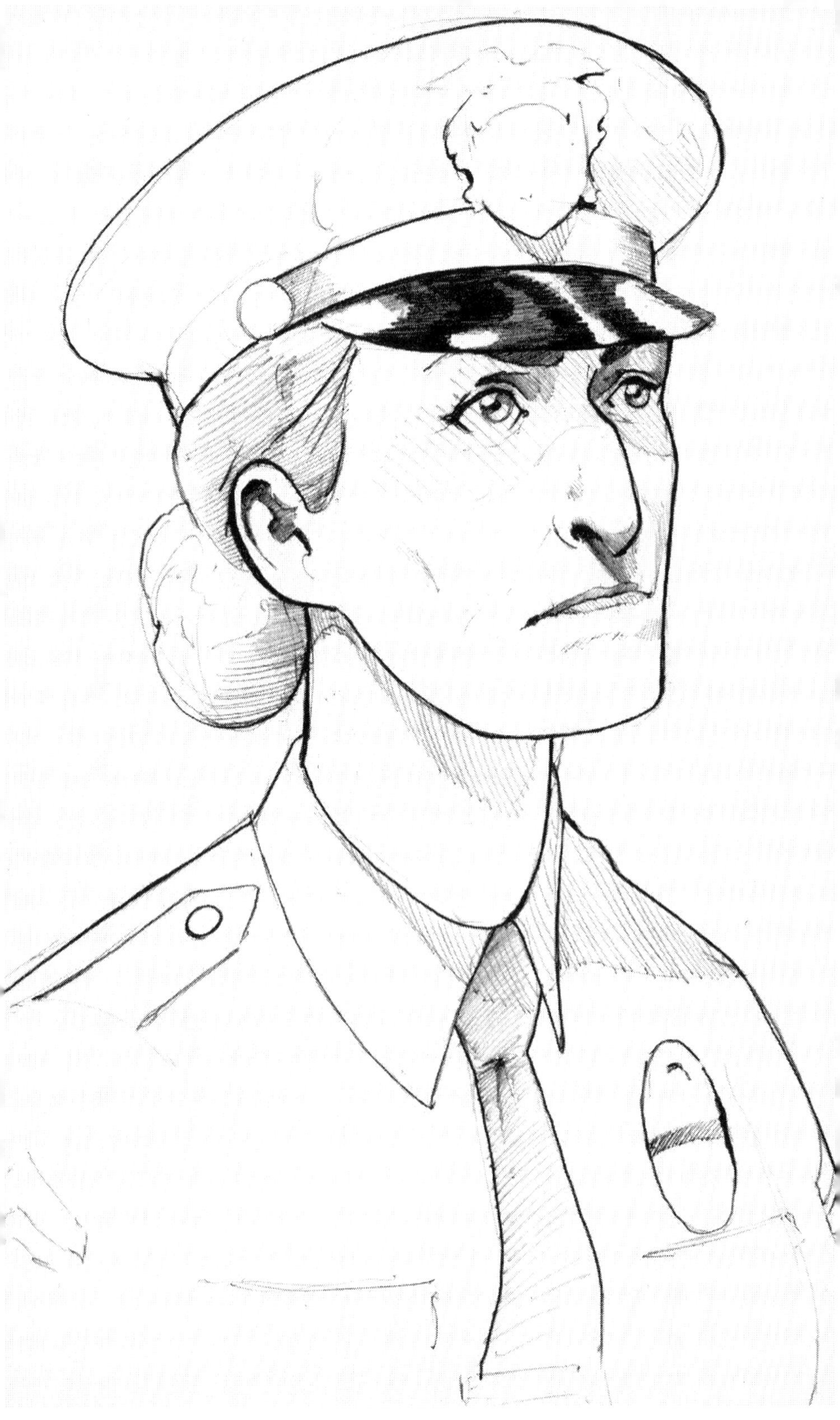

PURPLE MOON

Sometimes you close your eyes to a nightmare, and sometimes you wake up to one.
Case in point. Last night I woke up from a restless dream where large, swooping shapes chased me through a nightmarish version of the Neverglades: gutted storefronts, dead grass, inhuman beasties crawling out of cracks in the street. It freaked me out, and I was glad when I finally opened my eyes and escaped from that hellscape. It took me a few seconds to realize that my bedroom had turned purple.
I rubbed my eyes, still a bit delirious, and waited for the illusion to clear. I hoped I hadn't popped a blood vessel or something. But my eyes felt fine, and the room stubbornly remained its unusual color. There were little specks floating in the air, too - larger than dust motes, but just as wispy. I took a breath in and accidentally inhaled a cloud of the tiny things. They tasted like shreds of charcoal.
"Ruth?" I whispered. "I don't mean to wake you, honey, but…"
I reached out to touch her arm, but found my hand sinking into a sticky puddle. I looked over and my stomach did a somersault. Right where my wife had been lying, an angular globe of light hovered a few inches above the bed, dripping viscous black tendrils onto the sheets. The light had the same purple sheen as the rest of the bedroom. I withdrew my hand quickly and wiped it on my pillowcase, my heart pounding.
"Shit," I muttered. "Shit shit shit."
A thought struck me, and I leapt out of bed. I hurried down the hall to the boys' room. When I flung open the

door, there were two more dripping orbs floating in midair where Rory and Stephen were supposed to be. I slammed the door and leaned back against it, trying to gather my thoughts.

The Inspector, my brain insisted. *Get the Inspector.*

I scrambled back to my bedroom. Yesterday's jeans were draped across the dresser, so I rummaged through the pockets until I found my lighter and the Inspector's calling card. I didn't want to stay in this room - just glancing at that globe of light made my skin crawl - so I took my stuff and headed downstairs. Swaths of purple light gave the kitchen a sickly glow. I retreated to the sliding window and flicked the beaten-up lighter.

The tip lit up with a feeble spark, then went out.

"Come on, *come on*," I mumbled. I tried over a dozen times, but the lighter only gave off a few more pitiful sparks before dying completely. I chucked the useless thing into the corner. It rattled off the stove and disappeared underneath the fridge. Desperate, I placed the Inspector's card on one of the oven burners and turned on the heat. Nothing. The coils didn't even glow.

"Inspector," I said. I cleared my throat, then raised my voice - who was I going to wake, anyway? "Inspector, you'd better get your pasty ass over here, because my family's turned into a bunch of alien lava lamps and everything's gone purple -"

I stopped. For the first time, I'd caught a glimpse of the night sky through the back window, and I stepped closer so I could see it better. The moon had swelled in size, and its crater-riddled surface had turned as smooth as a sand dollar - except it was a vivid purple. There were no stars surrounding it. The sky itself wasn't black, or blue, or even that distinct shade of violet; it was just a void. A high-pitched ringing filled my head as I stared into it.

"I'm not in the Glade anymore," I said numbly.

Or maybe, a nasty voice whispered in my head, *you're just seeing it for the first time.*

*****

If the Inspector wasn't going to come to me, I would have to go to him. My first instinct was to check the station. I had no idea how widespread this was, but if the world had turned purple and all the townsfolk had been replaced by those sticky orbs, surely the Inspector would be on the case. I pulled on some clothes, grabbed a jacket from the closet, and headed out into the night. It was colder than it had been yesterday. The air out here was full of those little specks, which floated past my face on a breeze I couldn't feel.

After five minutes of struggling with the engine, I had to begrudgingly accept that my car wasn't going to start. I yanked my old mountain bike off the wall in the garage, praying the tires weren't completely shot; it had been years since I'd given the thing a whirl. But the bike stood steady, so I resumed the old stance, my fingers gripping the handlebars with a little more force than necessary. I kicked off and sped down the road.

The Glade didn't quite look like the hellscape from my dream, but the similarities were there. The purple light made everything seem slightly off and turned perfectly innocent cars and houses into grotesque shadows of themselves. I stared at them and not the void overhead, which threatened to give me a migraine if I looked at it for too long.

There wasn't a single soul out on the streets. I had never heard such utter silence before; no birds chirping, no distant cars, no rustle of leaves along the pavement. Even the clatter of my bike seemed muted. Was I the only one left?

The thought had barely crossed my mind when I felt a sudden buzzing in my pocket. The sensation scared the hell out of me and I almost took a tumble off the bicycle. Gliding to a stop in the closest driveway, I yanked the phone from my pocket. The screen was dark and dead, like everything else in this place, but somehow a call was still coming through. I held the black screen up to my ear.

"Hello?" I breathed.

"Hannigan?" said the voice on the other end. "Sweet Christ, is that really you?"

"Marconi!" I tucked the phone against my shoulder and glanced around the empty neighborhood. "God, I've never been so happy to hear your voice. Where the hell are you?"

"I'm at home. Where the hell are *you*?"

"Trying to find the Inspector. Are you seeing this?"

"I'm not sure what I'm seeing, Hannigan."

A low moaning floated down the street, like a wheezing foghorn, and I nearly dropped my cell. I ducked behind a peeling fence and peered through a crack in the wood. The flecks in the air had grown agitated, and there were... *things...* slithering along the pavement. I'm not even sure what to call them. They had too many scuttling legs to be snakes but were far too big to be centipedes. I cringed a little, my fingers curling around the phone, but the wriggling little beasts didn't get anywhere near me. They twisted down the road for a few feet before fading into a purple vapor and blowing away.

"Hannigan? You still there?"

"Quiet!" I hissed. "Something's coming!"

Marconi went silent in my hand, and good thing, too, because barely a second later another creature appeared on the stretch of road. It hadn't come from around the corner or anything; it had just folded out of the air, like an invisible origami starfish. I say starfish because the creature had several drooping limbs on all sides of its roundish body, and no eyes to speak of, but otherwise... well, the resemblance ended there. It trembled a bit, like a dog sniffing at the ground, then floated down the street in my direction. I pressed my back against the fence and tried to quiet my breathing.

The starfish drifted past me, still quivering, until it reached a house a little ways down the block. Like everything else, the house was washed in purple, but in a saner world I thought it might have been a pale green. The starfish veered sharply to the left and floated up the driveway. Its slimy limbs dragged behind it, leaving a faint trail of gunk on the pavement.

The creature phased through the front door as if it wasn't even there, then vanished. I waited half a minute to make sure the coast was clear. Not sure how the beastie would have spotted me, having no eyes and all, but I wasn't taking any chances this side of the looking glass. I lifted the phone to my ear and tiptoed over to my fallen bicycle.

"I'll call you back," I whispered. "Let me just find the Inspector first and I'll -"

A loud crunching filled the air, followed by a sickening squelch, and the phone went dead in my hand. I shoved the thing in my pocket and ran for the mountain bike. Leaping aboard, I kicked off the ground and pedaled down the street as fast as my out-of-shape physique could carry me.

The wet crunching slowly faded into the background, but the memory of it followed me, and I could feel the blood burning in my ears. I hadn't seen teeth on the alien starfish - hell, I hadn't even seen a *mouth* - but I'd seen enough nature documentaries to know what it sounded like when a predator gnawed on a dead carcass.

Whatever that thing had been, it was feeding.

* * * * *

The station was empty when I finally arrived, barring a single floating orb at the desk where Abigail Shannon usually sat. The rest of the night crew was nowhere to be seen. I ran through the halls, shouting the Inspector's name until I went hoarse, but it became pretty clear that I was on my own. Fear started to trickle in, but I told it to shut the hell up and made a beeline for the weapons locker instead. The room was protected by an electronic lock with a four-digit password. I typed in the usual numbers, but the screen remained dark. No beeping either. The dregs of fear slowly churned, giving way to panic.

Driven by desperation, I grabbed a paperweight from the closest desk and smashed the glass above the fire extinguisher. For the faintest of seconds I thought I heard the blip of an alarm overhead, but the sound - if it really had been a sound - bled away into that eerie silence. I reached in through the broken glass, seized the canister, and carried it back to the weapons locker. Then I got to work bashing at the lock.

Marconi would have flipped a shit if she saw me now, but I was too far gone to care. The fire extinguisher left a few dents in the metal lock but didn't seem to damage it much. Not at first anyway. After a particularly hefty swing that threatened to pop my shoulder out of its socket, I felt the keypad give - less than an inch, but it was a start. I ignored the aching in my limbs and continued to bash at the pad until the dented hunk of metal finally came loose. It fell to the floor with a muted clatter.

There would be hell to pay in the morning, I knew, but until then I had to focus on survival. As I grabbed a pistol and shoved ammo into the pockets of my jacket, I ran through my priorities: *Find the Inspector. Find Marconi. Get my family back. And stay the fuck away from Starfish and its little minions.* Easy enough, right? Except item one on that list was already proving more difficult than expected, and if I couldn't accomplish *that* much... I tried not to finish that thought.

I holstered the gun and inched past the dripping orb at the welcome desk. Then I pushed open the doors and strode out into the night. The moon overhead had somehow shrunk while I was inside - it was now crescent shaped, as if a cosmic spoon had swooped in and carved out a chunk off the top. My skin prickled, and I ran a thumb along the handle of the gun.

Find the Inspector. So far that mission was a bust, and I was officially out of ideas. Maybe Marconi would know where to go from here.

* * * * *

My phone buzzed again when I was half a mile away from Marconi's house. I yanked it out of my pocket and held it up to my ear, trying to keep the bike steady.

"Marconi?" I said. "Tell me you have good news."

For a few seconds the line was quiet, and I wasn't sure Marconi had heard me. Then her shaky voice came floating out of the speaker.

"Janine's not here," she said. "There's this... I don't know. Some kind of alien light bulb where she was sleeping. I got back from my shift and found it floating there. Hannigan, what the fuck is going on?"

"Hell if I know," I said. "The same thing happened with Ruth and the kids. I can't find the Inspector so I'm as in the dark as you are. Just stay put and I'll come find you. We can figure something out."

Marconi coughed. Not a little cough, but a hacking wheeze that sounded staticky over the phone connection.

"I don't feel so hot, Hannigan," she said.

"Just stay put," I repeated. "I'll be there in a minute - Marconi?"

There was a thump on the other end of the line, like a body hitting the floor. The phone went silent.

"Marconi!" I shouted, my heart racing.

Nothing. I swore and pedaled faster, taking corners a little sharper than necessary. As I drew closer to Marconi's house, I heard that same low moaning echo through the neighborhood. Little shadowy wisps scuttled along the ground, fading in and out of existence. I pedaled over them and burst them like balloons full of purple smoke.

I pulled up to Marconi's home and dropped my bike onto the lawn, making a beeline toward the front door. The house was a compact two-story affair, with a simple blue paintjob and gray-shuttered windows. The skittering shadows seemed to be on the same trajectory as me. I stomped through them and raced up the front steps, where I tried the doorknob. Locked. *Dammit.* I jiggled the knob half a dozen times before giving up and pounding on the door frame.

"Marconi, it's me!" I shouted. "Open up!"

But the door remained stubbornly closed. I remembered

that awful thump on the phone and barreled into the wood with my shoulder, hoping to break it open. I lacked the immense strength of the Inspector, however, and I only succeeded in bruising my shoulder. Pain shot down my arm and I took a staggering step back.

The low moaning cut out, and I turned to face the driveway. The air rippled a bit as a tentacled blob folded out of nothing, its many limbs drooping onto the ground. I stood stock still as the starfish creature quivered, floating a few inches toward me. I pulled the gun from its holster and brandished it cautiously in front of me.

The starfish stopped quivering. In the folds of its viscous skin, a flap lifted, and a blood red eye squinted out at me from the center. It had no pupil, no iris. Just a blank red patch. But I knew it was staring at me. I could feel the prickle of its gaze on my skin.

move human i have come to end

I nearly dropped my gun. "You talk?" I said.

i am many humans purple man i gather humanspeak

The words didn't issue from any mouth I could see but I could hear them clear as day, and they felt invasive in my eardrums, like the burrowing of that hive mind back at the old Glade radio station. I had to resist the urge to clap my hands over my ears.

"What do you mean, you're 'many humans'?" I asked. "You're a fucking starfish monster from outer space, you couldn't be anything *less* human."

The creature gyrated, its entire body spinning in a slow vertical so that its tendrils slapped wetly on the pavement.

purple man dares utter fuck against i the ender i who come to snuff all things

My thoughts turned to Marconi. I had no idea what had happened to her during our phone call, but *snuff all things* was pretty damn clear, and there was no way in hell I was letting this ball of ugly get past me. I lifted the gun and aimed it straight at the blank red eye.

i end all things big and small i even end you purple man

My finger tightened on the trigger, but there was no kickback, no blast of gunfire; the weapon sparked a bit and went dark. Like every other mechanism I'd tried since waking up in this nightmare, the gun was dead here. I reared back and lobbed the useless hunk of metal like a baseball. It struck the Ender next to its crimson eye and sank, burbling, into the folds of flesh.

purple man fears the end but i am not here for him

The creature drifted closer, its tendrils coiled up at the ends like curls of dripping black hair.

not yet not tonight

I could hear my heart pounding. "Stay the fuck away from Marconi!" I shouted, but the air swallowed my voice, made it sound thinner and more pitiful than I'd intended. The Ender hovered toward me, and I stepped backward, but soon I had backed up against Marconi's front door and there was nowhere left for me to go.

Run, Ruth whispered in my ear. But Ruth wasn't here, she was a fucking globe of light dripping onto our bedsheets back home. Ruth was gone and Marconi was gone and the town was gone and the Inspector was in the fucking wind. I had never felt angrier. Or more alone.

I looked up at the purple moon. The void hurt my eyes, but I looked up at it anyway, letting that awful ringing fill my head. The moon had shrunk again, this time to the faintest sliver of a crescent. If I stared at it long enough, would my mind start to crumble? Or had it already crumbled? Was I comatose in a hospital bed somewhere, and this was the fucked up purgatory my brain had constructed to torture me?

The sliver of moon grew smaller, vanishing bit by bit, until there was nothing left in the sky but the blankness of the void. I lost all awareness of the Ender, of Marconi's house, of the ground beneath my feet; gravity seemed to come undone, and I got the sense that if I jumped, I would float endlessly up into the sky, leaving purple streams of color in my wake.

Then the moon reappeared.

It was gradual at first, the sliver widening until it was rounder and more polished, as perfect as a sand dollar; then it shrunk again. It repeated this process, getting faster each time, until the movement became so rapid I could only describe it as blinking. And that's when the realization rushed through me like ice in my veins.

It's not a moon. It's an eye.

No sooner had the thought crossed my mind than I became aware of a shape looming in the void: a dark, hulking thing, outlined by stars, vaguely humanoid but larger than a planet. Even the Ender paused to look up at it. I felt the vague sensation of urine trickling down my leg as a six-fingered hand materialized in the sky above us. It was translucent, turning the air behind it into a purple smudge. And as it fell toward us, I could feel blood gushing from my ears and nose, could feel my lungs tightening as some invisible pressure squeezed them and turned every breath into utter agony.

NO IT IS NOT HIS END TIME YOU DARE YOU DARE

The Ender's voice had taken on a needly sort of whine, but I could barely hear it over the ringing that jostled back and forth inside my skull. I closed my eyes and clapped my hands over my bloody eardrums and roared - not at the sky, not at that giant falling hand. I just roared. I could feel the trembling in my throat but I couldn't hear a sound. I curled up and screamed and felt hot tears streaming down my face, tears that felt thick like blood, and I was afraid that if I opened my eyes my sight would be gone forever, but it didn't matter now, I would never open my eyes again, not with that planet-sized hand plummeting down to crush me into the barest of molecules -

"Mark. Open your eyes, Mark."

I did. At first I thought the world had shifted again, because everything was red now, and turned on its side. Then I realized I was keeled over on Marconi's front step. I tried to wipe the blood from my eyes but my hands refused to obey me, and when I looked down at them I saw they were shaking. My jeans were wet and streaked with blood and urine. The ringing had stopped, and when I looked up, my eyes burning and red and swimming with blood, I saw the reason why.

The Inspector had arrived.

Except I'd never seen an Inspector like this. Easily twenty feet tall, his skin prickling with little bright specks - *stars* - his cigar fuming like a chimney over our heads. The Ender's single red eye stared up at him with something like abject horror. High up above, the moon had vanished again from the sky. This time I suspected it wasn't coming back.

step aside purple king i must end it is my purpose

The starfish had started to spin in an angry circle, its eye blinking furiously. I pulled myself to a sitting position and stared at it.

"This is my domain," the Inspector said. His voice should have boomed across town, given his height, but the sound was oddly subdued. "I have given you permission to wander as you will and carry out your purpose. Touch this human, or either of the humans in that house, and I will revoke that permission. You can wander the netherwastes, scrounging for what little scraps you can find. Do I make myself clear?"

The Ender cowered, but its voice seemed no less bitter.

clear as crystal in humanspeak a great injustice this is for i the ender

"Don't talk of injustice to me, worm," the Inspector said. "You may speak the human tongue but you are little more than a parroting beast. Now go. Leave this place, or test the limits of my mercy."

The starfish made a series of psychic sputters before pivoting and folding out of existence. I blinked the redness out of my eyes, although behind it the world continued to remain as purple as ever. The Inspector stood there for a few minutes and stared at the spot where the Ender had been. Then he turned to face me. In that one motion, he went from being twenty feet tall to his usual seven feet, his skin becoming flat and gray once more.

"Mark," he said. "Oh Mark, I'm so sorry."

"Get the fuck away from me," I said, except blood dribbled from my tongue as I did, and it came out more like "Gedda fug way fromme." I scrambled backward and collided with Marconi's front door again. The Inspector knelt down, his trench coat spilling over his feet, and looked at me with those inscrutable purple eyes.

I spat a glob of blood into the grass. "You're not just some monster," I said, clearer this time. "Jesus *fuck*, you're bigger than this planet, one of your eyes is the size of the fucking moon! *DON'T FUCKING TOUCH ME!*"

The Inspector ignored my hysteria and placed a hand on my shin. I tried my best to kick him away, but one touch from him turned my whole body to jelly and sent me sprawling on the front stoop. I could feel a pleasing euphoria sweep through me, but I fought it. This wasn't me. This wasn't how I wanted to feel. The man in front of me was the farthest thing from a man it was possible to get and I wanted nothing to do with him. Not anymore.

"Please relax, Mark," the Inspector whispered to me, his comforting voice as false as everything else about him. "I need to tell you something. You can judge me when I'm finished."

"NO!" I screamed, but it was too late - his influence was working its way through me, pouring down every vein, tickling every nerve. I closed my eyes and found myself drifting. The pain squeezing my lungs lessened. The blood in my ears was gone. I took in a breath, and it was smooth, and easy, and warm.

"I want you to picture this, Mark, if you can," the Inspector said quietly. "Picture a world in its infancy. A world where the only life wriggles under volcanic rocks or burrows in caves at the bottom of the ocean. You cannot truly imagine such a world because it is not a world for humans. But I was there. I am not human."

Behind my eyelids, the world took shape, exactly as he had described: a wasteland of flowing lava and pits of boiling water. I shifted where I was lying but didn't open my eyes.

"The world was not created for me, but I inherited it, in a sense. I became its watcher. The being who birthed it was a fickle thing, a perfectionist, who took one look at its creation and abandoned it for other projects. Nobody except me took interest in this lump of rock. I found it fascinating. I watched as life grew, as tiny organisms became complex plants and creatures. I watched as the beasts you call dinosaurs took over the earth, and I watched as they died in agony from a fragment of space debris. I watched the rise of your race in its earliest stages, and perhaps that was the most fascinating era of all, because you were so different from everything that came before. You developed tools. You formed a society. You described your world through stories on cave walls. I watched all this unfold with the eye of a curious observer, like one of your scientists examining a specimen. But I watched from afar. I wanted to get closer. I wanted to interact with these beings I found so delightfully peculiar."

The Inspector went quiet. I opened my bleary eyes and saw him sitting on the stoop, facing away from me, his cigar puffing pure white smoke into the night.

"One day I decided to make myself known to them. They didn't know how to react. I don't think they even had a concept of gods, let alone beings like me. The strain of my presence broke them. Their brains collapsed, their bodies gave in, they fell to the ground writhing and foaming at the mouth. I did not fully understand the concept of death, not then, but I knew I had caused something that could not be undone. This filled me with what you might call shame, or regret, and I retreated. I resumed my watch from afar. The human race picked itself up and continued, and I stayed in my distant perch, afraid to step in again.

"But it became increasingly difficult. The more you grew, the more death I saw: some perpetrated among your own kind, some by the will of nature itself. I couldn't escape what I had done all those millennia ago, and yet it pained me to watch as so many bright lights dimmed and went out forever. I wanted to do something. But I feared that I could only bring destruction, that intervening again would only make things worse. So I watched. And waited. And all the while, I worried that I was watching you fascinating creatures inch closer and closer toward extinction.

"But you weren't the only ones occupying this world. Long ago, the empathic giants had torn open a rift from my world to yours, and a few cruel, hungry entities had taken the opportunity to slip through. They fed on your kind - some on your body, some on your spirit. And the more I watched, the more unease I felt. This was my jurisdiction, my responsibility. I may not have been able to stop the natural order of your world from killing humans, but I could very well prevent my own kind from doing the same. So I stopped being a watcher. I became the Inspector instead."

The Inspector turned to look at me. I stared into those eyes of his and tried to find a trace of humanity, something to make him less alien, but I couldn't. I looked into those pupils and all I could see was the moon.

"I am not like you," he said. "I squeezed myself into this body but my essence can only be contained so much. You saw what a little piece of me is capable of, back in the old radio station. You have no idea what it's like to walk around with a thousand nuclear bombs inside of you." He exhaled, letting out a single smoke ring. "My very presence is a danger to you, and Sheriff Marconi, and your family. The only reason you and the sheriff are here right now is because enough of my influence has rubbed off on you. You've spent so much time around me that all it takes is a little slip -" He made a gesture with one of his slender hands. "And you're behind the veil."

The Inspector turned back to face the sky. Something contorted in his profile, and for the first time that night, I thought I detected a trace of human emotion - the mask of a person hiding a deep well of misery.

"I just want to make a difference, Mark," he said. "Am I making a difference?"

I couldn't answer him. I was starting to come back to myself, minus the hysteria, but the Inspector still seemed to be in this unreachable place. I had glimpsed his true self before. Tonight I had seen it in its entirety. How was I supposed to take that? This man, this entity I had taken to be my friend, could crush me with a single flick of his finger. He could probably squeeze the entire world until it popped like a watermelon. And I was supposed to trust him? How could we possibly go back to the way we were before?

I turned away from the Inspector and glanced around the purple-hued neighborhood. So this was the world beyond the rift. After the bizarre dimensions created by the wendigo, I'd expected something a bit more... exotic. Not the same world I knew with a color filter. Plus it was a lot emptier than I'd anticipated. Given the number of entities we'd dealt with so far, I'd thought the place would be swarming. But aside from the Ender and its scuttling minions, this world felt utterly lifeless.

Then I felt it. A tremor. It was barely perceptible, but I could see it in the shivering blades of grass, the skittering of pebbles across Marconi's doorstep. The flecks of light swirled in an agitated spiral. Instinct drew my gaze upward, and in the depths of the empty sky, far, far in the distance, I saw a vast black shape stirring in the void.

The Inspector was suddenly at my side. "Time to go," he said. "I'll get the sheriff."

There was something off about his voice - fear? Could a being like him even comprehend the concept of fear? I rose to my feet as the Inspector barreled into Marconi's door and sent it crashing inward. He disappeared up a flight of stairs, his coat billowing behind him.

My eyes slid up to the sky, like a sailor searching for the North Star. The vast shape was still there. It was bulky, but long, like a whale with the body of an eel. As I watched, a forked tail swept lazily through the void. Ten seconds later a gust of wind blasted across the yard, whipping a cloud of those tiny specks in my face and forcing me to shield my eyes.

"I've got Olivia!" the Inspector shouted from behind me. I turned to see him dragging a half-conscious Marconi on his shoulder. His fedora tilted but remained stubbornly on his head as the winds continued to whip around us. I swayed where I was standing. A low bellowing filled the air, and I looked up to see the void whale opening its mouth, a gaping maw with no tongue and no teeth.

"Don't look at it, Mark!" the Inspector barked. I felt his slender hand wrap around my arm, and suddenly the world jerked away, and all my senses went dead. Then excruciating pain shot through me. It felt like my body was turning inside out, like all my blood and viscera and searing nerve endings had swapped with my skin and turned me into some grotesque anatomy dummy. I opened my mouth to scream, but my vocal chords were gone, and nothing came out but agonizing silence -

And then it was over. I broke free from the Inspector's grip and stumbled, gagging, onto Marconi's front lawn. It took me a second to realize: the grass was green again. The sky was blackish-blue and riddled with stars. All the purple had washed away, and even though I felt like I was about to heave up my insides, I couldn't help but let out a strangled laugh.

I got unsteadily to my feet and took in a deep breath of the crisp, piney air. Somewhere in the distance, I saw a pair of headlights cutting through the forest. The trees rustled and the wind felt cool on my face. An owl hooted, a cat yowled in some faraway yard, water burbled distantly through a series of waterfalls. I thought I even heard the blare of the alarm in the police station, several miles away.

Pacific Glade is alive, I thought. I'd never stopped to appreciate that before.

The Inspector knelt and placed a hand on Marconi's forehead. She shuddered a bit, but otherwise didn't react. Her glazed eyes stared out across the yard.

"The air beyond the rift didn't agree with her," the Inspector said. "Breathing too much of it put her under. She's conscious now, but it's going to take some time to get her back on her feet again."

He straightened up and stared at me. The fedora shielded his eyes, which I was grateful for. I didn't want to stare into those tiny moons again. I tried to force a smile but it didn't even reach the corners of my mouth.

"You are making a difference, you know," I said. "The Neverglades may be a blip in the scheme of things, but people are alive because of you. That's not small to me."

The Inspector's smile was thin. "But?" he said. "I'm sensing there's a caveat."

My pitiful attempt at a smile faded. I looked away from him, turning my eyes to the grass. "I just - I can't go back," I said. "To the way things were. Not yet at least."

The Inspector was quiet. "I understand," he said. He stepped past me onto the driveway, his cigar smoke billowing around his face. He stopped in the middle and just stared down the stretch of road. I was glad his back was turned. I didn't want to look at his face right now.

"I'll call you when I'm ready," I said. "But until then, I think we should get a little distance. Work our own cases. Marconi and I have been through enough to handle what goes bump in the night. I think we'll be okay for now."

"I'm sure you will," he said. He turned his head slightly, as if meaning to look back. But then he tilted his hat and walked down the length of driveway instead. The smoke from his cigar sank to the ground as he walked, enveloping each footstep in an acid green cloud.

I watched the Inspector go, then helped a dazed Marconi up the steps into her house. As I sat her down on the bed, I looked at Janine sleeping peacefully on the other pillow, and I thought of Ruth. I knew when I got home I'd find her safe and sound - no more dripping globes of light - but I couldn't shake that initial sinking I'd gotten in my gut when I'd seen what she'd become. Right then I just wanted to go home, slip under the covers, and hold her close. I needed that touch. I needed to remember what it meant to be human.

Marconi settled in, nestling up against Janine almost unconsciously, and I turned my eyes to the bedroom window. The moon was rising. Small and white, it hovered in the darkening sky, a little sliver of a crescent in all that darkness. In the light it cast, I could make out the Inspector's slender form wandering down the streets of town, hands shoved in his pockets.

I watched him go, stark in his loneliness, until he disappeared into the tangle of houses down the block. Then I headed downstairs and grabbed my bike from the front lawn. I pedaled home in the other direction, tires whirring, the moonlight guiding my way.

ON THE MOUNTAIN OF MADNESS

Pebbles skittered off my windshield as I spun my cruiser around the bend, coming way too close to plummeting off the edge. I yanked the wheel to the right and tried to steady the car. I could hear my tires chewing up the dirt, feel the rumble as the cruiser left man-made pavement for the crude rocky soil of the mountain path.

"Hannigan, if you try a maneuver like that again, I will fucking *murder* you."

I lifted the radio to my mouth. "Roger that, sheriff. I'll leave the fancy tricks to the pros."

"I want to catch this guy as much as you, Hannigan," said Marconi's crackly voice. "But if it comes down to his life or yours, I expect you to choose your own pasty ass. Capiche?"

"Loud and clear." I placed the radio down and tried to focus on the road ahead. Barlow's car had a few hundred feet on mine, but I could see it each time I rounded another corner of the mountain: a beaten blue Ford slipping between the trees, rumbling like its engine was stuffed with rocks. It was a miracle the piece of shit hadn't fallen apart by now.

I rumbled over the bumpy trail as fast as I dared. Marconi was right - it wasn't worth it to blow a tire or go careening into a tree for this guy, no matter what he'd done. There was only one route up Mount Palmer anyway. Sooner or later Barlow would run out of road, or gas, or that rust bucket of his would finally go wheels up, and we'd have him. That was the easy part. Taking down the thing inside of him was another story. Marconi was only a few minutes behind me, so if I could hold Barlow off for long enough, at least I'd have backup.

I just hoped it would be enough.

I rounded the corner, the mountain plateaued, and a building rose up suddenly in front of me: a ruin of blackened stone towers, like a castle in miniature. Three spires at the corners jutted up into the open sky. The fourth had collapsed on itself in a spectacular pile of rubble. All the windows were smashed except one. It was a stained-glass depiction of a woman in a nun's habit, her outstretched hands covered in what looked like blood. With no light to shine through, every pane in the window was a deep obsidian black.

The tilted sign above the entrance read MOUNT PALMER INSANE ASYLUM.

"What the hell…?" I muttered.

Then Barlow's car barreled out of nowhere and smashed into my cruiser, knocking me sideways. The seatbelt dug into my neck and squeezed the breath out of me. I spun the wheel and tried to mash the brakes, but we were spinning out of control now, dirt whipping in furious clouds around us. I fumbled for the radio to call Marconi. When I glanced out the window again, I found myself staring at the pitch black - and rapidly enlarging – stained-glass woman.

"Fucking shit," I said.

Then my car collided with the window and sent the glass shattering inward. My head bashed against the side window. Darkness bloomed behind my eyes, eating at the edges of my vision, and no matter how hard I tried I couldn't fight it. I collapsed onto the steering wheel.

The last thing I saw before I checked out: a shimmering in the air, like water rippling across the sky, and a figure in a flowing black outfit approaching me. Its head was oddly shaped, like it was wearing an angular hat with a long, heavy veil. I closed my bleary eyes as the figure knelt down and peered into my windshield.

"Well now," a harsh voice said. "This won't do."

The rest was darkness.

* * * * *

I woke to a soft, maddening glow, a buzzing strip of light that sent barbs of pain through the front of my skull. I looked through squinted eyes at the source of the brightness. It was a medical lamp, like the one at my dentist's office, but stained a deep yellow and spotted with the corpses of tiny flies. In the darkness outside the light's reach, I saw three figures: one perched in a chair by my side, one bustling back and forth with sharp, pronounced footsteps, and one standing utterly still by a black shape that could have been a doorway. Awareness crept over me, but slowly.

There was an accident. Barlow's car. Marconi must have taken me to the hospital...

I shifted where I was lying, wincing as my brain prickled with pain. "Where's Marconi?" I asked the sitting figure - presumably the doctor. The voice that slipped out of me was faint and dry, barely more than a croak.

The doctor leaned over, so that the lamplight fell over his face and gleamed off of his thin glasses. Tufts of gray hair sprouted around his ears and in patches along his balding scalp. I couldn't see much of his nose underneath his medical mask, but what I could see was red and scabby. The mouth beneath the mask curled up and crinkled the blue paper.

"My, my," he said in a surprisingly silky voice. "It awakes."

The rapping footsteps approached us. "Finally," said a sharp, familiar voice. I peered through the lamplight and made out the vague outline of a woman in a nun's habit. At first I had the baffling impression that the top half of her face was missing. It took me a few seconds to realize she was wearing a black veil over her eyes. The eyeless nun tilted her head and tsked down at me.

"Sister Martha found you in the yard," the doctor said. "A rather unfortunate accident. Your car struck the side of our building and broke a valuable stained-glass window. We've moved the vehicle to avoid disturbing the other patients."

"He destroyed the image of Our Lady Dorcas," Sister Martha fumed. "I know you could hardly care, *doctor*, but our glorious Lady is now in pieces across the kitchen floor. All because of some... some deranged hooligan in a Flash Gordon costume."

"What?" I said, still groggy. "But Barlow... Marconi and I were chasing Barlow up the mountain." My head gave a particularly sharp throb. "He looks like a man but he isn't. He has these, these suckers for fingers, and he sticks them to your head and sucks out your brain until you go totally crazy."

The doctor turned his glasses to Sister Martha, who shook her head disapprovingly. "Dangerous *and* utterly mad," she said. "I don't know where you keep finding them, Dr. Renfield."

The lamp flickered and buzzed as Renfield turned back to me. "Well," he said softly. "I suppose, given time, all madmen find their way to our doors."

"I'm not mad," I insisted. "Christ, get Marconi, she'll explain everything. Who the hell are you people anyway?"

Sister Martha strode forward and struck me across the face with the back of her hand. "Hush your blasphemous tongue," she seethed.

I lifted a hand to touch my stinging cheek, or at least I tried to - when I looked down, I saw that my limbs were bound to the table by a series of crude metal shackles. Cold soberness washed over me. I jiggled my arms inside of the shackles, but they were locked up tight. The metal dug into my wrist and left an ugly red welt.

"There's something rotten in this one," Dr. Renfield said in that unsettlingly quiet voice. "A little touch of sickness in the brain." He traced my forehead with a cold finger. I tried to wriggle away from him, but the shackles kept me from getting far. He found a spot on my temple and tapped it three times.

"Nothing a few snips won't fix," he mused. "Deacon! Get my tools from the office, if you please."

The third shape, who hadn't moved so far, opened the door and disappeared down a dark hallway. I could see a single electric torch set into the wall before the door swung shut and brought darkness rushing back.

"It's a simple enough surgery," the doctor said to me, withdrawing a pen from his pocket. He removed the cap, licked the tip, and leaned in to scrawl a tiny X on my forehead. I winced as the point of the pen dug into my skin.

"We just make a tiny incision - here," he said. "Then we drill into the skull and carefully remove the diseased brain tissue. It's a tried and true method. Once the source of the madness has been excised, you'll be on the road to recovery in no time." His voice was low and soothing, as if he was casually discussing the weather instead of how he was going to *fucking lobotomize me.*

"What kind of crack doctor are you?" I croaked. "Did I take a wrong turn and wind up in the fucking Twilight Zone? I need a bandage and a shit ton of ibuprofen, not brain surgery. Let alone brain surgery that went out of fashion in the fucking thirties."

Sister Martha struck me again, this time across the mouth. Pain blossomed in my jaw and joined the incessant throbbing in my head.

"I don't care what you say, Doctor," she said in disgust. "There is no curing madness like this. It would more merciful to send him to his Maker."

"Why Sister Martha, I'm surprised at you," the doctor said. He leaned in closer and peered at me, staring down over the top of his scabby nose. I still couldn't see his eyes in the glare of the lamp, and suddenly I was struck by a horrible thought. When Marconi and I had found Barlow in the midst of one of his "feedings," he'd been crouched over a prone body, suckers out and slurping the sweet sanity out of his victim. I'd startled him with a warning gunshot, and when he looked up, there was no humanity in his eyes - just discs of spinning orange, like slivers of molten lava.

We already knew that entities from beyond the rift could hop from vessel to vessel, wearing out human bodies like a pair of old jeans. Had the thing inside Barlow jumped into Dr. Renfield? If I couldn't see his eyes, how could I know for sure?

"Don't fucking touch me," I said. I struggled uselessly against my restraints, but it didn't matter - the doctor was reaching over to me now, his knobby fingers tracing the bumps on my forehead. I pictured the horrible suckers on the tips of Barlow's fingers and wondered if that was coming next, if the doctor's light touch would transform into something a hundred times more monstrous. I closed my eyes and took in a rattly breath.

There was a sudden boom as the door flung open. I lifted my eyelids a crack to see the third shape bursting back in, slumped over and out of breath. "Doctor! Sister Martha!" he wheezed. His voice was young - probably still in his teens - and it carried the slightest trace of an accent, although I couldn't quite place it.

"What is it?" the nun barked.

"There's - there's been a row," the boy stammered. "Merrow got loose in the east wing and punched out two orderlies. Now the patients are fighting. It's horrible, Sister, just horrible. I think I heard a bone breaking."

"In the name of all things holy," Sister Martha said. "I don't care how mad they are, I will *not* tolerate this behavior. Not in my asylum." She strode past the boy's shadow and slipped into the hallway, her habit flowing out behind her.

"You ought to come too, Dr. Renfield," the boy said shakily. "It sounded bad. I think you may need to treat the wounded."

The doctor's hand lifted from my head - with some reluctance, I thought. "If you say so, Deacon," he said. He rose from his seat, stretching almost six feet tall, his frame stooped and bony. For a second I was reminded of another tall slender figure, and I shuddered before I could stop myself. I watched as Renfield, in no apparent hurry, passed Deacon and disappeared after Sister Martha.

I expected the boy to go rushing after the others, but he just stood there, a solitary figure in the dark. I lay on the medical table and listened as the footsteps grew fainter and fainter until they faded entirely from earshot. At once Deacon rushed forward and produced a tarnished silver key, which he began jiggling in the lock of my foot cuffs.

"Are you hurt?" he whispered. The accent in his voice had disappeared. "Did the doctor start operating on you?"

"No, I'm fine," I said. "What are you…?"

"I don't think you're mad," Deacon replied. "I'm going to get you out of here before those monsters come back."

"Oh thank god," I breathed. "Did you start that fight?"

"It doesn't take much to set Merrow over the edge," Deacon said, wrenching at the cuff. "I pushed his buttons a little until - he - snapped - there!" The shackle on my left ankle came away with a clatter. The boy hurried around the table and began working on the other foot. In a minute or two I was free and rubbing at my tender wrists.

"Come on!" Deacon said, grabbing my hand. The lamplight fell over his face for the first time, and I saw a young face - not quite a kid, like I'd suspected, but a guy in his early 20s or so. He had messy brown hair, cheeks dotted with dark freckles, and a pair of milky white eyes that stared at my face without seeing me. My rescuer was blind.

I swung my legs hastily over the hospital bed and let Deacon drag me to the door. Despite his lack of sight, he moved with sureness in each step, not even bumping into the door frame as he pulled me into the hallway and led me past the line of electric torches. The bulbs flickered as we passed them. I looked around, hoping to get my bearings somehow, but there was nothing distinctive about this hall - just cold gray bricks and a series of dark doorways.

"Where are we going?" I asked.

"Sister Martha's office," he answered. "It's the only room in the entire asylum that has a phone. We'll need to call for outside help if we're going to get out of this place."

"Music to my ears," I muttered. "Hey, how'd you know I'm not crazy?"

"Because you're like me," he said. "You're not from this time, right?"

"Excuse me?" I said. But on some level, I did know what he was talking about. I think Sister Martha's "Flash Gordon" comment had gotten the ball rolling, but it wasn't until the doctor had started his whole lobotomy shtick that it had really struck me: I'd crashed through another portal and gone tumbling back in time. Crazy in theory, but hey, crazier things happened in the Neverglades all the time.

"I came from the year 1986," Deacon told me. "I was hiking the mountains with my friend Meg when we found the ruins of the asylum. I couldn't see them, of course, but Meg described them to me. She's always been my second set of eyes. We thought we'd explore the place, you know, just for fun, but when we got inside we were surrounded by voices. I didn't know what was going on. Meg started freaking out and somebody ripped her hand away from mine, and then my eyes were gone. I was totally in the dark.

"I stayed quiet, mainly because I had to. I guess they assumed I wasn't crazy. Dr. Renfield saw I was blind and kind of... took me under his wing. He never asked where I had come from. I pretended to be a foreigner so it wouldn't draw too much suspicion if I said anything strange, you know - anything that would be out of place for the time period. The doctor let me be, as long as I carried his tools and cleaned his chambers and whatnot. When I had time to myself I felt my way around the asylum, looking for Meg."

Deacon went quiet for a moment. "That was three years ago," he said. "They took my friend away and I haven't heard from her since. She could be dead for all I know."

"Jesus," I said.

For the first time, I heard the sounds of distant screaming: high-pitched, miserable wails, echoing off the walls. The screams of the mad. I thought of Barlow's victims, how they'd been found slack-jawed and rocking by themselves in the corner, mumbling nonsense under their breath. Even in our day and age, there was no cure for that kind of madness. I couldn't imagine how these kinds of people were treated in an era when brain surgery was a totally acceptable substitute for therapy.

"When are you from?" Deacon asked.

"Um," I said. "Twenty first century. I'm a detective. I was chasing a - a criminal up into the mountains. He crashed his car into mine and I ended up here. No clue where he went." Even as I said it, I could feel the cool tickle of Dr. Renfield's fingers tracing my forehead.

Deacon stopped suddenly outside a door that looked no different from all the others, bar a spiky black crucifix dangling from a nail in the center. The implication was clear: stay far the fuck away. I didn't want to think of how that spiteful old woman would react if she caught us snooping up here. It wouldn't be pretty.

"I've been here so long I know almost every nook and cranny, but beyond this point I really am blind," Deacon said. "You're going to have to take it from here."

"What am I looking for?" I asked, placing my hand on the door.

"This is the early 1900's, so try to find a rotary phone," he said. "Just dial the operator and phone the police. I don't know if they'll take us seriously, but if we can get friends on the outside, we may stand a chance."

"Gotcha," I said, looking over my shoulder. The lights flickered and the air was heavy with distant screams, but it didn't sound like anyone was nearby, and that was good enough for me. I pushed open the door and slipped inside the room.

For an office, the place was pretty barren. A desk with a plastic placemat and an old ham radio sat in the middle of the room, surrounded by wooden chairs and a few sparse bookshelves. There was a slight crackle in the air, and it took me a second to realize the radio was on. The static filled my ears as I approached. The sound got my head throbbing again, so I adjusted the frequency until the static became nothing but low background noise.

I'd just drawn my hand back from the dial when another sound cut through the soft wall of static: a child's singsong voice, reciting a nursery rhyme. Or what sounded like a nursery rhyme. My hand froze, and chills skittered up and down my arms.

> *"Sticks and stone may break my bones,*
> *swords and spikes impale me*
> *insects crawl inside my throat*
> *and eat the soft tissue of my belly*
> *leaving sticky webs with clumps of eggs*
> *to sprout inside me and burst out*
> *in swarms of spiders from my eyes*
> *and mouth and ears and every imaginable*
> *orifice, until my bloated corpse splits*
> *at the seams."*

The voice stopped, and I reached out with a trembling hand to turn off the radio - but then a piercing giggle issued from the speakers and stopped me dead. *"Remember me, detective?"* the voice of the legion laughed.

I stabbed at the OFF button and the machine went dark. I backed away from it, shaking, debating whether I should pick up the damn thing and smash it against the wall. The voice in the radio was supposed to be dead. I'd seen the Inspector... I'd seen the thing's beating heart destroyed in a wall of fire. Had my little time slip brought it back somehow? Was this a version of it from an earlier time period? But then how could it remember who I was? The wound on my head resumed its dull, painful throbbing, pulsing with each pound of my heart.

I jumped as the door creaked open and Deacon poked his head inside. "Any luck?" he whispered.

I opened my mouth, but whatever I'd been about to say dried up - because the radio was gone. Instead, the desk now held a yellow rotary phone, a bucket of paper clips, and a stack of lined paper held by a stone angel paperweight. Hesitantly, I lifted the phone to my ear, but there was no sound on the other end of the line. I tried dialing 9-1-1 but my fingers got caught in the rotary, and when I finally managed to get the right numbers, I was rewarded with more resounding silence. I placed the phone back and tried to steady my breathing.

"The lines are down," I heard myself saying. "We'll have to try something else."

Deacon swore. "There may be a way out in the service tunnels," he said. "It'll be a long walk back to town, assuming we get past the guards and the doctor and Sister Martha without getting caught. But one step at a time."

I opened one of the drawers with numb fingers and found myself staring at a pile of yellowed papers. It looked like a stack of patient files. I picked them up and leafed through them, not sure what I was looking for. Grayscale photographs stared back at me from each sheet: pairs of tiny black eyes, some angry, some morose, others just empty. I stopped at a photo of a young woman with frizzy hair and a wide, terrified expression on her face.

"Your friend," I said to Deacon. "Is her name Meghan Rosenberg?"

"What?" he said. "Yeah, it is. Why?"

"Because I think I found her file," I replied. I traced the lines of printed text with my fingers. For a few uneasy seconds it looked like the letters were skittering under my touch, like tiny black insects, but I blinked a few times and the sensation passed.

"It says here that she's in room 37," I said.

"That's in the east tower," Deacon said. "I never had access to the upper stories so I couldn't check those rooms." His voice grew quiet, and I turned to see that his face had gone pale. "Detective... I can't just leave her. Not if I know where she is."

I looked back down and found myself staring at another open drawer - one I could swear I hadn't touched. Nestled on a blanket of velvet was an old-fashioned revolver. I reached in and touched the sleek, black metal. It was cold. I lifted the gun and examined it in the lamplight. There was a tag dangling from the barrel, so I flipped it over and read the single line of scrawled text:

you get three shots. use them well.

I blinked, and the tag was gone.

"Detective!" Deacon hissed. "The doctor and Sister Martha are going to be back any minute!"

I came to my senses with a jerk. "Right," I said. I tucked the revolver into the empty holster on my belt. It slid in snug and easy, as if it had always belonged there. My nerves on edge, I closed the drawer and followed Deacon out into the hallway.

"Let's find your friend and get out of here," I said in a low voice. "I don't like what this place is doing to me."

Deacon nodded and set off down the hall. His footsteps were barely audible, despite his hurried pace. I followed him, hand playing nervously at the holster of the stolen revolver. My head was aching again and every shadow seemed to slip away from me when I turned to look. I just wanted to find Marconi and get the hell out of this place, but there was no chance of me getting anywhere without Deacon's help, and no Meg meant no Deacon. So this was a necessary detour. Hopefully it would also be a quick one.

*****

The wails grew louder the further in we went. Each patient's cell had a small barred window in the center, and hands would emerge from the darkness as we approached: some reaching out for us, others rattling the bars as if they could snap them in half. I saw a few grimy faces peering out at us, their eyes wide and bloodshot. One person - the long scraggly hair made me think it was a woman, but I couldn't be sure - grinned at me with yellowed teeth, then lobbed a hunk of bloody mucus through the bars. I veered toward the middle of the hallway to avoid the ensuing splat.

Deacon led me up a few short flights of stairs, winding through hall after identical hall, until at last he stopped at a small wooden door. "The east tower," he said under his breath. "But it's locked, and I've got no idea where we could find the key."

"Stand back," I said. I drifted back a few inches, tensed my legs, and launched a kick at the space above the doorknob. The door wasn't nearly as sturdy as it looked. My foot smashed through the wood with a loud splintery crack, leaving a hole just big enough to fit my hand. I stuck it through and jimmied the lock from the other side. The door came loose and opened with a tremendous creak.

"Someone's bound to have heard that," Deacon said nervously. "We've got to hurry." He squeezed past me and stumbled up the flight of stairs, his fingers scraping against the wall. I placed a tentative hand on the revolver and hurried after him.

The stairs wound up in a haphazard spiral before opening up into a large circular room. Dark cell doors surrounded us on all sides, broken only by the occasional stained-glass window. Each one depicted a hunched figure in various states of agony or self-flagellation, watched over by a horde of robed men. My skin crawled at the sight.

"I can't read the numbers," Deacon said frantically from the center of the room. "Help me find her, Detective."

I tore my eyes away from the windows and approached the closest cell door. A flat white panel on the front read 31. Nothing stirred inside, so I left it alone and hurried past the next several doors. When I reached number 37, I placed my hand on the cold metal and peered between the bars. There wasn't much light up here, but I could make out a young woman with frizzy hair slumped in the corner, rocking back and forth. She was moaning, so low and deep I almost didn't notice it at first. Her bloodshot eyes stared at a fixed spot on the far wall.

"I found her," I whispered to Deacon. "But she doesn't look pretty."

"Just get her out of there," he pleaded.

There was no padlock or anything on the cell, just a large bolt driven into the door frame. I yanked it loose with a loud scrape and opened the door ever so slightly. Meg apparently hadn't noticed the sound; she just continued to rock in place, moaning under her breath. I was just about to step inside and drag her out when a sudden hiss of outrage stopped me in my tracks.

I turned and saw Sister Martha standing at the foot of the stairs, her habit spilling around her feet, her eyes still hidden behind that loose black veil. She advanced toward us, her mouth set in a hardened line. I reached absurdly for the revolver for a moment, then lowered my hand. Deacon, pale and sweaty, stumbled away from her.

"I never did trust you, you little wretch," the nun spat at him. "God knows what the old doctor saw in you." Her head whipped up to look at me, and I could feel the rage burning in her unseen eyes. "And *you*. The doctor's latest little project. Thought you were going to get free reign of my asylum, did you? That you were going to free my wards, have yourself a nice little riot? Oh no, no, dear Lord, not while I'm alive." She pointed at the closest stained-glass window with a crooked finger. "Your punishment will make theirs look like the sweet grace of God."

I took a step forward. "What are you gonna do to me, you old bitch?" I said. "Slap me again? You don't have your shackles anymore. Any power you had down there is gone."

An angry cry rose in her throat. She stormed over to me, habit flapping, and reared back to give me another almighty whack. I leaned to the side and avoided it easily - but then her hand swung back around and struck me square in the jaw. My head exploded in pain again and I staggered back a few inches.

She advanced on me again, but before she could strike, I grabbed the folds of her veil and ripped it clean off. Underneath, one hazel eye glared back at me. The other was gone. A charred and wrinkled cavity was the only thing left of her left eye socket. She snatched the threads of the veil out of my hand and gave me a violent shove back, her withered lips curling into a snarl. I stumbled and went sprawling against the door.

Deacon appeared in front of me, his small frame standing between me and the fire-scarred nun. He lifted a hand to fend her off, but he couldn't see her coming, and she dodged his reach with the speed of a much younger woman. Then her hands closed around his neck and the young man started to sputter. I felt ice trickle through me as I saw Deacon's veins pop in red rivers underneath his skin, as something silver - not orange - started to spin in Sister Martha's eye.

Bang!

I hadn't even realized I'd raised the gun until the kickback bashed my skull against the door. Pain swam in my eyes, but I could see enough to make out Sister Martha staggering backwards, hands pressed against a seeping red hole in her gut. Her mouth was open in an O of surprise, her one remaining eye wide and hazel - no gleam of silver anywhere. I lowered the revolver and tried to fight the churning in my stomach.

A screech came from the cell behind me, and I was shoved aside as the door flew open, a hunched, frizzy-haired shape lunging out from inside. *Meg*. She continued to shriek as she charged at the staggering nun, her fingers spasming. Sister Martha couldn't even lift her hands to defend herself. Meg slammed into her and began railing on the old woman, driving her back, striking at her arms and head with clawlike hands. The nun wailed and clutched at her wound. I tried to heave myself off the floor to get between them but promptly tripped over Deacon, who'd fallen prone to the ground, gasping and wheezing.

I scrambled to my feet. Meg had launched herself at Sister Martha, sending both women crashing against - and through - one of the large stained-glass windows. I could only watch as the glass exploded outward, as their flailing bodies flew together into the stormy sky, before gravity took hold. I didn't run to the window to watch them fall. I only stood, numb, waiting for the inevitable crunch of bones against pavement.

I didn't have to wait long.

"*What the fuck was that?*" Deacon screamed.

I reached down and lugged him to his feet. He had started to shake and I tried to tell him to get it together, but then the wind whistled through the shattered window and something papery brushed against my hand. I looked down and saw that the little tag had reappeared on the barrel of the gun. The wind whipped it back and forth, and I saw that the line scrawled across it had changed:

you get two shots. down one shell

"Come on," I said to Deacon. "Come on!" I yanked at his arm and turned him to face me. His milky eyes spun in his skull, staring everywhere except at my face. I slapped him and barked, "We have to go!"

His trembling abated, at least somewhat. He took in a few struggling breaths and stared blankly at the wall.

"The service tunnels," he mumbled. "That's our only shot."

"Can you get us there?" I asked, fighting the impulse to shake his shoulders.

"Yeah," he said. "But if Renfield gets wind of what happened to Sister Martha he'll have them locked down tight. We have to hurry."

A sob broke from his throat, but I didn't give him the time to mourn. I simply grabbed his arm and dragged him down the spiral stairs, through the splintery door, and into the dim hall of cells. Back into the heart of that screaming madness.

* * * * *

Deacon led me down more twisting passageways than seemed physically possible; the ruins of the asylum hadn't looked nearly this big on the outside. Eventually the cells gave way to offices and storage closets and that awful incessant wailing receded into the background. We clambered across chipped gray bricks and down a few narrow flights of stairs. I didn't like the idea of going further underground - it felt too much like descending into a tomb - but if there really was a way out down here, I could put aside a little claustrophobia and suck it up.

"Down here," Deacon said, leading me into a dimly lit basement. "Just around the corner and - *oof!*"

He had collided with a tall, lanky figure that had been crouching at the bottom of the stairs. Deacon only had time to let out a cry of surprise before the figure wrapped him in a pair of spindly arms and dragged him back into the darkness.

"Hey!" I shouted, whipping the gun out of its holster. I clambered down the remaining steps and hurried into the depths of the basement. The figure had stopped by the wall and yanked the chain on a dust-covered lightbulb, spreading a pale yellow wash over everything. In the light I recognized the lanky figure as Dr. Renfield. One of his hands was holding Deacon's shoulder in a vise-like grip; the other held a scalpel to his throat. Both hands were flecked with tiny spots of blood.

"Sssh!" the doctor whispered as Deacon tried to struggle. "Hush, boy. You made quite the mess upstairs. I had to get my hands dirty picking up the pieces. You know how much I hate getting these hands dirty."

"Let him go!" I barked. I lifted the revolver, but Renfield only tsked.

"A man in your condition shouldn't have a firearm," he said in that infuriatingly quiet voice. "So unstable. You should put that away, before things get even messier."

"Too late," Deacon said in a strangled voice. The doctor lifted the scalpel to his Adam's apple, but the young man kept talking. "You want to see a mess? Go outside. Find Sister Martha. She's probably just a splat on the ground by now. No picking up those pieces."

The doctor tried to hide it, but I could see that he was visibly shaken, and the hand on Deacon's shoulder loosened just a touch. Deacon moved before I could. He elbowed Renfield in the ribs and threw his head back, bashing the doctor in the mouth. Renfield's grip slipped as he stumbled back, his free hand flying up to his broken jaw.

Deacon took advantage of the distraction to clamber away, and I approached the doctor, who had backed up against the far wall of the basement. Up close, I could see past his thick glasses, and the eyes that stared down at me were a beady black - not orange. Renfield wasn't the brain sucker. Not that it mattered. I lifted the revolver and placed the barrel in the center of his forehead.

"I can cure your madness," he said through his bloody teeth. "I can fix you. Why won't you let me fix you?"

Every instinct in me wanted to plant a bullet in his skull. I compromised by bashing him across the head instead. Renfield hit the wall and slumped immediately, one pane of his glasses cracked. Curled up on the ground, he looked like a marionette doll after a child had dumped it unceremoniously in the corner. I found myself filled with a sudden surge of rage and disgust, so I sucked in a gob of saliva and spat onto his scabby cheeks.

"Get over here!" Deacon called from behind me. "I've got the tunnel door open!"

I re-holstered the gun and turned away from the fallen doctor. Deacon had wrestled open a great metal door at the far end of the basement, revealing another set of stairs that led down into a dark, dank tunnel. Even from here I could smell the lovely odor of sewage wafting up from below.

"Don't tell me how it looks," he said. "Just help me navigate."

I nodded, before realizing how pointless that was. "Sure," I said. I took his arm and guided him down the stairs, so that we stepped together into the wide, low passage. The place was lit up, but just barely, by the occasional electric light embedded in the ceiling.

"I've never been down here but I've heard that goods from town come up this way all the time," Deacon said. "It must get out somewhere near the base of the mountain. Just keep heading downward and we should eventually find the exit."

"Wish I had more than a 'should' to go on," I muttered. Deacon didn't reply - really, what was there to say? - so I helped guide his hand to the tunnel wall, and we started down the grimy stone path.

The sounds of the asylum had faded to nothing over our heads, leaving only the thunk of our footsteps and a light dripping sound that always seemed to come from just up ahead. We walked and we walked, Deacon keeping his hand on the bricks, and the ground continued to slope downward, and the stench grew stronger with each corner we turned. Every so often I thought I saw a dark shape darting along the ceiling, and I would whip my head around - but if anything else was in here with us, it was faster than my eyes could catch.

I was so focused on the scuttling little things that I didn't notice the low rumbling until we were several hundred feet in. I didn't stop, although I placed my own hand against the wall to feel the tremors. They were quiet, but getting steadily louder. Something was approaching us.

"How big do these tunnels get?" I asked Deacon. "Big enough to fit a truck through?"

"Probably," he said. "Some of the boxes they lug up here must be pretty big. Why do you ask?"

"There's something -" I started to say, but I was cut off when the ground trembled so much it almost knocked me off my feet. I stood still and stared ahead. This stretch of tunnel ended at an intersection a couple dozen feet away.

The source of the noise was close - maybe just around the corner.

Then a looming shadow emerged from the left-hand branch, and a horrific shape squeezed itself into view. I held my breath. Crawling on hands and knees, each movement heavy enough to send chunks falling from the ceiling, was the wendigo Marconi had killed.

Its globular mass of eyes spun and whirled, looking in every direction but mine. My heart leapt into my throat and I flattened myself against the wall. I could hear each thump of my pulse as the being lumbered past the tunnel opening, its bulky shape so big it scraped against the walls and ceiling. I sank to the floor and waited for the tremors to die down.

Something crinkled in my pocket as I pressed against the wall, and I pulled it out into the light. The Inspector's calling card. I fumbled for my lighter before realizing that the doctor must have confiscated it, and besides, did I really want to use the thing anyway? I folded the card in my fist and slipped it back into my pocket.

"Detective?" Deacon asked. He stopped in place, tilting his head slightly, like he was listening for vibrations. He turned and stared vacantly in my general direction. "What are you doing on the floor? We have to keep moving."

"You don't feel that?" I said. "That rumbling?"

"I don't feel anything," he said. "Come on."

I rose to my feet. The wendigo had vanished back into the tunnel, but the rumbling, though distant, still shook the pebbles around my feet. I watched them skitter for a bit, then looked up at Deacon. The guy was looking back at me, his milky eyes blank, his brow furrowed and confused.

"It's not real," I realized, and I felt like slapping myself. "None of this shit is real."

Deacon's slight frown grew more pronounced. "What are you talking about?"

"This whole time I thought it was the doctor," I said. "Because he touched my forehead. But you touched me too, didn't you? You grabbed my hand when we were escaping. That's direct skin to skin contact. And that's all this thing needs to work its mojo."

"This *thing*?" Deacon said. He took a step back - cautious, slight, but I saw it.

"I've been going crazy all day," I went on. "Watching things change and disappear in front of my eyes. Seeing a whole menagerie of old faces. The time eater. That fucker in the radio. Even the Christing wendigo, but you know what? None of them are real. The only thing that's real is the brain sucker, and if I kill it, maybe I'll get my fucking brain back."

Deacon's hands began to tremble. "You're starting to scare me, Detective."

"Am I?" I said. "Good. Because I don't have sympathy for alien body squatters hiding behind a blind man's eyes."

I pulled the revolver out of my holster, slowly, and thumbed the safety off. Deacon couldn't see what I was doing, but he heard the metallic click, and his face went deathly pale.

"If you're still in there, Deacon, I'm sorry," I said. "But I can't let this thing escape."

He turned tail to run, but the second bullet clipped him square in the back - just above his heart. He collapsed onto the tunnel floor. I lowered the smoking revolver and inched cautiously toward his slumped body. Blood seeped into the dirt around him, barely visible in the dim electric lights. With the tip of the gun, I lifted his arm and flipped the body onto its back.

The milky eyes had stopped spinning. I waited for them to flare a bright orange, for the creature inside to make its flight, but the seconds passed and the body didn't stir. I wondered if I had actually killed the thing after all. If it was gone, wouldn't my madness be too?

Then a slight draft blew through the tunnel, coming out of nowhere, and I felt something familiar tickle my hand. I looked down and saw that goddamn tag fluttering against my thumb. Lifting it up, I squinted at the tiny scribbled text.

you get one shot. burn in hell

"No," I mumbled. "No no no no *no.*"

I fell back on my ass and let the revolver drop to the ground. Bulbs flickered overhead, and the tunnel rumbled with the wendigo's distant footsteps. Inches away, Deacon's blood slowly turned the dirt a brownish red. I sat and watched as the dark tendrils seeped toward me like stretching fingers.

"Fuck," I blurted. "Oh fuck, Deacon. I'm sorry."

The bloody fingers were splitting into branches now, like some spiky subway map etching onto the soil. I scrambled to my feet and snatched up the revolver. The footsteps thudded again, making the walls tremble, so I picked a direction at random and began to run. The tunnel arched around me, cold and chalky, like a hollowed-out bone. My own footsteps thumped against the dirt, a second out of sync with my heartbeat.

I'm not sure when I noticed the tunnel getting wider, but after a few minutes of running it struck me suddenly that the electric lights were well over my head, when before I could have knocked my noggin against them. The walls, too, were farther away, and the bricks had given way to a smooth gray stone. Was I about to emerge in some sort of reservoir? I wracked my brains, trying to picture the geography of Mount Palmer, but the only map I could form in my head was that crisscross of blood spilling across the ground a few intersections back. I swallowed the image back and pressed onward.

The lights soon grew so high that I could barely see where I was going - each step was lit by a faint yellow glow, but just barely. Eventually the way forward became so murky I had to slow my pace. Which turned out to be a very good thing, because when I rounded the next corner, the ground suddenly dropped away into a gaping chasm. I skidded to a halt and threw myself backward to avoid tumbling over the edge.

I hit the ground with an *oof,* and for a second I thought I had conked my head, because I was literally seeing stars. But it wasn't just stars. It was moons, and planets, and galaxies, far away but also impossibly close, looming above me in a purplish black abyss. My head throbbed as a large blue planet arced through the closest patch of darkness, its slender rings spinning like razor blades.

I couldn't stare at it, it was going to drive me absolutely crazy, so I pulled myself to my feet and tried to run back the way I had come. But the second my foot touched down, the ground rippled like a pool of shallow water. I had a second to register this as weird before the floor abruptly froze over and shattered into dusty fragments. I tripped backward, and the ground exploded at my step, sending dim shards in every direction. There was no sound, no crash - just the barest of whispers. Each step caused another shatter, and soon I was teetering above that purplish expanse of space.

I had the barest of islands left, so I stayed utterly still, not even daring to breathe. The revolver was like ice in my hand. I stood and stared at the galaxies swirling past my head. Another ringed planet spun in slow circles underneath me, its disc grooved like an old record. I shivered and shivered and clutched the gun and wracked my brain for a course of action, but there was no up or down here, no plan of escape, just the unending cosmos, the cosmos and me: a tiny molecule in the body of something much, much bigger.

My head throbbed as something shifted in the cosmic vastness. The stars slid aside, pushed by a shadowy hand; a vague outline appeared amid the planets, larger than all of them, so large I couldn't even perceive its bottom. I'd been behind the rift and seen planetary-sized beings, but this new figure dwarfed them in comparison. It was galactic. Its eyes were clusters of purple stars. Wispy galaxies streamed from the area that might have been its mouth - almost like smoke from the universe's largest cigar.

The cosmic shadow shifted again, more of its form appearing in the blackness: a thin-brimmed hat, lanky arms, a coat of rippling galaxies descending into the abyss with no apparent end. Pain arced through my head, and I lifted the revolver with trembling fingers.

It's inside me, I realized. *I'm the source of the madness. The brain sucker was inside me the entire time.*

I cocked the gun and placed the tip of the barrel against my temple. One shot left. One bullet and the brain sucker would be dead; one bullet and this mad universe would be destroyed. I didn't even care that I'd be going with it. I was diseased, and this was the only cure. Water trickled from the corners of my eyes. It dripped onto my lips and my chapped tongue licked off the salt: one last taste of the world before the lights went out.

I slipped my finger around the trigger, tightened my muscles - and a voice floated from the depths of space. A voice calling my name. A voice I knew. I froze, cold metal still pressed against my temple.

The universe bled away like dripping paint, the planets sagging, the galaxies fading out: a sea of dying fireflies. The cosmic shadow grew blurry around the edges. Its form wobbled and changed shape, becoming smaller, a bit stouter. Weakness swept over me, and I fell backwards, back into the abyss - except my back collided with a cold stone floor. The gun clattered out of my hands and promptly flickered out of existence.

Bricks folded out of space, enfolding me in four towering walls, broken only by a few windows and a single bright doorway. A familiar shadow stood on the threshold. I stared at it, my throat dry, my limbs numb and shaking ever so slightly. The shadow hurried forward and lifted its own gun, but it didn't point the thing at me - it swept the pistol around the room, peering into every dark corner. Then it lowered the gun and knelt down by my side.

"Hannigan," Marconi said. "The fuck happened to you?"

I opened my mouth, but the only sound that came out

was a dry rattle.

At last, I managed to rasp out, "Barlow?"

"I got him," Marconi said. "Three bullets in the head. I don't know how you walked away from that crash, Hannigan, but Barlow was struggling to get out of the driver's seat when I plugged him. The guy was practically mashed against the windshield. I waited for some sort of slug to slither out of his ear but I think the brain-sucking monster thing inside of him is dead." She stuck out an arm and helped me up. I got unsteadily to my feet, staring around the empty room. The floor was littered with rubble and shattered glass. I was back in the ruins of the Mount Palmer Insane Asylum.

Dizziness swept over me, and I grabbed onto Marconi's arm. She held me up and started guiding me toward the exit.

"How did you get away from that mess, anyway?" she asked me. "You've got a little blood on your head but I don't see a scratch anywhere on you."

I swallowed back a painful lump and croaked out, "Long story."

We emerged onto the asylum's front lawn, which was overgrown with long blades of browning grass. I looked to the left and my stomach turned. Barlow's car had sandwiched my cruiser against the outer wall of the building. My car was a crumpled mess, and Barlow's issued a cloud of acrid black smoke from its exposed engine. Lester Barlow himself was slumped in the driver's seat with three puckered holes in his forehead.

"You're gonna need a new car, Hannigan," the sheriff said.

I didn't answer. If Marconi had killed the thing inside Barlow… then it hadn't followed me into the past after all? Then how could I explain all those objects appearing and disappearing, all those phantoms from my past rearing their ugly heads?

Maybe I hadn't gone back in time at all. Maybe the whole thing had just happened in my head. Maybe the crash had knocked me into a pocket universe, like the wendigo's, and my brain had populated the world as I went along - complete with all sorts of glitches and echoes, like a computer program gone bad.

The Inspector would have known. But the Inspector wasn't here.

Marconi was talking again, something about paging the station to pick up Barlow's body, but I barely heard. I couldn't stop looking back at the crumbling ruins of the asylum. The skies in the present day were clear and cloudless, but the sun was starting to sink below the towers, and it glinted off the glass in each shattered window. I stared at the gaping hole in the eastern tower and thought of Meg and Sister Martha crashing through it. Had that really happened? Had any of it?

Marconi helped me into her cruiser and got behind the wheel. The car rumbled forward along the dirt path, but I was looking backward still, back at the decrepit building and all its darkness. The screams of the insane had gone silent years ago. There was nothing but nature out here - nature and this lurking, empty shell, a scar on the face of the mountain.

The towers glowed a soft orange against the sun, like a fire burning on the rooftop. I watched them for as long as I could. Then Marconi's cruiser plunged into the tree line, and the leaves blocked out the sky, and whatever remained of Mount Palmer Insane Asylum vanished into the murky past.

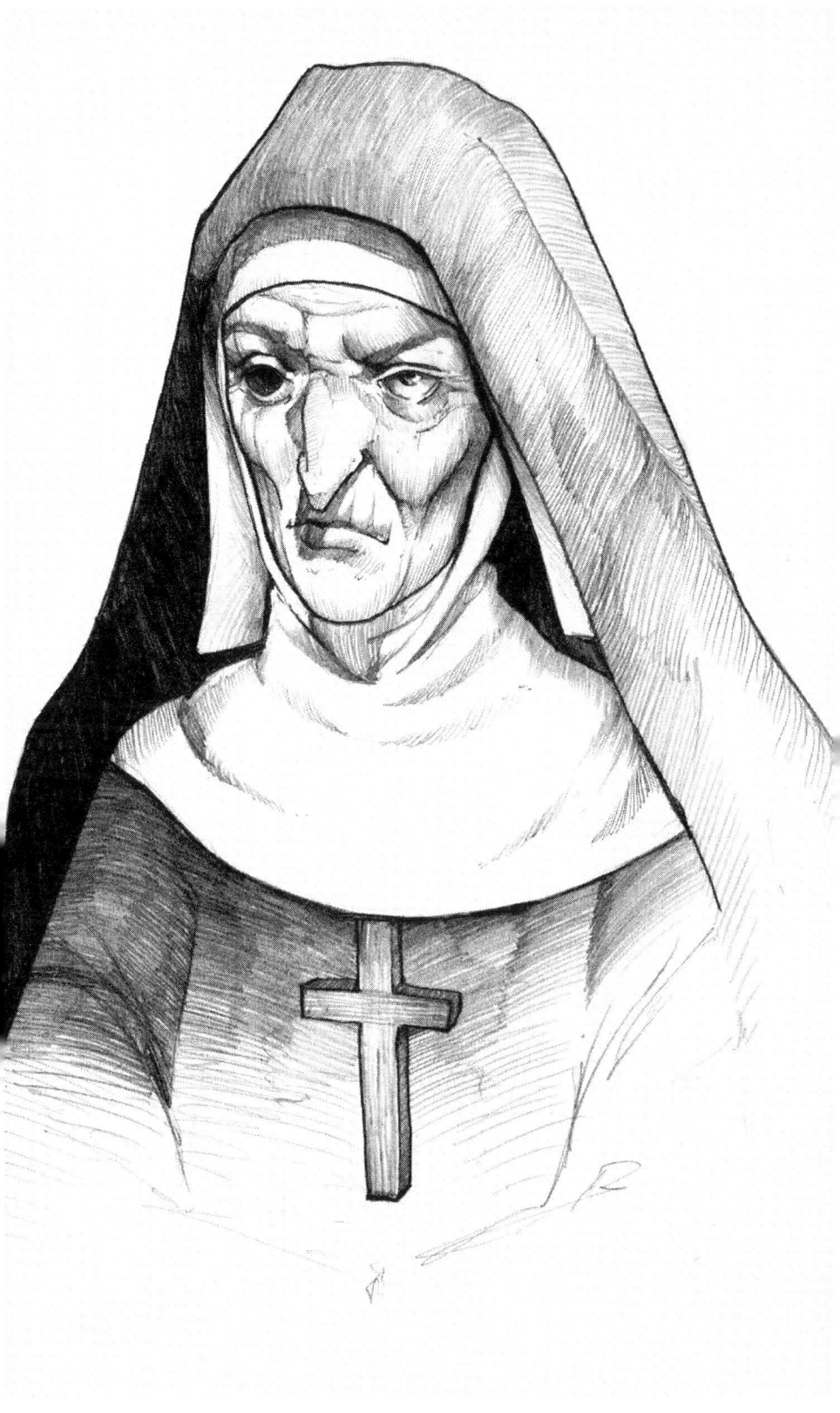

Lucid Dreams

In a small town like Pacific Glade, death isn't always faceless. It hits you especially hard when you're a cop. That body dragged into the coroner's office, that victim slumped and broken behind the lines of police tape - that could be your neighbor, or your kid's algebra teacher, or that sweet old lady you pass every week at the grocery store. Death doesn't just come for the people on TV. Death slips by you every day, so close you can feel the breeze on your cheeks as it passes, and leaves your world a little emptier. Sometimes you notice; sometimes you don't. But it changes you either way.

My father-in-law, Peter Lambrecht, died on an early spring morning. He was gray-haired and stooped, but spry for his age, and the carved wooden cane he walked with was mostly for show. He'd brag to anyone who'd listen about how he'd won the stick off a stranger at the Hanging Rock. "Had 'em sulking in the corner like a raccoon in an empty trashcan," he'd say. "Never seen the cards hate a man the way they did that day. He was strung up and he knew it. Threw his hand on the table and stormed out. But not before leavin' me this beauty." Then he'd show it off by dancing a little jig.

He called it his wizard's staff. It was his prized possession, his lucky talisman. But even luck can't stop death when it's barreling toward you at eighty miles an hour.

He'd just stepped outside to grab the paper, leaning sturdily against his lucky staff, plodding through the dewy grass to the mailbox. The morning air was cold and his joints must have been aching, but he pressed stubbornly onward, all the way to the street. The newspaper boy had shoved the thing in deep and he had to set the cane aside to yank it out. I don't know if he heard the engine getting closer. When he set his mind to something, my dear old father-in-law tended to get lost in his own thoughts, and it wasn't uncommon to see him glaze-eyed and staring off into space.

The driver of the car was named Vera Hanscomb. She was going fast, way faster than her crappy old minivan was probably built to handle, but there was a wailing baby in the backseat with a spreading rash and two small children who were yelling over each other about God knows what. Poor harried Vera turned back for just a second to put the kids in their place, but her hand slipped as she did so, and the minivan lurched onto the sidewalk like a drunken man. It was only for a second. But one second was all it took.

The van struck Peter head on and sent him flying across the yard. The coroner told me he was dead even before he struck the side of his neighbor's house. *Broken back*, he'd said, *among other things*. I didn't need to know the details. All I knew was that there would be no more jigs, no more stories. Just glazed eyes forever.

Vera knew what she had done, but she panicked and hightailed it away from the scene with her three screaming children in tow. She might have gotten away, too, if another neighbor hadn't seen the whole thing and phoned in her license to the police. In no time she was surrounded by cruisers, sirens blaring and lights flashing. The terrified mother left the vehicle with her hands up and tears streaming down her cheeks.

They took her and the children down to the station, where Vera wept and shook and confessed to the whole thing, her whole body heaving with sobs. Calls were made, officers were sent to bring in the body, everyone was running around trying to keep the situation from getting any worse. It was a big fucking mess.

In all the confusion, everyone forgot about the rashy little infant, whose wailing had given way to a soft, pained whimper. In a matter of hours the baby was dead. Vera didn't even notice until she tried rocking the tiny corpse awake. If she hadn't broken before, that was the crack that split her open. People say her anguished cries could be heard for miles.

Karma, some might say. A life for a life. Which is bullshit, of course, because no cosmic force was watching over that road. None that cared, anyway. Death came and death went and left two big holes where it had been, and that was it. The story went on. This time it was missing a couple of players.

Nico Sanchez was the one who called us at home, and Ruth was the one who answered. I didn't know what they were discussing at first. But I saw Ruth's smile slip, saw her warm persona falter for just a moment, and I knew enough. She composed herself quickly and listened to what Sanchez had to say. But that half second slip had said it all, and even though I never saw her cry, not even at the funeral, I knew it was taking everything she had to keep herself composed.

She did it though. She smiled at the mourners and told them stories and hugged them close and eased their pain, even when she herself was hurting. Because that was Ruth. I was the cop, but she had always been the fighter.

* * * * *

The wake was a quiet affair. Peter had been one of those rare souls who'd actually moved to the Glade and stayed here. Something about the place seemed to discourage visitors from staying long. But not Peter. He loved the trees, loved the cool summers and the way the sun set so strangely. So he planted himself down, and before long it was like he'd lived here all his life.

The consequence of this was that most of his family lived outside of Pacific Glade, and they apparently had no desire to come here, not even to see him off. Ruth's cousin Trina was the only member of the Lambrecht clan to show up on the day of the wake. The rest of the mourners, few as they were, were neighbors and friends: fellow Gladers here to honor one of their own.

The Locklear funeral home wasn't extravagant, but Ruth had worked with the family to drape the visitation room in violet banners - Peter's favorite color - and lay out a table of small refreshments. I grabbed a glass of water and eyed the vegetable platter, wondering if it would be distasteful to munch away during my father-in-law's wake. Ruth wandered by me, and I took the opportunity to leave the food and join her by Peter's casket.

The dead are just sleeping, I thought, and not for the first time. Ruth's dad looked like he'd simply nodded off for a bit. The coroner had set his limbs straight and given his cheeks a blush he'd never had in life. I've seen plenty of corpses, and after the whole embalming thing most of them looked like waxy mannequins. Peter looked like he might wake up at any moment.

A familiar stick lay with him in the casket. The cane had survived what its owner had not. Whole and unbroken, it now rested under Peter's cold hands. His talisman would go to the grave with him.

"Did I ever tell you he took me flying?" I said. "Back when we were engaged. He rented a helicopter somehow and flew us all over the Glade. I had no idea he knew how to pilot one of those things. He would do all these dips and dives that scared the shit out of me, but every time he would laugh that wheezy, good-natured laugh of his and I knew we weren't in any real danger."

I took a sip from my glass. "At one point he even let me take over. And looking down at everything.... God, Ruth, it was incredible, it was like being one of the birds. You never really appreciate the trees until you see them from up there. And the lakes and the rivers and the highways cutting through the forest - they looked like one big nervous system, like this huge engine keeping the Glade in motion. It puts things in perspective, you know?"

Ruth didn't look at me. She swished the water in her own glass and stared down at her father's body.

"I never knew he flew," she said. "But it doesn't surprise me. Dad always did seem to be reaching for the sky."

I kissed her hair and held her close for a moment. She leaned her head against mine and sighed. That was the moment I expected the tears to flow, for all the sadness to come gushing out, but after a few seconds she gently detached herself and went to talk with her cousin. I listened to her hushed voice but couldn't make out a word of the conversation.

The wake went on for another couple of hours as mourners straggled in and out. I finally gave in and went for the hors d'oeuvres - they had barely been touched, which seemed like a waste to me - and was in the process of biting into a canape when my son Rory approached, holding a cup of water. He was small for his age, and the suit we'd rented for him looked absurdly big on his tiny shoulders. He picked at his cuffs and stared up at me. It looked like he wanted to say something.

"What is it, Rory?"

He bit his lip, eyes wide and, I thought, a little bit scared. For a second I thought he wasn't going to speak at all. Then, under his breath, he mumbled, "I saw Grampa."

"I know," I said. "It's not easy to see him lying there like that, but -"

Rory shook his head vigorously. "I don't mean in the coffin," he said. "I mean *outside.*"

A tiny chill went through me, but I suppressed it. I smiled down at my son and patted his shoulder in what I hoped was a reassuring way. "I'm sure it's nothing," I said. "But why don't you show me anyway?"

Rory bit his lip again, but nodded. He led me over to the window by the refreshment table. Placing down his cup, he raised a finger and pointed through the glass. "Grampa was out there," he muttered. "In the graveyard. He just stood there and stared at me."

I leaned closer and peered out the window. Locklear Cemetery was solemn in the dusk light, a sea of jutting tombstones and monuments. The place was deserted. I started to feel a twinge of relief - Rory's overactive imagination was probably getting the better of him again - but then I saw a slight figure standing in the shadow of a tall obelisk. It was too dark to make out much about him, but he appeared to be wearing a pressed black suit, and in his hands he clutched a very distinctive wooden cane.

I shot a startled look at Peter's casket. The wizard's staff lay there, as always, held beneath those pale dead hands. When I looked back, the figure in the shadow was gone.

"Did you see him?" Rory asked nervously.

"I… no," I said. "There's someone out there, but it's obviously not Grampa. Probably just some guy paying his respects to a dead relative." I reached out and ruffled Rory's hair, even though it felt forced to me, and probably Rory too. He looked unconvinced. A slight frown tugged at his mouth, his eyes still locked on the window.

I looked back outside with him. There was no dark figure anymore, and even if there had been, that didn't mean Rory and I had seen a ghost. A lot of old people walked on canes - so what if the guy out there had one that looked an awful lot like Peter's?

But this was the Neverglades we were talking about. Weird shit central. And I had a bad feeling that whatever we'd seen out there was just the beginning.

* * * * *

Two weeks passed without incident, and over time I gradually forgot about the specter Rory and I had seen. I had my hands full with other cases. Nothing weird, for once - just human crimes with human criminals. A man had been killed in his home with a pair of garden shears and I was pretty sure I knew who'd done it, but I didn't have the evidence to make an arrest yet. Nine o' clock Thursday night found me at the Beaver Street Diner, rummaging through stacks of paperwork and trying to spot a thread in this whole tangled mess.

I was so wrapped up in my work that, at first, I didn't notice the faint smell of tobacco entering the diner. It was only when a long shadow fell across the table that I looked up and noticed my visitor standing there. His cigar smoke was a normal shade of gray and his skin didn't look quite so pallid, but he was still the weirdest looking patron in the diner by a long mile.

"Inspector," I said. "It's... been awhile."

He gestured to the empty booth opposite me with a tilt of his head. "May I sit?"

"I suppose." I gathered the papers I'd strewn across the table and stuffed them back into their manila folder. The Inspector took a seat with that unsettling grace of his. He wove his hands together and leaned forward, the tip of his cigar glowing.

"I know we haven't spoken in quite some time," he said quietly, "and I know you probably have no interest in pleasantries. So I'll cut to the chase. I've found a new case, and I'd like your help solving it."

A waitress wandered over and asked the Inspector if he'd like a cup of coffee, but he waved a vague hand in her direction and she turned back to the counter, looking mildly dazed. I watched her go with an unpleasant clenching in my stomach.

"Can you not do that shit?" I muttered. "I still have nightmares about that little freak show you put on behind the rift. I don't need you showing off your fucking god powers."

The Inspector looked hurt, and for a second I felt guilty - but only for a second. It was hard to feel empathy for a being who was literally bigger than a planet. He sat silently in the other booth, still puffing out that toxic smoke, still staring with those eerie purple eyes. Eventually he broke the stare and looked out the window into the parking lot.

"I understand where you're coming from, Mark," he said. "But I just want to help."

"So help then." I drummed my fingers on the folder of case files. "What's this case of yours, and why haven't I heard of it?"

"It's not a homicide," he said, turning back to me. "So it wouldn't have found its way to your desk." He reached into his sleeve and withdrew a series of photographs, which he scattered on the table. "In the past several weeks, there have been eight separate suicides in town. None of them showed any signs of depression before the fact. When I questioned their families, I learned that several of the victims had become obsessed with dead relatives before they killed themselves - poring through photo albums, visiting gravestones, digging up old heirlooms from the attic. Three days of this obsession, and then death." He began arranging the photos with his slender fingers. "All eight of them drowned themselves in their bathtubs."

I eyed the photos with some hesitation. To my dismay, I recognized a few of the faces. Chester Maines, Nicole Kramer, Veronica Stapleton, Mike Schneider - they were all familiar fixtures around town. Chester managed the supermarket on Brook Street, Nicole was our senior librarian, Veronica led the local Girl Scout troop, and Mike ran the auto shop down in the center of town. I'd just seen him the other month to get my new cruiser checked. He'd been a real pleasant guy, always smiling, with a bright laugh and a mouth full of pearly whites. The idea of him killing himself seemed next to impossible.

"Okay," I said, taking a deep breath. "Okay, that definitely is on the weird side. But what do you need me for?"

"You know this town, Mark," the Inspector said. "You know these people better than I ever could. Is there anything that links them together? Any commonality that could help us understand why they might do this?"

I examined the line of photographs. All of the faces, even the ones I didn't know, looked like neighbors to me. The pictures were exactly what the news would show when their deaths were reported to the public: smiling mouths turned to the camera, rosy cheeks, laughter in their eyes. The news didn't want death to be faceless. It's like the newscasters wanted to say, *Look. Look at this happiness, because that's all you get. That happiness is dead. Now it's just emptiness: empty rooms, empty hearts, empty homes...*

"Hang on," I said. "I have an idea."

I flipped through my case files and pulled out a map of the Neverglades, which I'd been using to mull over the garden shears killer's potential hideouts. I grabbed my pen and marked an X over the supermarket on Brook Street. Then I drew another X over the public library. The Inspector watched me work, pensive smoke billowing from his mouth.

"What are you doing?" he asked.

"Each X marks a place where the victims lived or worked," I said, placing another above Veronica Stapleton's house. "If this thing is widespread, then maybe there's a sphere of influence. An epicenter. It could be like the entity in the radio, broadcasting... I don't know. Some kind of suicide wave."

Another X, over Mike's auto shop. Four marks hardly made a pattern, though, and I struggled to think of what I was missing. Then a thought came to mind: Rory pointing out the window, and a strange figure with a dead man's cane lurking in the shadows of the gravestones. I reached out and scrawled a final X over Locklear Cemetery.

"What happened there?" the Inspector asked, frowning.

"Dead relatives," I replied. "You said the victims all got obsessed with dead relatives. Well, that's where my son saw my father-in-law up and walking - at his own wake." I looked up at the Inspector. "I saw him too."

The Inspector leaned back in the booth and ran a thumb along the brim of his fedora. "Interesting," he mused.

"Perhaps the victims all saw their dead relatives before they…"

He didn't finish, but I got the implication.

"I'm not feeling particularly suicidal, so don't worry about me," I said. "Let's just see where our epicenter is."

I took the pen and drew a rough, wobbly circle through the five X's. Inside the circle was a shapeless mass of trees, and inside them, clear and blue and perfectly round, was…

"Lake Lucid. The epicenter is Lake Lucid."

The Inspector shot upright in his seat. "Of course," he said. "Of course! Mark, do you know the main water supply for those five locations?"

"Well, I can't speak for most of them," I said. "But I know the Locklear funeral home uses filtered water from the lake. It's barely a mile from the shore."

The Inspector rose from his seat and began pacing beside the table. A few amused patrons looked over at him, but he either didn't notice them or didn't care. "The water's been contaminated," he muttered. "When consumed it induces hallucinations, obsession, depression. Enough exposure and the victims drown themselves in it." He stopped and turned to face me. "I think I know exactly what contaminant we're dealing with."

"Do you, now?" I said.

"You've known me long enough, Mark," he replied. "Of course I do. Now come on - we must get down to the lake and stop this thing before its influence spreads across the entire Glade."

He spun around and strode out of the diner, his coat flapping behind him as he walked. I watched him go, and in spite of myself, I smiled. He looked so gung-ho when he caught the scent on a case. He kind of reminded me of me, actually, back when I'd first joined the force - all swagger and confidence and full of the stuff of justice.

He's a monster, my brain whispered. *He could crush you and your family without blinking an eye.* But that little warning voice was getting easier to ignore. Monster or not, he was here to help, and deep down - or not so deep down, really - I think a part of me had missed the guy.

* * * * *

Lake Lucid was dark and starless when the Inspector and I arrived. I pulled my cruiser into the parking lot and stepped out into the cool night. The moon was hidden behind a thick layer of clouds and the surface of the lake had a strange murky sheen I'd never seen before. We approached the shore and watched the wavelets lap at the sand.

"So the suicide wave is coming from somewhere… down there," I said. I looked skeptically at the grimy water. "I hate to break it to you, Inspector, but unless you've got scuba gear tucked away in some secret pocket dimension, we may be at a dead end here."

The Inspector stared thoughtfully at the moonless sky. Thin smoke drifted from the end of his cigar. Then he turned to me and scrutinized my face. I didn't like it. It made me think of a scientist squinting at a disappointing test subject.

"Hold still," he said at last.

"Wait, what are you -"

The Inspector removed his cigar and blew a cloud of blue smoke into my face. I coughed and sputtered - the smell was rancid, like rotten fish. Then a searing pain stabbed into my neck, and the breath whooshed out of me in a gasp. Trying to draw in air was suddenly like gulping in a vacuum. I lurched forward and plunged into the lake, my body flailing. I hit the water with a tremendous splash and sank beneath the surface.

The lake was cold and murky, and through the cracks of my eyes I could only make out a tangle of weeds and a few darting fish. Water rushed into my mouth, but instead of choking me, it slurped into my lungs with a cool, sated sensation. I clapped a hand to my neck and felt a series of tiny slits that hadn't been there before. They flapped outward with each breath, releasing a stream of bubbles.

There was another splash as the Inspector dove in after me. He floated in the murk, the tails of his trench coat splayed like a manta ray. He still hadn't let go of that damn cigar. The glowing orange tip somehow refused to go out.

"*Gills?*" I shouted. My voice burbled outward in another stream of bubbles, muted by the water. "You gave me fucking *gills?* This is exactly the kind of shit I'm talking about. You can't just play God and fuck around with my body like this."

"I'll remove them when we're done," the Inspector said, a touch defensive. "Besides, it was necessary. You couldn't possibly hold your breath long enough to accomplish what needs to be done here."

I gingerly touched the slits in my neck. "A little warning would have been nice," I grumbled.

The Inspector responded by kicking his legs and swimming further into the lake. "Follow me," he said distantly. "If I'm right, this thing is buried deep. We're going to have to dive all the way to the center."

I swiveled in place and swam after him. I'd fully expected my sodden clothes to slow me down, but whatever the Inspector had done to my body had apparently made them waterproof. It had also made me a better swimmer. I slipped through the lake like a human torpedo, my fingers brushing through strands of underwater plant life and disrupting tiny schools of fish. The Inspector clung to the floor of the lake, so I did too. We sent clouds of sand whipping around us as we passed.

After a minute or two of swimming, the ground sloped down sharply, and I noticed a dark shape hovering in the gloom just in front of us. *Alligator*, my brain panicked, before I told it that was stupid. The shape grew clearer as we approached. It had four limbs, a small head, and wasn't moving an inch - and it was wearing a soggy black suit. Panic swept through me again, and this time it didn't subside. I swung my arms around and came to a clumsy halt.

"Jesus!" I cried. Bubbles shot in a stream from my mouth.

The Inspector turned to look back at me. "Mark?" he said. "What do you see?" His eyes were still a piercing purple, even in the murky water.

"It's my father-in-law," I stammered. "His body, I mean. It's just floating there."

Peter's corpse was pale and bloated, his open eyes staring off into the clouded lake. I watched as the currents from the Inspector's passage spun him slowly in a circle, his wispy hair floating out in all directions. The urge to puke came over me but I swallowed it down.

"There's nothing there," the Inspector said, staring past Peter's body. "The lake is making you hallucinate, Mark. It's just the contaminant doing its work."

"Yeah," I said. "Yeah, of course." But the body sure as hell looked real, and I was afraid that if I reached out and touched it, my hand would brush against the threads of his decaying clothes. I shimmied past him, keeping my eyes averted, and followed the Inspector deeper into the lake. The water was getting colder down here, although it would have been ten times worse if my clothes had been sopping wet.

It became clear that Peter's body wasn't the only one floating in Lake Lucid. The Inspector and I passed a second corpse, then a third, then a pair of them who had drifted into one another and gotten tangled. Their faces were pallid, but I recognized them. They were the suicides from the Inspector's pictures. I knew they weren't real, I knew I shouldn't look, but I couldn't help myself. Their bodies were so small in death. Even Mike Schneider, the burly auto mechanic, had a drained feeling about him. I kicked my legs and did my best to maneuver past the drowned.

Then I recognized other faces. A mangled Edgar Guerrera - the first victim from the time eater case. A headless Harvey Jackson. A bullet-riddled Lester Barlow. The pattern was clear. My stomach lurched as I wove my way through a sea of all the people I hadn't saved. They drifted by me, unseeing, waterlogged and empty.

A small corpse floated my way, much smaller than the rest. Black strands of hair blotted out his face. The currents moved his body, the hairs shifted, and I found myself staring into the dead face of my son. Rory floated there with all the rest, his mouth open in dull surprise. Behind him, Ruth revolved slowly, and Stephen drifted with his arms spread out like a bird. I started to shake. It wasn't because of the chill in the water.

"It's my family," I said dimly. "They're here, Inspector. They're just like all the others."

"You're stronger than that, Mark," the Inspector said from up ahead. This time he didn't turn around. "Don't let a shadow scare you. The real danger is up ahead."

I tried to look away, but Ruth's vacant eyes turned in my direction then, frozen in an expression of hurt surprise. I wanted to reach out and grab her hand. Would I lose myself if I did? Would I end up just like my drowned neighbors, consumed by obsessive memories of my loved ones?

"There!" the Inspector shouted. "I see it!"

I withdrew my hand, startled - I hadn't realized I'd been stretching it out toward Ruth, my fingers curled. This time I managed to tear my eyes away. I twisted my body and kicked away from the illusion of my family, leaving them behind in a cloud of swirling sand.

The Inspector had stopped a few yards ahead and was now floating in place. I swam over to him. Down on the floor of the lake, in the tangle of floating weeds, a bright salmon-pink shape was pulsing in the sand. It had the curved carapace of a crab, but the sucker was *huge* - maybe the size of a small horse. Six broad claws extended from its body and drifted lazily through the water. It seemed to be glowing slightly. I peered a little closer and saw that the glow was actually a cloud of neon pink smoke, issuing from holes in the creature's shell.

"That's one ugly motherfucker," I said quietly. "Is it giving off a pheromone or something?"

"Or something," the Inspector said. "The dream crab secretes a gas that causes visions and intense mood swings. It likes to squat at the bottom of ponds and lakes until it's tainted the water supply; then it burrows into the ground and finds a new home." He frowned. "It's a stupid creature. I can't fathom how it managed to pass through the rift, unless…"

"Uh oh," I interrupted. "I think it spotted us."

The sand around the crab had started to roil, shooting great dusty clouds out into the water. A ring of beady eyes popped open along the circumference of the shell. I drifted back as a low chittering noise rippled through the lake and sent goosebumps popping up and down my arms.

"Get behind me," the Inspector warned. "It's about to -"

One of the pink claws suddenly rocketed forward on a string of sticky sinew, like a ball on a rubber band. The Inspector and I leaped aside. I found myself spinning, going head over heels, as the ensuing ripple buffeted my body aside. There was a loud *snap* as the claw closed on the spot where I had just been.

I heard the next attack before I saw it. The chittering grew louder, a thrum went through the water, and then the second claw was shooting straight at me. I got my bearings just in time to kick my legs and avoid the ensuing snap. The air around me thickened with that pink smog, blurring my vision and hiding the giant crab from my sight. I floundered for a bit as the claw retreated for round three.

This was bad. The water muffled the sound of the creature's movements and the smog kept me from seeing anything more than ten feet from my face. The gun on my waist wouldn't do shit underwater and I wasn't sure how helpful it would be even if I could use it. That carapace looked thick. Bullets might not even leave a dent on that thing.

The waters stirred again, sand rising up in a spiral, and I knew the next attack was imminent. I spun around and tried to get my bearings, but there was no sign of the crab anywhere, nothing but that noxious pink smoke and the awful chittering. I braced myself and tensed my muscles and waited for the creature to strike.

But when the smog parted, it wasn't the giant crab I saw – it was the Inspector. His coat was splayed out behind him and his lips were locked tight around his cigar. Rearing back, he puffed his cheeks and blew. A storm of purple smoke burst from the tip of the cigar and crashed into the pink cloud. The smog dispersed, turning into little curled wisps, then vanishing. Then the purple tornado swept downward and burrowed into the creature who had been hiding there.

The chittering turned to a screech as the smoke coiled up and slipped inside the holes in the shell. I had no idea what was happening underneath but I'm sure it wasn't pretty. The ring of eyes began to pop, one by one, leaving bloody streaks in the water. The claws flailed for a bit after that, but the fight was gone. Eventually it slumped on the floor of the lake, gave a final rattle, and went quiet.

The purple smoke emerged from the holes and billowed back to the Inspector's cigar. I watched as he sucked it all back in one long, heavy breath. The last of the smoke vanished into its tip, which glowed a brief violet, and then the waters were clear again. I stared down at the crab's unmoving shell.

"Fucking Christ," I said. "Remind me never to piss you off. Is it dead?"

"I melted its internal organs," the Inspector said. You know, as if that was a perfectly ordinary thing to do.

He swooped down to the creature's limp body. I tensed up, fully expecting the thing to snap back to life and cleave the Inspector in two, but it really did seem to be dead. The Inspector pushed aside its corpse with minimal effort and peered down into the sand. He brushed his fingers along the lakebed, a slight frown on his face.

"Hmm," he said, so quiet I barely heard him. "Take a look at this, Mark."

I swam over and squinted at the ground beneath him. The Inspector had brushed the sand off of a circular metal plate, a real high-tech gizmo with circuitry patterns across the front and a single bulb in the center flashing a low, pale green. Etched above the bulb was a simple red logo: **CAPRA**.

"I've seen that before," I muttered. "Where have I seen that?"

"In the forest," the Inspector replied. "I found a capsule with this logo near the entrance to the giant's universe. It's strange, isn't it? Two CAPRA devices. Two ancient creatures that haven't been seen on this side of the rift in millennia." He went quiet, staring down at the metal disk.

"But what is CAPRA?" I asked. "And what the hell is this stuff doing at the bottom of Lake Lucid?"

"I don't know," the Inspector said. "But I think I know where we can start looking for answers."

He lifted the device out of the sand. As he did so, a thick metal wire appeared, trailing down from the lip of the plate and into the lakebed. The Inspector gave it a yank, and several feet of taut wire popped up out of the ground. We looked at each other, then off into the deeper reaches of the lake.

"Follow the wire," I said. "Why do I get the feeling this is a seriously bad idea?"

"It may be," the Inspector admitted, "but right now it's the best opportunity we have." His cigar tip glowed brightly for a second. The light flickered oddly in his eyes.

"Strange things have been happening in this town," he said. "Strange even for me. But I think the answer to everything lies at the end of this trail."

"Lead the way, then," I said.

The Inspector obliged by yanking more wire out of the sand and pulling himself along it, hand over hand. I skirted the giant crab corpse and floated along after him. The fish were scarce down here - probably driven off by the dream crab, or maybe even eaten - so aside from a few straggly weeds, we were alone. There was no sound except the soft rippling of water in our ears. We could have been in another world entirely.

* * * * *

The wire led to a pipe - on the smaller side, but large enough for a man to squeeze through if he was so inclined. I had a sinking feeling that was the Inspector's plan. He stuck his head into the pipe and peered silently into the darkness.

"It goes on for at least a mile," he said. "The wire follows it all the way."

I sighed. "Fine. I'll guess we'll go spelunking. But if that thing bottlenecks when we're halfway through, I swear to God…"

The Inspector ignored me, slipping inside the pipe and out of sight. I reluctantly followed him, chasing the speck of his cigar, which glowed a vivid orange in the otherwise pitch blackness. The water seeping through my mouth had a vaguely sterile taste, and I tried not to dwell on what kinds of chemicals I was ingesting.

The pipe didn't bottleneck. As we swam, it sloped upward, the water going from chilly to lukewarm to uncomfortably hot. I was worried it was going to start boiling when a light suddenly appeared in front of us. The pipe widened into a wide-open pool, and the Inspector and I finally burst out of the water. I let out a gasp as the gills on my neck flapped shut and sealed back into smooth skin.

The Inspector was already climbing out of the pool, still following the wire. I clambered after him, shaking the dampness out of my hair. The Inspector's hoodoo had kept me from getting soaked but I still felt a bit waterlogged. At least I wasn't dripping onto the floor.

The room we'd emerged in was pretty small aside from the pool, which stretched from wall to wall. Everything else was a tangle of machinery that looked way too advanced for a dummy like me. The wire wound across the tiles and ended in a console covered with buttons and switches. I drifted closer and saw that there were tiny TV screens embedded in the console. Most of them showed empty water, but on one I very distinctly saw the dead carapace of the crab the Inspector had killed.

"Shit," I breathed. "They were watching us?"

"They must have seen us and run for help," the Inspector said. "Someone was in here not too long ago." He pointed to a dark puddle on the floor where a coffee mug had fallen and shattered. The puddle was still steaming.

"I vote we get the fuck out of here," I said. "Before they come back."

The Inspector swept his eyes around the room, then made a beeline for a plain white door I hadn't seen. We slipped out into a bright hallway with rows of blank doors and a checkered tile floor. Before I could look around too much, I heard the sounds of footsteps approaching from around the corner. The Inspector must have heard too. He swept past me and hurried toward another door at the end of the hall. Together we burst through it into a sweeping open space that looked like a sleek hotel lobby, with huge windows forming a curved wall around us.

The Inspector and I ducked behind a reception desk, all seven feet of him somehow squeezing into the tiny space. We huddled there and listened for the approaching footsteps. They got steadily louder, then a door opened, and the footsteps grew muted. I waited as long as I dared. Then I poked my head over the desk. I could hear voices from some distant room, but otherwise we were alone.

I stood up to get a better look at the space, the Inspector rising beside me. The lobby was filled with plush chairs and potted ferns. Through the enormous windows, I saw a long stretch of pavement surrounded by grass and ending in a metal gate. It occurred to me suddenly that we were in a totally unfamiliar - and potentially dangerous - place with no exit route.

I grabbed my cell phone, which had somehow survived a dunk in Lake Lucid, and checked the GPS. Assuming my phone's circuits hadn't gotten scrambled, we were standing in a nameless building on the edge of the lake, a few miles into the Catamount Forest. I dialed Marconi's number and held the phone up to my ear.

"Hannigan?" she said, picking up on the third ring.

"Sssh!" I whispered. "I'm in a tight spot, Marconi, and I need an escape plan. Can you take a cruiser and meet me at these coordinates in fifteen minutes?" I told her where we were, and I heard a pencil scratching as she scribbled it down.

"Hey, Hannigan," she said suddenly. "It's not like you to run off on a crazy mission without me. Is *he* with you?"

I glanced over at the Inspector. "Yeah. There's a whole story here but I don't have time to tell it now. Just meet me where I told you."

"You got it, Detective," she said. Then the phone went silent.

I tucked it into my pocket and turned to the Inspector. "C'mon," I said. "We've got fifteen minutes. Let's figure out what this place is and get the hell out of here."

The Inspector lifted a slender finger and pointed to a series of gilded letters on the wall above us. I spun around and backed up a bit. The words were a metallic gold and seemed to glimmer, even though there was no moonlight.

CLIMATE ASSOCIATION FOR THE PACIFIC REGIONAL AREA

~ A SUBSIDIARY OF ROSEN CORP ~

"'Climate Association'?" I said. "Why do I get the feeling that's a front for something much more sinister?"

"Because it probably is," the Inspector said. "Come on. Let's go further in."

We snuck through the lobby and down a nondescript hallway. Door after door stretched out as far as I could see. I tried the first one, but it was locked - of course. The Inspector stepped forward and made a clicking sound with his teeth. Something inside the lock imitated the sound, and the door cracked open.

"You're just full of surprises, aren't you?" I said.

The room inside was your standard laboratory fare, although it was dark and I couldn't make out much except a few spindly microscopes. The next room was largely the same, and the next, and the next, and for a minute I thought we wouldn't find anything remotely incriminating. Then I opened one door and found myself staring at a storage room full of wooden boxes. Stamped across each of them were the words CAUTION: EXPLOSIVES.

"Well," the Inspector said. "That's a bit concerning."

"You're telling me," I muttered.

I closed the door. We pressed onward, creeping through corridor after corridor, passing more locked doors and the occasional bit of wall decoration: mainly landscape portraits and pictures of nameless figures in lab coats. At one point we passed an aquarium filled with lazily drifting rainbow fish. A few corners past the aquarium, the hall ended in a set of imposing double doors, marked with yellow warning signs that practically shouted EMPLOYEES ONLY. I drew closer to them cautiously. The Inspector drifted ahead of me and lifted a hand up to the glass window.

A loud sound ripped through the air - I can only describe it as a VORP - and the Inspector was suddenly blasted forward. The projectile singed my cheek as it whooshed by. I clapped a hand to the searing skin, wincing. A thought flitted into my head - *that's gonna leave a mark* - but right then I had more pressing concerns than a little burn. I watched helplessly as the Inspector's body flew through the air, struck the double doors, and exploded into a thousand tiny purple particles.

"*No!*" I screamed.

The air crackled behind me, and I turned to see a very large and very deadly-looking weapon held inches from my temple. It was a gun straight out of some sci-fi flick, with a long chrome barrel and a yellow orb at the tip that sparked with bursts of electricity. The woman holding it looked about my age, although her cheeks were lined with premature wrinkles. She wore glasses, a white lab coat, and had a mane of long blond hair tied back into a ponytail. A single golden hair curled across her forehead like a question mark. About a dozen men in armored black suits and faceless masks stood behind her, holding assault rifles that looked far less sci-fi but no less deadly.

"I suggest you come with me," the woman said in a husky voice. "Our tall friend will probably piece himself together again, but something tells me you won't be as successful unscrambling your atoms." Her finger tightened on the trigger, and the crackling intensified. "Drop your weapon and put your hands behind your head."

I bent over cautiously and placed my pistol on the tiles. What choice did I have? I straightened up, hands raised, and rested my palms on the back of my head. One of the masked men hurried forward and snatched the gun from the ground. After a few tense seconds, the woman lowered her weapon a fraction.

"Turn around and walk through those doors," she said. "Do exactly as I tell you and your safety is guaranteed. If you try to escape, or do anything else funny, I won't hesitate to fire this thing. Do I make myself clear?"

"Clear as crystal," I muttered.

My burnt cheek throbbed as she nudged me forward with the tip of her gun. Hands still behind my head, I walked as slowly as I dared toward the set of double doors. Each footstep clacked on the tiles like panes of breaking glass. I reached the doors and pushed through them with my shoulder, emerging in a dimly lit hall lined with windowless doors.

"Third door on the right," the woman said. "Step inside and don't move a muscle. I'll be right behind you the entire time."

I did as she said and approached the door. The yellow WARNING sign plastered across it did little to ease my already churning stomach. I turned the handle, pushed it open, and walked inside. Fluorescent lights in the ceiling flickered on as I entered. Despite the ominous sign out front, the room looked like another fairly nondescript science lab, complete with beakers and microscopes and an equation-riddled whiteboard. A large circular shape in the corner sat hidden under a gray blanket.

"You two stand guard out here," I heard the woman say. "The rest of you, spread out. If there are any more intruders around here, they won't get far."

There was a shuffle as the masked men did what she instructed, and then the woman was in the room with me, closing the door behind her. The only sound was the crackle of her laser gun. She kept it trained on me as she circled around the room, her eyes sharp and blue behind her thin glasses. Neither of us spoke for several seconds. Then her shoulders relaxed and she let out a breathy laugh. I didn't move, not even when she powered down the gun, placed it on the counter, and approached me with an outstretched hand. Every muscle in my body sensed a trap.

"Sorry for all the theatrics, but we can't be too careful," she said. "I know who you are, Detective Hannigan. I've heard all about you. It's a thrill to finally meet you face to face." She gestured for me to take her hand and smiled. "I'm Valentina Koeppel. I run this facility."

I didn't shake her hand, but I did lower my arms. Her smile was earnest and her eyes had softened, but just seconds ago she'd had me at blaster-point, so pardon me if I had fucking trust issues.

"'Theatrics'?" I echoed at last. "You blew up my friend. You call that 'theatrics'?"

Valentina's fingers curled up. "He'll be fine," she said. "The Inspector's a big boy. It'll take more than an atom blaster to keep him down for long." She turned around, strode to a lab stool, and took a seat, her legs crossed. "Which is why we don't have much time to talk."

"I'm not sure what you think I have to say to you," I said. "Jesus Christ, you blew him up, don't you get that? I don't care if he'll glue himself back together. What makes you think I'm going to get all buddy buddy with someone who blows up my friends?"

"I needed to speak with you," she said with an infuriating calmness. "And there was no chance of that happening with him around. So I removed him. Temporarily. You're blowing this way out of proportion."

"Am I?" I said. I took a step toward her. "Why don't you tell that to the eight people who just killed themselves because of the contaminated lake water? Or those campers who got their juices sucked out by the wendigo? Because both of those scenarios had your ugly stamp on them. Kinda hard to fake innocent when you leave behind a fucking calling card."

Valentina was quiet, and for a second I thought I'd stumped her. But she simply uncrossed her legs and sighed as if she was disappointed in me.

"Why would I want to 'fake innocent'?" she said. "I'm proud of what we've accomplished in Pacific Glade. Did you know we were the first humans on the entire *planet* to find tangible evidence of another world? Even better, the first to make contact with life on the other side? It's not always intelligent, and it's not always benevolent. But we learn more with every experiment. Soon we may even be able to cross through the rift ourselves."

"You don't want to do that," I blurted, before I could stop myself.

Valentina raised an eyebrow. The smile that had dimmed returned, this time a fraction wider. She reached into the pocket of her lab coat and withdrew a tiny tablet computer. Her fingernails clacked furiously as she began to type.

"Of course," she said. "I forgot you'd been behind the rift, Detective. What was it like? Was it populated? Was their world like ours, or was the environment utterly alien? Tell me as much as you remember."

"It was purple," I said. "Everything was the same, except purple... wait, why am I telling you this, anyway? I don't have to tell you anything."

Valentina looked up from her tablet. "Of course you don't," she said. "But I think you will. We have a lot to learn from each other, Detective, and it would be in your best interest to think of me as an ally. I can offer you resources - information, weapons, technology - that would aid you in your investigations."

"My... investigations?" I said. A skeptical laugh escaped from my mouth. "You mean the investigations *you* were responsible for? There wouldn't have *been* any cases to look into if you and your corporate goons hadn't invited monsters to town."

Valentina frowned. "You don't think we brought them all here, do you? Reality is thin in the Glade. Sometimes things get through, and sometimes we deal with them. Other times we welcome them in and try to learn from them. Everything we do is in the pursuit of knowledge and understanding."

"I fail to see how killing a whole bunch of civilians fits into this mission statement of yours," I said.

She pursed her lips and crossed her legs again. "The collateral damage was... regrettable," she said. "But any scientific advances of this scale require some sacrifice. We learned a great deal from the entity in the radio waves before it went haywire. It told us about the empathic giants and how they could naturally cross between dimensions. It told us how to channel the power of the rift to enhance human ability. Most of the test subjects didn't last, but we achieved tremendous success with one Marcy McKenna. I believe you knew her?"

"I have no idea who you're talking about," I said.

Valentina looked surprised, then laughed. "No, I suppose you wouldn't."

"What the hell are you even trying to accomplish here?" I asked. "Whatever's behind that rift isn't interested in making friends. They're cruel and hungry and think we're like insects. Best case scenario, they kill you fast. Better than having your body hijacked or your life force slowly sucked out through your brain."

"But don't you see, Detective?" she said. "Making friends is *exactly* what you've done." She leaned forward, something glinting in her eyes. "How else would you describe this rapport you've formed with the Inspector?"

I faltered. I hated to admit it, but she actually had a point there. She balanced on the edge of her stool, shoes dangling idly above the tiles.

"The Inspector's an exception," I said at last.

"He's the missing link," she said. "The bridge between us and that world. If we can work with him, there's no limit to the things we can learn." Her excitement was growing, her eyes lighting up. "Just think of what we could accomplish with a being like that on our side!"

"You don't know anything about him," I said. "He's never going to help you. Not after what you've done."

Valentina settled back against the counter. "No," she said. "Probably not. Which is why we need you, Detective Hannigan."

"Come again?"

"Observe him," she said. "Share his knowledge with us. Tell us about his powers and his weaknesses. Learn what you can about him and the world he comes from. No piece of information is too small or too insignificant."

"I'm not being your fucking double agent," I spat.

"This isn't about loyalty," she said, frowning. "This about what's best for this town - for the entire human race."

"What's best for this town?" I echoed. "What an absolute crock of shit. Was it good for the town when your radio monster melted people's brains? How about those people who killed themselves because you placed a hallucinatory monster at the bottom of the lake? Those were my neighbors, my friends. They didn't deserve what they got." I took in a shaky breath and clenched my fists. "You're putting the entire Glade in danger, and for what? Science? This isn't sacrifice, it's a slaughter."

"The problem," she said calmly, "is that you're not seeing the larger picture here. Our research is not theoretical. We know the rift is dangerous, and we know that one day - maybe tomorrow, maybe in a month, maybe in a thousand years - something will come through that threatens everything we've ever known. And when that day comes, we must be prepared." She peered at me above the rim of her glasses. "Sometimes lives get lost in the name of progress. This is nothing new. I thought you, as a cop, would understand that much."

I was silent for a moment. A clock ticked somewhere in the background; the masked guards shuffled their feet outside the door. I mulled over her words and stared at the blanket-covered object in the corner.

"Yeah, I've killed people as a cop," I said quietly. "But it's a tragedy every time. That's a family missing a father, or a mother, or a child. It's someone's story coming to an end. And even if it's necessary, even if it means saving my life or the lives of the people around me, it still hurts. They all mean something to me. They're not just data on some spreadsheet."

Valentina said nothing. She sat utterly still on the lab stool, looking at me as if she'd never seen anything stranger in her entire life.

"If you don't help us," she said, "we'll have to continue observing the Inspector from afar. And that means more monsters. More pointless deaths. More tragedy. Will you be able to live with yourself, knowing that on some level, all that blood is on *your* hands?"

I gritted my teeth. "You bitch," I growled. "Don't try to twist this around and blame this shit on me -"

I stopped. The room had suddenly started to rumble, like a train was going by on the other side of the wall. I reached out and gripped the closest counter. Valentina looked up at the ceiling, alarmed, as little flecks of plaster came loose and sprinkled around her like snowflakes.

"Goddammit," she muttered. "I thought we'd have more time."

The air in the center of the room suddenly contracted, warping the tables and chairs and creating a loud sucking sound. Bits of purple goo spat out of the center of the contraction and floated in the air like they'd struck an invisible wall. Valentina and I watched as the gunk condensed on itself, growing mass, becoming long and thin and sprouting outstretched limbs. My heart leapt as the goo molded into a trench coat and a wide-brimmed fedora - still purple and dripping, but unmistakable.

Valentina's eyes were fixed on the newly reforming Inspector. I took advantage of the distraction to run forward and snatch her blaster from its spot on the counter. Valentina jumped and fumbled for the gun, but I darted backward out of reach, training the barrel at her chest. I flicked a switch on the side and the tip began to crackle with yellow lightning.

"Make a move," I breathed. "I fucking dare you."

She froze in place and stared at me. She didn't look scared, or angry - just curious, as if she wanted to see what I'd do. I tightened my grip on the handle and glanced at the blob that was the Inspector. He had started to shed the blanket of purple goo, gray skin exposed on his face and hands. His feet touched down on the floor of the lab. His coat dripped in violet puddles on the tiles as he turned his head and stared at Valentina. His cigar was back, and curls of hot red smoke issued from his mouth.

"Inspector," I said. "You made it back in one piece."

The tall figure said nothing, did nothing, only stared at Valentina with rage burning quietly in his eyes. I didn't like her in the slightest, but I didn't exactly want the Inspector to splatter her guts across the walls - or whatever else he was capable of. I cleared my throat.

"We gotta go," I said. "Leave her for now. We can deal with her later."

The Inspector didn't speak, but he nodded slowly. Good enough.

I figured we could probably muscle past the guards if necessary, but I had a fucking laser gun in my hands, and it would be a waste not to use it. I turned the barrel to the door and tightened my finger around the trigger. The device let out a low hum, like a nest of cicadas, before letting out another ear-splitting VORP and unleashing a blast of light. The door utterly disintegrated, leaving behind a jagged circular hole. Through it, I saw the two guards slumped on the floor, having been blasted into the far wall. They looked burnt and unconscious but otherwise alive.

"Come on," I said, scrambling through the hole.

We didn't exactly have the element of surprise, but we did have an atom blaster, so I guess it sort of balanced out. The Inspector glided past me and made a beeline for the double doors. I followed him, but not before shooting a glance back at Valentina. She was still perched on her stool, although she had her tablet in her hand, and I was sure she had already called for backup. Her eyes locked on mine.

This whole meeting clearly hadn't gone as she'd intended. But even so, she didn't look upset, or even disappointed. It looked like she was thinking - like she was already calculating what the next move would be. I didn't like that look. So I turned away and ran after the Inspector's retreating back, even as the halls lit up with red alarms, even as sirens began to blare like foghorns in my eardrums.

It was only a matter of time before the guards in black would be on us. But I had this big fucking gun, and I had the Inspector, and maybe that would be just enough to make it through the onslaught unscathed.

I just hoped Marconi was waiting for us on the outside.

* * * * *

The first wave of guards hit us right as we were passing the aquarium. They came pouring out of hidden doorways, visors pulled low, lethal-looking rifles clutched in their hands. One of them barked a command to stop, but the Inspector didn't even hesitate. He ripped the cigar from his lips and flicked it at the glass. The tip flared briefly, then exploded. Water came gushing through the hole along with a deluge of brightly colored fish. The guards were knocked off their feet and swept down the length of hallway, swearing as they did so.

The water rushed toward us, but instead of knocking us over too, it broke into two waves and missed us completely. The Inspector stood impassively between the walls of water. As I watched, the cigar shot back to him like a boomerang and planted itself firmly in his mouth.

"Nice trick, Moses," I said. "Now let's get the fuck out of here."

We hurried through the halls, ducking around the corner as another set of guards rushed past. My fingers itched on the atom blaster, but I was reluctant to actually fire the thing at a human being - plus there was no guarantee it was even powered up after that last discharge. The orb at the tip was still crackling but I thought the sound was a bit dimmer than it had been before.

The Inspector lifted his hand and beckoned for me to follow him. We moved through the halls as fast as we dared. At one point we ran past a large set of glass doors, and I skidded to a halt, staring at what lay behind them. The doors were bolted shut but they led outside. A small stretch of ground jutted from the threshold and ended in a helipad. Sitting pretty on the pavement was a sleek black helicopter.

"Inspector!" I hissed, stopping him. "Look. My father-in-law taught me to fly those things. It was ages ago, but still. I can probably pilot that baby out of here."

The Inspector looked outside and frowned. The smoke gushing from his cigar was an alarming shade of yellow.

"Sheriff Marconi's waiting for us," he rasped - maybe his vocal chords hadn't fully reformed yet. "If we take another route of escape, they'll find her. Don't forget that she's been beyond the rift too. She's just as valuable to them as you are."

I hesitated, but not for long. The Inspector was right. I hefted the blaster and hurried past the glass doors, leaving the helipad behind.

The lobby was miraculously empty, but when we burst through the front doors and dashed out onto the pavement, we found ourselves suddenly faced with a squad of armed men. I skidded to a halt and whirled around, but now the lobby was swarming with guards. They spilled through the doors and surrounded us on all sides. I felt my heart sink as I whipped the blaster back and forth. I could probably take out a swath of them, but there were too many to handle with just one weapon, and it would only take one well-placed bullet to drop me.

"Place the gun down and put your hands up!" barked one of the masked men.

"Enough of this," the Inspector muttered.

He raised his hands, palms up, and clenched his fists. At once the ground erupted. A solid column of dirt and grass shot from the cracks in the pavement and barreled into the first line of guards, sending them flying. The rest of them immediately opened fire on the Inspector. I threw myself on the ground as bullets whizzed over my head and sank into the Inspector's body like putty. Unmoved and unhurt, he swung his arms to the right and took out another dozen men with a second column of earth. They cried out in pain and surprise. I watched as they flew through the air and struck the ground, moaning.

"Now, Mark!" the Inspector shouted.

Startled, I got clumsily to my feet and swung the blaster toward the facility gate. Only two guards were left standing, but they paled when they saw the weapon in my hands. I thumbed the switch on the side and set the tip a-crackle with yellow lightning.

"Move or I blast you," I said shakily. "I'm not going to ask twice."

I tightened my finger on the trigger, the weapon's hum grew louder, and the guards - deciding they wanted to live another day - threw themselves aside. The blast escaped from the gun and slammed into the gate, disintegrating it on impact. The Inspector strode forward at once. He glided through the gaping hole, dirt and pebbles still swirling around his feet. I gripped the smoking gun and hurried after him.

The Inspector sped up once we were past the gate, and I quickened my pace as well, shooting a nervous glance behind me. It wouldn't take long for the guards to get back on their feet and come after us. We had a head start, but they had more men and more guns. Our escape hinged entirely on Marconi.

We raced down a crude stretch of pavement into the heart of the forest. My heart was pounding and I cursed myself for not staying in better shape. Just when I thought I couldn't run any further, the rumble of an engine rose suddenly from the forest, and a police cruiser with dark headlights appeared. The car skidded to a halt in front of us and kicked up a cloud of dirt.

"Get in!" Marconi shouted.

The Inspector and I leaped into the backseat and swung the door shut - just as a bullet zoomed through the trees and shattered the window. A few more bullets thunked into the side of the cruiser, but Marconi was already peeling rubber in the other direction, headlights glaring. I clutched my seat as we rocketed down the road. The car rumbled like a washing machine as it drove over the uneven gravel.

"Jesus, Hannigan," Marconi called back to me. "How do you always get yourself into the deepest shit?"

I didn't answer. I could hear shouting and a few more bursts of gunfire, but for now it sounded like we were gaining distance. Then I remembered the helicopter, and I turned my eyes to the night sky, squinting for any black shape hidden in all that darkness. If they were following us by air, they were well hidden. I couldn't see anything in the sky except a few stars struggling to poke through the dense layer of clouds.

"Let's get back into town," I said finally. "They don't want us getting away but I have a feeling they won't follow us into the Glade. A bunch of civilians getting an eyeful of their masked army would totally blow their cover."

"I'm real curious as to who 'they' are, and why 'they' want to put a bullet in you two so bad," Marconi said. "Get talking, Hannigan."

So I walked through what we had seen in the facility and what Valentina Koeppel had told me. Marconi listened without saying a word. The Inspector didn't seem to hear a thing I was saying; his eyes were turned toward the shattered window, lost and distracted. I peered through the hole with him. In the distance, I thought I saw a long bungalow-type structure, partially hidden by the trees. Was that CAPRA headquarters? I stared at the low shape and wondered what kind of strange science was going on inside.

I knew so little about the organization or what it was really after. Valentina had said an awful lot in that lab room, but in the end, she hadn't told me much at all.

* * * * *

It was well past midnight when I finally got home, but a light was still on in one of the downstairs windows, and I opened the front door with some apprehension. *Valentina beat me here*, I thought absurdly. But as I crossed the kitchen quietly and peered into the den, I saw Rory curled up on the couch, reading a comic book by lamplight.

"Hey, sport," I said. Rory jumped and almost dropped the comic. His eyes were bleary, I noticed, like he'd been fighting sleep until I came home. I sat down next to him and patted him on the knee.

"Whatcha doing up?" I asked. "You're going to be hurting at school tomorrow if you don't get to bed."

Rory was quiet for a moment. Then he put aside his comic book and said, "I couldn't sleep. I keep thinking about Grampa."

I had been so preoccupied by psychic crabs and shadowy organizations that I'd almost forgotten where this whole investigation had begun. Rory didn't just look weary from the sleep, he looked world-weary. It was a strange expression to see on a twelve-year-old.

"If you're worried about… what we saw at Grampa's funeral," I said, "you don't have to be. I have a feeling we're done seeing ghosts around here."

But Rory shook his head. "I'm not worried about *that*," he said, like the idea was stupid. "I just keep thinking about the last time I saw him. He came over on Easter and told us stories about when he was growing up, you know, outside the Glade. They were really good stories. And it's dumb, but…" He stopped and sniffled a little. "I want to hear more of his stories. But I know I can't. And I keep thinking, like - I knew him, but I didn't really know him, you know? And now I won't ever know him. Not really."

I pulled Rory into a tight hug. He let out one tiny sob, but was otherwise quiet. I held him close and patted his back and thought about what I'd told Valentina: how every death was a story ending, a book being closed for good. Rory understood that now, in ways Valentina and her scientists never could.

We stayed up for another hour or so, curled up on the couch, sharing stories about Peter and what we remembered of him. Eventually Rory's eyes drooped, and I laid his head gently on the cushion. Then I shuffled upstairs, opened my bedroom door, and slid under the covers. Ruth's hand closed around mine. I nestled up against her, comforted by her warmth, by her steady presence, and together we slipped into sleep.

Every life is a story, and we never know how many pages are left in ours. So we bookmark moments to come back to. That night with Rory, that moment of closeness of Ruth - those were some of my bookmarks. And when the pages finally ran out, when my story reached its peak, those were the moments I clung to.

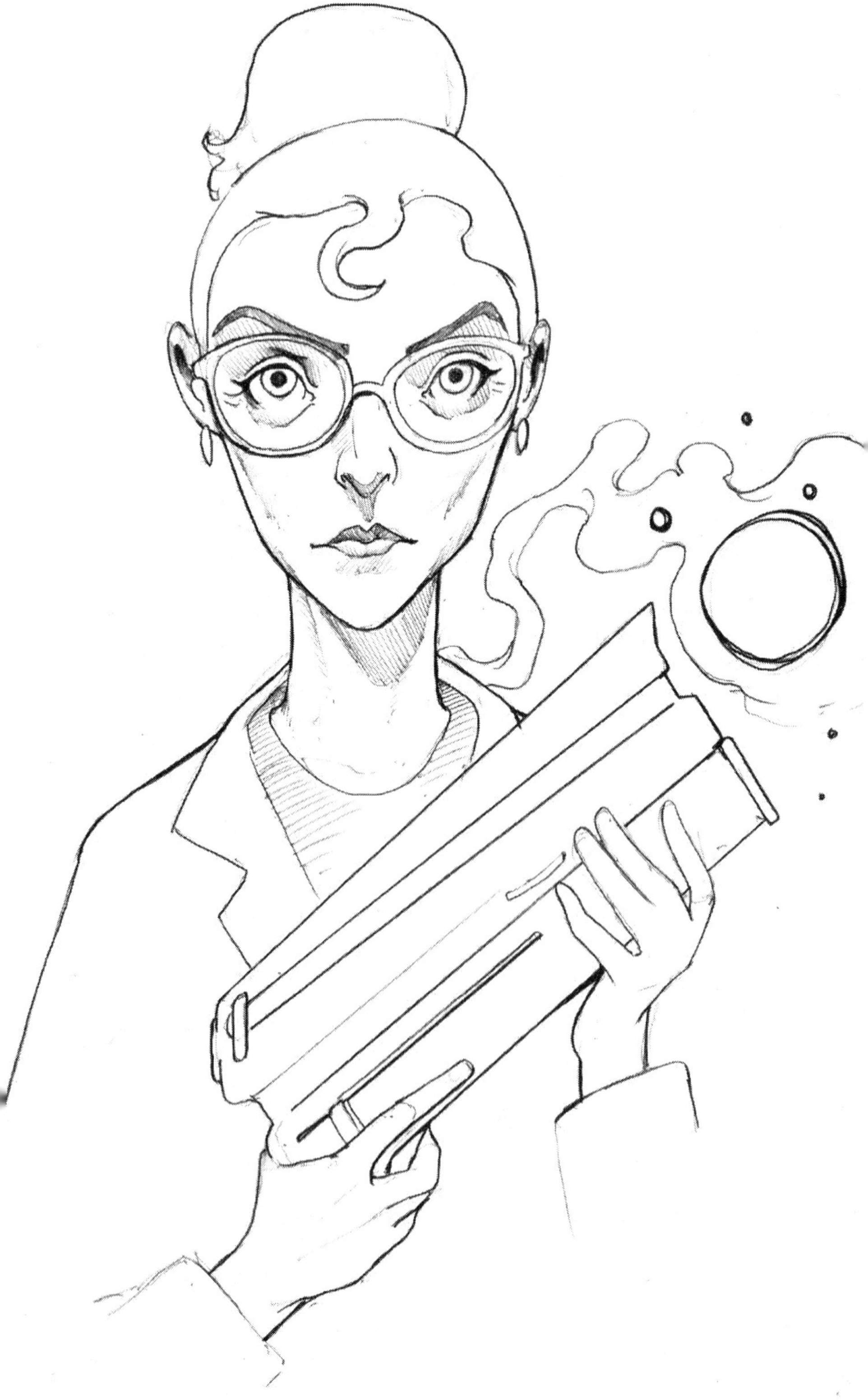

DEVOUR

Two weeks after our great escape from their facility, Marconi and I were investigating CAPRA at the station when the whole fucking world fell apart.

We'd dug into the organization as far as we could go, and our efforts had turned up zilch - nothing to incriminate them, at any rate. For all intents and purposes, the Climate Association for the Pacific Regional Area was a government agency founded in 1985 that regulated water levels and maintained our public parks and forests. That was it. There was nothing anywhere to indicate that they were tearing giant holes in the universe to let in all sorts of beasties.

"Take a look at this," Marconi said, passing me a newspaper clipping. It was a blurry photograph of a bunch of scientists gathered outside the front gates of CAPRA headquarters. At the front of the pack was a young Valentina Koeppel. Her face was smooth and wrinkle-free, her eyes bright behind her glasses.

"I had to dig this one out of the archives," Marconi said. "For *some* reason, Uncle Sam's climate brigade coming to town didn't exactly make headlines. That's her, isn't it?"

"Yeah," I replied. "I wonder if -"

But a loud, sudden rumble cut me off. A tremor shook the station and almost knocked the two of us off our feet. I grabbed the corner of my desk as a filing cabinet toppled over and went sliding across the room. My computer monitor flipped backward and shattered. Everything had gone slanted, turning the floor of my office into a carnival slide. Marconi reached out and grabbed my arm to keep from slipping.

"Earthquake?" I shouted over the rumble.

"No shit," she shouted back. "But I've never seen one this bad."

We clutched at the desk and stayed low as we waited for the quaking to stop. It took about five minutes for the tremors to subside completely. Marconi and I shared an uneasy look. The floor was still tilted at an awkward angle, so we had to clamber upward to reach the door and climb into the main lobby.

The station was in shambles. There was an enormous crack running through the floor, with desks and chairs sticking up from inside. Dust floated through the air, and people were stumbling through the haze, coughing loudly. I heard a choked gasp of pain from up front and hurried toward the source of the noise. Abigail Shannon was lying on the ground, her leg pinned by a fallen rafter. There was a blood-soaked patch on the shin of her pants and a tiny protrusion that could have been a broken bone.

Nico Sanchez ran by me, and I grabbed him by the arm. "Get that thing off of her and splint her leg," I ordered. "I'm going to see if anyone else is injured."

His face was pale, but Sanchez nodded and knelt down to lift the piece of tangled metal. I looked around and waved a hand through the air to try and clear the dust. I spotted a few people on the floor and stumbled toward them, but they weren't hurt, only shaken, so I helped them to their feet and continued making the rounds. Most of them were okay. Only Abigail had suffered a severe injury, and even that wasn't life threatening. I went back and helped Sanchez load her onto a makeshift stretcher.

The phone lines were down, along with our cell phones, so we couldn't call for an ambulance. Sanchez and I looked at each other, then picked up the stretcher and pushed through the front doors of the station. We had a few bigger cruisers specifically designed to carry injured passengers; one of those would have to do. Abigail hissed in pain as we carried her outside.

We were ten steps into the parking lot when Sanchez stopped dead. I almost tripped and spilled Abigail onto the pavement. "What the fuck?" I shouted to him, but he wasn't listening. His eyes were turned to the sky. The color had utterly drained from his face.

I looked up, and I understood.

There was an enormous tear in the sky, a jagged gash across the clouds that cut off the bottom half of the sun. The edges of the gash glowed a faint purple. Inside was nothing but void. I stared into the emptiness and saw something large and dark stirring in its depths, and a familiar icy dread rushed through my entire body.

"*Shit*," Marconi breathed. She had joined us in the parking lot, and she wasn't staring at the rip in the sky. I looked downward and drew in a sharp intake of breath.

The Neverglades had turned into a disaster zone. The streets had heaved upward like a ripple in water and frozen in lurching, lumpy formations. Trees had fallen on cars and power lines; houses had collapsed on themselves. Now that I was focused on the world below the rift, I could hear the distant blare of car alarms and people shouting for help. My stomach churned.

"Ruth," I uttered, at the same second Marconi said, "Janine!"

I got my shit together long enough to help Sanchez load Abigail into the back of the emergency cruiser. Then I turned to Marconi and yanked the Inspector's calling card out of my pocket.

"I'm going to find my family," I said, handing her the card. "I'm sure the Inspector already knows what's going on, but if you don't run into him, light that card on fire and he'll come running. I have a feeling we're going to need him soon enough."

Marconi took the card and stared at it for a moment. "Be careful, Hannigan," she said. "This might not be the only quake we get today. If it's even half as bad as the last one..."

"I'll be fine," I said. "I can take care of myself. Just make sure Janine is okay."

She nodded, and we both set off to our separate cruisers. Sanchez had already left with the wounded Abigail, so I revved the engine and rolled out of the parking lot. On my right, Marconi's car took a sharp turn and headed down the road toward her house. I pulled into the street and immediately found myself faced with a bump two feet high. The road beyond it didn't look much better. I planted my foot on the gas and flew over the first bump, then the next, my body rattling back and forth inside the vehicle.

It was going to be a shaky ride. There was a ton of debris blocking the road and I had to swerve dangerously to avoid it. At one point I came to a screeching halt when the pavement in front of me suddenly dropped away into a narrow chasm that hadn't been there the day before. I spun the wheel and turned around, searching for a detour.

All the while I had to keep my eyes low, since looking up at the rift made a familiar throbbing pulse behind my eyelids. I wasn't going to be any help to anyone with a splitting migraine. So I focused on the here and now: on Pacific Glade, my town in shambles. People were emerging from their battered houses, some clutching wounded limbs, others staring in fear up at the void. The ground let out another ominous rumble as something dark and unknowable shifted in all that nothing.

Time is running out, I thought.

* * * * *

My heart sank when I turned onto my street and caught the first glimpse of my house - or what was left of it. The entire second floor had collapsed in on itself, leaving a mess of broken rafters and chunks of roofing. There was a jagged gash in our front lawn where the ground had split apart. I urged the car to go faster.

As I pulled into the driveway, I saw a solitary figure standing in the front yard. Ruth. Her deep blue summer dress whipped around her in the wind. I brought the car to a hasty halt and leaped out of the front seat. Ruth rushed toward me at once, throwing her arms around me. There was a cut on her cheek, but it was barely more than a sliver, and otherwise she seemed to be unhurt.

"You're safe," she gasped. "Oh thank God, you're safe."

"What about the boys?" I asked, letting go reluctantly. "Are they okay?"

Ruth hesitated. Her eyes didn't give away what she was thinking, but the longer the silence went on, the deeper my stomach dropped. Finally she turned and began walking toward the front steps. She looked back to make sure I was following.

"Just come inside, honey," was all she said.

I climbed the steps after her, feeling a little numb. The inside of our house was just as destroyed as the outside. The refrigerator had toppled over and unleashed a splatter of broken eggs and soupy leftovers. Our kitchen counter had been cleaved straight down the middle. In the living room, the TV lay in a pile of splintered glass. Every picture frame had fallen from the walls and shattered.

Stephen was standing by the couch, apparently unharmed, and the sight of him sent such a surge of relief through me that I almost didn't notice Rory. My younger son was laid out on the cushions, his messy hair strewn with pebbly bits of rubble. One hand rested on his chest; the other dangled limply over the edge of the couch.

He's sleeping, I told myself. *He's just sleeping.* But when I reached down to touch Rory's hand, I saw the dent in his forehead: a bloody wound of matted hair and brain matter. His skin was cold. I gripped his hand and felt a heaving sensation in my stomach. Someone was sobbing, and it took a second to realize it was me.

"We were just playing video games in my room," Stephen said, as if in a daze. "I went downstairs to grab a snack. If I'd waited an extra minute or two, I could've... I mean..." He couldn't bring himself to finish. His fingers clutched at the arm of the couch, knuckles white.

I couldn't see anymore. My eyes were too blurred with tears. I tried to wipe them away, but they kept on spilling, and why shouldn't they? My son was gone. Just a few weeks ago he'd been sitting on that same couch, reading a comic book way past his bedtime. I remembered how world-weary he'd looked then. Now he didn't look weary at all. Just small.

Footsteps crunched across the rubble. Out of the corner of my eye, I saw it was Ruth. She drew close and cupped my face in her hands.

"Mark," she said. "Mark, *look at me.*"

I turned my teary eyes to her. The wind from the broken windows caught her hair and sent dust billowing around us. Ruth looked into my eyes and I saw myself reflected in that hardened hazel. Her cheeks were dry, barring the blood from that sliver of a cut. My wife wasn't crying. I had no idea how she managed to hold in so much pain.

"There's nothing we can do for Rory," she said gently. "But there are others who need help right now. Friends, family, neighbors. That earthquake was a big one and people are bound to be hurt." When I said nothing, she leaned forward and placed her forehead against mine.

"We'll mourn later," she whispered. "But for now we have to help where we can."

I clutched at her arm. "How?" I breathed. "How can you be so calm, when he's… when he's…" I couldn't finish the thought. Another sob escaped from my throat.

Ruth lifted her head from mine, then looked to Stephen. Our son was staring down at his brother with a profound hollowness in his eyes. One of his hands rested on the couch cushion, inches from Rory's blood-matted hair.

"When my father died," Ruth said, "I realized that death doesn't pull punches. It can come out of nowhere and knock you clean off your feet. And it's so, so easy to stay knocked down. To give into loss and anguish. Getting up again is the hardest thing in the world." She turned back to face me.

"I love our son," she said, and her voice hitched. "God, Mark, I love him so much. And I am absolutely devastated that he's gone. But this isn't the time to stay knocked down. There are people out there who need me more than Rory does. There are other families with kids who *can* be saved. So I'm going to do whatever I can to save them. I'm not letting death get the last word today."

She left me standing in our blasted living room and retreated to the side hallway. When she returned, she was holding the first aid kit we always kept stashed in the hall closet. Stephen watched her silently as she crossed the room and planted a dry kiss on my lips. I kissed her back, and was deeply sorry when she backed away.

"I saw what's in the sky," she said. "I know this is the kind of thing you and the Inspector handle. So I'll leave you to do what you have to do." She reached out and grasped my hand. "But Mark - please stay safe."

"I will," I said.

That was the last thing I ever said to my wife, and it was a bald-faced lie. How shitty is that? But it was a lie we'd built our lives around from the beginning. This wasn't a safe world. Not even close. If this job had taught us anything, it's that tomorrow was a gift, not a guarantee. So in this crazy, dangerous world, why wouldn't I want to come home to a safe house, a safe family, and nestle safely into bed with the woman I loved?

It may have been a lie, but at least it had been a beautiful one.

* * * * *

I met Marconi outside the Hanging Rock twenty minutes later. The Inspector trailed behind her, cigar wisping into the sky in clouds of light blue smoke. I don't think I'd even seen him so pale - not even when we were working the wendigo case. His eyes seemed glued to the massive rip above us.

It was early, but even at this time of day the Hanging Rock should have been bustling with mid-afternoon customers: work-weary employees enjoying a drink or two away from their jobs. Not anymore. The Rock had caved in on itself, leaving two sloping halves and a whole ton of splintered rubble. If anyone was left inside, they'd probably been crushed by the debris. Rory's bashed-in forehead floated behind my eyelids. I blinked it away furiously.

"How's Janine?" I asked, my voice hoarse.

"You'll never believe it," Marconi replied. "When the shaking started, she got knocked off her feet and sprained a wrist breaking her fall. That's it. The house didn't even get too damaged except for a few broken plates. We were lucky."

"Lucky," I repeated. "Yeah."

I knew what was coming, and I should have been ready, but it still hurt when Marconi said it: "How about you? Is your family okay?"

I swallowed a painful lump and tried to clear my throat. I looked off toward the wreckage of the Rock, at the mounds of wood and stone, and tried to remember what Ruth had said. *I'm not letting death get the last word today.*

"Ruth and Stephen are fine," I said quietly. "Rory... Rory didn't make it."

It took Marconi a moment. "Oh," she said. "Oh, *Jesus*. Your son? Christ, Mark, are you saying Rory -"

"He's dead," the Inspector said curtly. The words stabbed into me like shards of glass, and I recoiled. God, what a time for the Inspector to remind me he wasn't human.

"He's dead, and he won't be the only one," the Inspector went on. "The earthquake is bound to have taken a few others. The rift will take the rest." He stared at us with those cold purple eyes, his cigar tip burning. "There is no time to be delicate, officers - we're not talking about a few dead bodies here. We're not even talking about genocide. This is *extinction*."

He lifted his hand and stuck one thin finger into the sky. We looked up, up into the void, and I felt a twinge of pain bloom in my temple. The void wasn't empty. That looming shadow from before was there, and it was bigger now, its shape vast and dark and unmistakable. It opened its jaws and let out a low moan that sent another tremble through the ground.

"Is that... is that a whale?" Marconi said. "A fucking space whale?"

"It's the Leviathan," the Inspector said in a hollow voice. "The star eater, the all-consuming beast. It only exists to devour. It doesn't care that your world is covered with specks of life, it doesn't care about the Rorys or Janines, it just plows through the cosmos and swallows worlds whole. If it gets through that rift, everything is over. Everything."

"I saw that thing before," I said. "In the purple world. How did it open the rift?"

"It didn't," the Inspector said darkly. "The Leviathan can't cross universes on its own. Which means it had outside help."

I cast a sharp look at Marconi. "You don't think..." I said.

She nodded. "CAPRA."

"I can't fathom why any humans would be so colossally stupid as to welcome in the Leviathan," the Inspector said. "But I agree with you both. I have a feeling our friends at the facility are responsible for this mess."

Something in the wind turned. The sadness inside me shifted, grew hot and roiling, and suddenly I realized I was angry. Before I had been directionless. I couldn't blame Rory's death on an earthquake, or a falling rafter, or even a monster from outer space. But I could blame an arrogant scientist who'd already proven that she saw human beings as expendable.

I could blame Valentina Koeppel.

I turned abruptly and walked to my cruiser. The ruins of the Hanging Rock cast a long shadow over me. As I pulled open the driver's door, I ran a hand along the holster on my hip. My thumb brushed the dented metal handle of my pistol.

"Hannigan?" Marconi said. There was a touch of worry in her voice.

"Come on," I replied, sounding calmer than I felt. "We've got a gate to crash."

* * * * *

The gate, as it turned out, was already bent into pieces of twisted metal when we arrived. The earthquake had really done a number on CAPRA HQ. Most of the pavement out front had been split into shards and the roof of the compound seemed to have caved in on one side, making the building look like a large creature trying to lope its way out of the lake. Still, there were lights on in the windows. Somebody had apparently thought ahead and built a backup generator.

"Look!" the Inspector said, pointing through my windshield. A narrow structure stood on the roof's highest point, like a tiny radio tower. A single red beam issued from the tip and ran all the way up to the rip above.

I picked up the radio and called Marconi's cruiser. "You seeing this?"

"I think we found our guys," she crackled back.

We parked our cars under the cover of the trees and approached the entrance, weapons drawn. The forest was dark, but the purple glow of the rift revealed the outline of two armed men standing by the mangled remains of the gate. Marconi signaled to me, and we circled around them, keeping our pistols raised. They hadn't seen us yet. For once in my goddamn life, the element of surprise was on our side.

"Hey!" one of them shouted, and both lifted their assault rifles. The Inspector had appeared in the road in front of them. His eyes were burning like dots of cold fire and his coat whipped behind him in a sudden gust of wind.

The guards prepared to fire, but Marconi and I leapt out of the tree line and got them each in a headlock, making them sputter. One of them pulled the trigger and sent a volley of bullets into the air that missed the Inspector by miles. It took a bit of flailing, but eventually the men went quiet, their eyes rolling back in their heads. Marconi and I dragged them into the forest and stuffed them behind a fallen log.

"Do you think anybody inside heard that gunfire?" she asked me.

"Probably," I said. "We'd better move fast."

The Inspector had already strolled over the tangled gate and was approaching the front doors. I noticed a tiny camera on the roof swivel in its perch and follow his movements. Angry blood rushed through me, and I placed a bullet in the center of the lens. The camera whipped around with a spray of shattered glass.

"They've got eyes on us," I said. "Move, move, move!"

The Inspector lifted a hand, and the doors crumpled inward like they'd been turned into cardboard. Another gesture and they blasted across the inside of the lobby. They struck the golden C in CLIMATE with a *clang* that echoed throughout the room. The ensuing crash as they fell to the floor was loud enough to wake the dead.

"If they didn't know we were coming, they know now," Marconi muttered to me. We followed the Inspector indoors. Sure enough, a keening alarm split our eardrums as soon as we crossed the threshold. Red warning lights flashed across the walls. I could hear the sounds of distant yelling and the clomping of heavy boots.

"Into the labs," I said. "We have to find Koeppel."

"To get her to close the rift?" Marconi asked.

I stared down at the pistol in my hand. The metal felt cold under my fingers.

"Yeah," I said. "Something like that."

Footsteps were approaching, so we ducked down the same hallway as before and hurried past the locked laboratory doors. The water had washed away, but the aquarium was still empty, yellow caution tape stretched across the gap in the glass. At one point we had to stop abruptly and dart down another hall as a swarm of armed guards ran past. The Inspector waited for them to disappear, then gestured for us to move.

I wasn't sure how we were going to find Valentina, exactly, but then I heard a familiar breathy laugh, and I skidded to a halt outside another laboratory door. The sign on the front read QUANTUM PARTICLE RESEARCH LAB. Behind the door, a crowd of happy voices laughed and cheered and applauded as somebody gave a victory speech. My blood began to boil. These scientists didn't care that my son had died. They had made a major fucking breakthrough and that was all that mattered. Someone pop the goddamn champagne.

I kicked open the door. The scientist standing at the nearest desk looked up at me, surprised, but I didn't give him the time to shout for help. I raised my pistol and squeezed the trigger. The powder lit, the bullet rocketed out of the chamber, and the man's head whipped backwards. A puckered red hole appeared in the center of his forehead. He seemed to sway, his lab coat billowing out, before his whole body just went limp and collapsed onto the floor. Blood pooled, slow and sticky, onto the tiles.

Someone at the back of the room let out a cry of outrage, but the cry turned to a burbled sputter when I turned and planted another bullet in their throat. Chaos erupted. There was a flurry of white lab coats as the scientists ducked behind desks, tables, chairs - wherever they could find cover. I strode around the room and picked them off one by one. They cowered, they screamed, they held up their hands in pitiful protest, but I ignored their pleas. I could feel something dark surging inside of me, something not altogether alien, and I didn't fight it. I let the cold anger fill my veins.

There was a ringing in my ears, and it wasn't until a felt a sharp tugging on my arm that I realized Marconi was screaming my name. I continued to unload my gun into the corpse at my feet until the barrel clicked and I was firing empty air. I kept pulling the trigger until a sharp blow on my cheek knocked me against the wall. Marconi had slugged me in the face.

"Jesus, Hannigan!" she shouted. "Are you a cop or a fucking psychopath?"

I dabbed at the blood on my lip, my fingers coming away a vivid red. For a second Marconi's words started to sink in. Then I heard a clatter from behind me, and I turned to see another figure in a lab coat slipping out the door, her long blond ponytail whipping behind her.

"Koeppel," I seethed.

I dodged around Marconi and chased the fleeing scientist, who had just enough of a head start. I fumbled for some extra ammo as I ran, slipping it clumsily into the gun. Then I fired three shots at Valentina's retreating back. All three missed, but the last one was only by inches; I saw it rip through the folds of her lab coat before she ducked around the corner and disappeared.

I followed her down another hallway, just in time to see a door closing about halfway down the corridor. My shoes pounded on the tiles as I ran over to it and yanked it open. It was the same room where she'd taken me the last time I was here, or at least it looked awfully similar. All the little details were the same, down to the glass beakers and the microscopes and the large shape in the corner, hidden under a gray blanket.

Valentina spun around as she heard me enter. I fired another shot into the wall just above her head. She ducked down and huddled against the blanketed shape, her tablet clutched in one pale hand.

"Call for help and I'll put a bullet in your brain," I said. "Now put the device down and slide it over to me."

Valentina did, slowly, keeping her other hand raised. She pushed the tablet across the tiles. I lifted my leg and stomped on the transparent screen. The glass crunched and shattered as I drove my foot into the floor, leaving little piles of glassy dust.

"Do you have any kids, Dr. Koeppel?" I asked.

She hesitated. "A daughter," she said at last. "Vanessa. She left the Glade at eighteen and went to study physics in Chicago. No idea where she went from there. I haven't heard from her in years."

"This morning I had two sons," I said. "Now I only have one. Your little earthquake knocked down our house and bashed his head open."

Valentina didn't say a word, which saved her life; if she'd offered some insincere apology or started yammering about "collateral damage" and "the greater good" I'd have plugged her between the eyes. She stared up at me, inscrutable as ever behind her glasses, her hands still lifted in tense surrender. I tightened my grip on my gun.

"You're thinking I'm gonna go on some revenge crusade," I said. "That I'm gonna track down your daughter and make you feel what it's like to lose a kid. But you've got it all wrong. I'm not going to kill Vanessa. You did that yourself, the second you opened that rift and let in the Leviathan." I curled my finger around the trigger. "Thanks to you, we're all going to die. If you happen to die sooner rather than later, well... it's no skin off my back."

There was a click as a gun cocked somewhere behind me. I turned my head slightly to see Marconi standing there, her pistol raised and pointed straight at my back. The Inspector hovered behind her. His expression was flat, but there was something disapproving in his eyes.

I laughed. "You're gonna shoot me, sheriff?" I said. "A giant space whale's about to eat the entire world, you think a couple more dead bodies is gonna make a damn bit of difference?"

"I don't care if the world is ending," she said in a surprisingly quiet voice. "Drop your gun, Hannigan."

I looked at the cowering scientist with loathing. "Give me one reason why I should let her live."

"Because we need her," Marconi said. "And because this isn't you, Hannigan. I know you. You're a stubborn son of a bitch but you're not a killer. You're letting yourself be controlled by grief and anger and when you finally cool the fuck down you're going to see that. Now drop your fucking gun."

"I'd listen to her, Mark," the Inspector said in a low voice.

My finger twitched on the trigger. It would be so, so easy to just squeeze the damn thing and send her brains splattering against the wall. The strangest feeling of deja vu came over me; I had been here before, or somewhere like here. That dark anger surged inside me, but I gritted my teeth, trying to swallow it down.

With immense effort, I reached out and placed my gun on the counter beside me. The Inspector darted forward and grabbed it. My heart was thudding like a jackhammer and I could barely look at Valentina without seeing red.

"Make yourself useful, then," I said. "Close the fucking hole in the sky."

Valentina jumped up at once and yanked at the massive gray blanket. It slid off the circular shape and hit the floor with a *fwump*. Underneath was a large control panel with a mirror-like object jutting from the top. Inside the frame, reflected on a strange metallic surface, I could see a reddish bird's eye view of the rift. Even on the screen the sight of the void sent a dull thrumming through my brain.

Valentina's fingers danced across the panel, pressing the buttons at speeds I couldn't even begin to follow. Window after window popped open, asking for confirmation, authorization, password, finger recognition. Valentina bypassed them all with the dexterity of someone who's worked with computers all her life. Eventually the device grew dim, the red light faded, and the beam retracted from the rift. We stood and watched, waiting for the rip to seal. But the seconds passed and the gash in the sky remained as stark and present as ever.

"I don't understand," Valentina said with a trace of panic. "The splicer is powered down, I swear. I don't know why the rift is still open."

"Turning off the device won't work," the Inspector said. "That beam was like a butter knife sawing at human skin. Scrape at it enough and yes, you'll break through. But if you remove the knife, it doesn't heal the wound. It just stops the sawing."

Marconi and I exchanged an uneasy look. "So how do we close it?" she asked.

"The same way you'd close any deep wound," the Inspector said. "You cauterize it. If we could channel enough energy, we might be able to seal the rift. But it would require an immense amount of explosive force. And…" He paused. "It would have to be done from the other side. Throwing energy at the rift from down here would only make it bigger."

"So we're going to need some sort of bomb," I mused. "And a way to get it inside the rift…"

I paused. The Inspector and I looked at each other, and *bam*, the puzzle pieces fell right into place. For a moment I forgot about my rage toward Valentina.

"The helicopter," I said, just as the Inspector said, "The explosives."

"Excuse me?" Marconi said. "Is anyone going to tell me what's going on here?" She'd lowered her gun, that usual disgruntled tone coming into her voice.

"Right here in the facility, we have a source of energy and a way to move it," the Inspector said. "But we have to move quickly. There's no telling how close the Leviathan may have gotten by now."

I grabbed Valentina by the arm - she made a brief effort to wriggle away, then gave up - and marched her out of the lab. The Inspector swooped by me and glided down the hall as if he knew exactly where we were going. Marconi eyed me skeptically, but she followed me as I led Valentina after the Inspector and into the heart of CAPRA.

I kept expecting guards to show up and open fire, but the halls were eerily empty, and no one disturbed us as we made our way down the corridor. When we finally reached our destination, I let Valentina go and pushed her toward the door. There was a keypad and eye scanner on the side that hadn't been there the last time we'd broken in.

Valentina tapped in the code, scanned her eyeball, and opened the door. We found ourselves staring at those same big blocky letters from before - CAUTION: EXPLOSIVES. We stepped inside, drifting carefully among the cartons. Marconi whistled. The boxes stretched off into the dark corners of the room, each emblazoned with that same black warning.

"There's a hundred sticks of dynamite in each container," Valentina said. "And this is specialty stuff. One stick alone could destroy an entire city block." She eyed the Inspector warily and said, "Would that provide the amount of energy you need?"

"And then some," the Inspector muttered.

I bent down and peered between the cracks on the closest box, making out a stack of chalky red tubes. I withdrew quickly and took a hasty step back. "Why does CAPRA need so many fucking explosives, anyway?" I asked Valentina.

She stared into the sea of boxes. "Backup plan," she said tersely. "In case things go wrong."

"Like now?" Marconi asked.

Valentina nodded. "Like now."

She assured us that the containers were safe to move, so we reluctantly got to work dragging them out of storage. The Inspector lifted a few boxes like they were made of tissue paper, but I was barely able to lug one of them on my own. Marconi and Valentina grabbed one each and together we followed the Inspector out into the hall. He seemed to remember the way better than I did, so I let him lead us through the winding passages. The doors flew open at his approach as if they'd been triggered by motion sensors.

It didn't take long for us to find the door leading out to the helipad. The helicopter still sat there, all sleek and black finish, its massive blades hovering like dragonfly wings at rest. I was beginning to think we were actually going to get away with this when the clomping footsteps of guards echoed around the corner.

"Freeze!" a voice barked from behind us.

The Inspector didn't even turn around. He swung his hand back, and a sudden wall of stone sprouted from the floor of the corridor, thudding into the ceiling. Another swarm came barreling around the corner, but the Inspector waved his hand and sent a second wall shooting upward. There was a chorus of gunfire as the guards unloaded on the Inspector's makeshift barriers. I tightened my grip on the box and hurried toward the helipad.

"We're surrounded," I panted. "How the hell are we going to get out of here?"

"One step at a time, Hannigan," Marconi said. "Let's close that rift before we worry about anything else."

We burst into the cool morning air and were immediately hit by a blast of wind from above. The Leviathan had stirred in the void, sending ripples through the sky. Every step we took was on rumbling ground. We lugged our boxes to the helicopter as carefully as we dared and deposited them in the back. When Valentina placed down hers, she reached inside and withdrew a long, snaky fuse. She placed it on the floor of the cockpit and backed away gingerly.

"I'm not sure you've thought this through," Valentina said, once we'd all gotten clear of the explosives. "We can't just fly this thing via remote control. Someone's going to have to be on the inside to light the fuse."

"You wanted to see behind the rift, didn't you, Dr. Koeppel?" I said. "Well, congrats. Here's your fucking chance."

"What?" she asked, startled.

"You're going to take that helicopter, and you're going to fly it up into that tear," I said. "It'll be easy. The autopilot will take care of the tough stuff. Then, once you get inside, you're going to light that fuse and blow this baby to kingdom come. *Boom.* One big explosion, and the rift will be sealed."

For a second I thought Valentina was about to run, but she must have realized she wouldn't get far. A strange heaviness came over her face. She turned her eyes up to the rift, where the Leviathan was letting out another great yawn in the distance. The ground rumbled again, a few seconds longer than the last time.

"I suppose I don't have much of a choice," she said. "This is really it, isn't it? If I don't go up there and detonate enough energy to close the rift, we're doomed. We're all doomed."

There was a rustle as the Inspector stepped forward. His fedora was tilted up, revealing those piercing purple eyes, and the smoke from his cigar curled in lilac spirals.

"I came to Pacific Glade to serve humanity," he said to Valentina. "As did you, in your own way. Everything you did, you did in the name of progress, of understanding. You wanted to know more so you could *do* more, so you could improve the human experience. But your curiosity pushed you too far. And that, that being up there -" He gestured with a slender finger. "That hungry beast will undo all the hard work you've ever done. Your life will have amounted to nothing. But if you do this, your life will mean everything. You will singlehandedly save the human race. All that work you've put in, to make the world a better, safer place - that work goes on. Isn't that what matters?"

Valentina looked at him, then at Marconi, then at me. The wind grabbed her hair and sent it billowing around her face. I stared into her eyes and wondered what she was thinking. But she didn't say a word - she only nodded. The ground gave another rumble, and she began walking toward the cockpit.

The three of us watched as Valentina climbed aboard and headed for the dashboard. She stared at the controls for a moment, then took a seat and flicked a switch. The blades whipped to life, picking up speed until they were a circular gray blur. Then the helicopter began to rise. Guards pounded against the wall somewhere in the distance, but I could barely hear them over the whir of the blades and the animal roar of the engine.

The Inspector, Marconi, and I stood and watched as the last hope for humanity lifted off the helipad. The wind whipped around us and blew pebbles into my face. For a minute I actually dared to believe this crazy idea would work. But as the helicopter swung around, giving me one last look at Valentina's face, a worrying sensation twisted my gut. Something was wrong.

It was the gleam in her eye. The tiniest of smirks. Not at all the expression of someone embarking on a suicide mission. And I knew, in a split second, that Valentina had no intentions of flying up into that rift. She was taking this helicopter full of explosives and piloting it far, far away from here. Probably to find her daughter one last time. She was going to leave the whole world to be devoured.

I acted before I could stop myself. Bounding forward, I leapt off the rubbery surface of the helipad and heaved myself into the cockpit. Marconi's cry alerted Valentina, who glanced back at me, taken off guard. I took advantage of her confusion to scramble to my feet and charge her. She reached into her lab coat, probably to draw some unseen weapon, but I grabbed her skull and bashed it against the dashboard. Her hand fell, and she dropped to the floor, moaning.

The helicopter had started to tilt, so I leapt at the cyclic stick and yanked it back. The cockpit steadied and righted itself. I hadn't flown since those long-ago days with Peter, but the instincts came rushing back, and I settled into the controls with a surprising sense of ease. We were still rising. I took a seat and adjusted the collective lever to increase our ascent. Valentina had slumped against the side of the cockpit, apparently unconscious.

I let myself look down. Marconi had a stunned expression on her face, like someone had wound back and punched her in the chest, but I could barely see her from here - her body was shrinking beneath the shadow of the helicopter. The Inspector stared up at me from beside her. His eyes were hidden beneath the shade of his fedora, and his mouth was drawn in an expressionless line, but there was something solemn about his cigar smoke. It was a dark, billowy maroon, and it floated up after me like a hand waving goodbye.

I swallowed and forced myself to look away. We were getting closer to the rift now, purple light spilling from the gash in the sky. I scanned the control panel and pressed a promising looking button. Two reinforced doors slid shut on both sides of the helicopter, muting all sounds from outside and sealing us into the cockpit. My heart thudded as we rose higher and higher. Then - a shudder, a tearing sound, like someone ripping a piece of paper - and we were past the barrier.

The world outside the windshield turned into a mind-splitting void, and I heard a creak as the glass adjusted to the sudden vacuum. If it shattered then we were fucking doomed. But the windshield held, and my migraine lessened, and I was able to stare out into the nothingness.

Except it wasn't totally nothing. The Leviathan filled most of the void above us, its mouth gradually opening like a whale preparing to inhale krill. This close, I saw that its body extended farther than I'd originally thought. It rippled back into the abyss, huge yet snakelike, its tail drifting lazily through the starless sky. The sheer size of it sent a tremble through my body. What chance did we stand against this thing? If we didn't seal the rift, I had no doubt those jaws could open wide and swallow the entire world.

The air behind me seemed to contract, and when I dared a look backward, I saw a familiar starfish shape folding into existence. Its solid red eye opened wide, and its tentacles curled up on the ends like tiny muscles flexing.

hello purple man i have come to end

"What the hell is that thing?" Valentina shrieked.

I hadn't realized she'd woken up. While I'd been distracted by the Leviathan, she'd crawled toward the pile of explosives and pulled a tiny blaster out of the folds in her coat. She aimed it at the Ender with shaky hands. I felt a surge of fear rush through me.

"Don't!" I shouted. "If you break the windshield, we're done for!"

Valentina ignored me and fired off a single shot. It was a spark of brilliant light, like the atom blaster in miniature, and I had no doubt it would vaporize the glass in a heartbeat. But it had been a good shot. The light bullet struck the Ender dead on and sent a splatter of black liquid across the cockpit. The creature didn't fall though, and when it turned to face Valentina, I could see livid veins popping across its starfish skin.

purple bitch dares to attack i the ender this will not do

The beastie moved faster than I would have thought, flinging itself on Valentina's face and wrapping its tentacles around her head. She shrieked. For a second I was afraid she'd let off another shot and kill us all, but the blaster fell from her hand and clattered across the floor. She flailed for a bit, then went quiet, as if the Ender had injected her with some sort of sedative.

A horrible gnashing filled the air, like a set of sharp teeth grinding together, and a sudden spurt of blood splashed across the doors. I nearly screamed myself as the Ender gnawed at Valentina's neck, its body inflating in and out like a puffer fish. She didn't make a noise as it drained her dry. Then it turned to face me, blood dripping from its tentacles, leaving Valentina's pale corpse behind it.

I'd like to say my last thoughts were about Ruth, or Rory, or Stephen. I'd like to say my whole life flashed before my eyes. That's what happens in the movies, right? The hero gets one moment of peace before the big finale. But I was no hero. Sure, I had saved a few folks, and stopped plenty more from dying painful deaths, but a lot of that boiled down to the Inspector. He was the real hero here. And truth was, the Neverglades needed him a hell of a lot more than they needed me. At least I could go out saving the people I loved.

In the end, all I thought was: *I hope it doesn't hurt.*

The Ender's sticky tentacles slapped against my face, and I could feel its suckers sinking into my skin. I fought the incoming wave of wooziness and pulled my lighter out of my pocket. For a second I was afraid it wouldn't light up here, but the helicopter was airtight, and the little flame burst into life. I leaned down and touched it gently to the fuse. The thin rope burned away, the spark crawling across the ground toward the pile of wooden boxes.

I looked away and stared into the maw of the Leviathan. Those great jaws were open wide now, so impossibly wide that they blocked out all view of the void. Tiny specks glimmered inside the creature's cosmic gullet. Despite the hissing of the fuse, despite the suckers digging into my skull, I found myself smiling.

"What do you know," I said. "It's full of stars."

The Ender's teeth suddenly stabbed into my neck, and it hurt, all right. Oh GOD did it hurt. I staggered against the window and left a spatter of blood on the glass. That fucking starfish bit like a mini-shark. I could feel my consciousness draining, but I forced my eyes open and stared blearily out of the cockpit. I stumbled forward until I was practically slumped against the control panel.

The fuse behind me went quiet, and in that fraction of a second, the world turned kaleidoscopic. I gazed into the Leviathan's glittering universe and thought I saw a tiny speck of purple amid all those stars. The cockpit was as silent as the Glade on a cold winter night.

Then the explosives lit, fire blossomed around me, and I was gone.

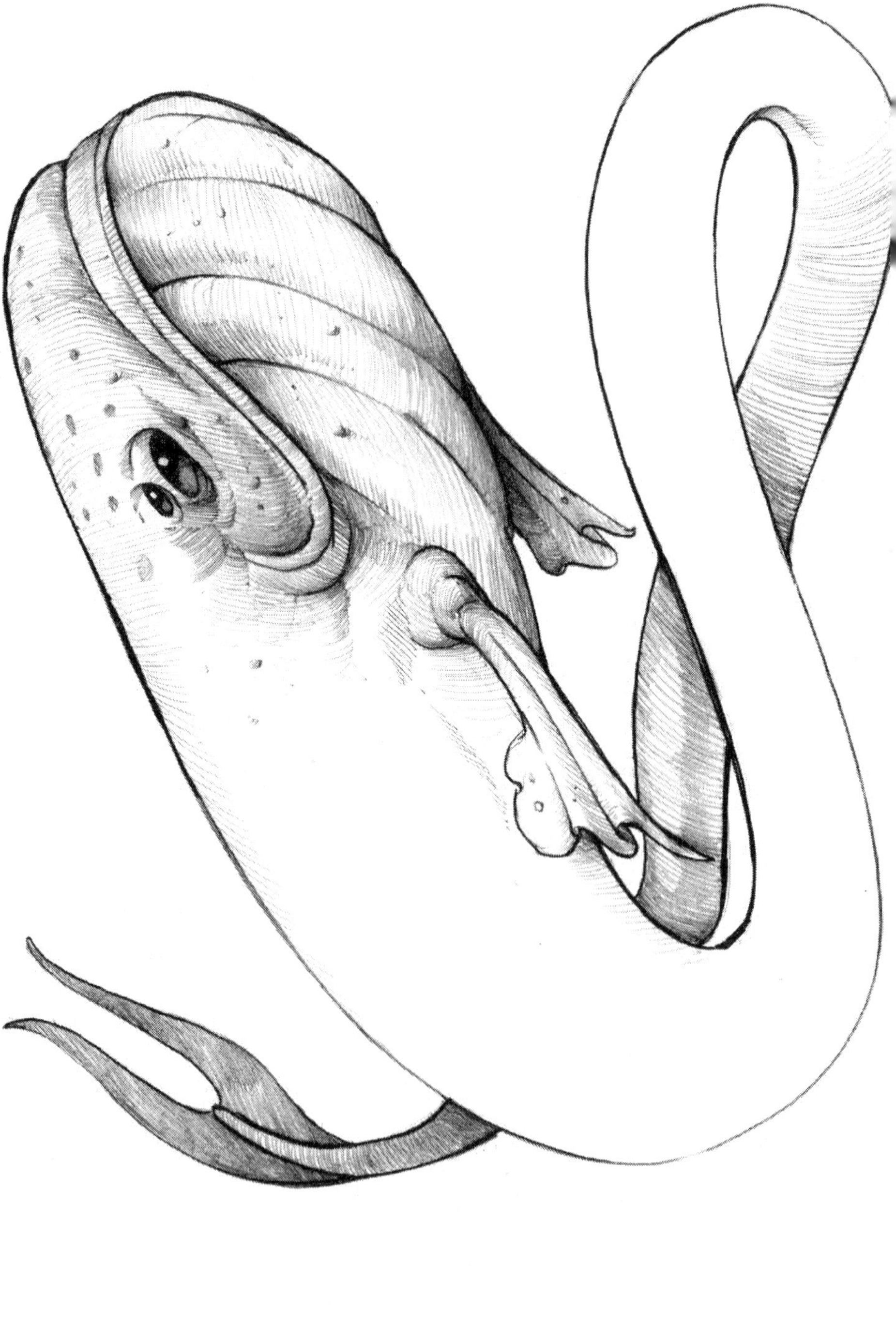

Fallen Night

Picture, if you will, a quiet day in the Neverglades.

The morning sun floats behind a thick cover of clouds, barely visible as a disc of glowing white. What little light it spreads washes over mountains, forests, roads that cut through stretches of country broken by wandering animals and the occasional rundown house. Follow the roads, and no matter the direction, you'll find yourself winding back into town. Folks with beat-up Jeeps journey to the supermarket, mothers push strollers down overgrown sidewalks, policemen sit in windowless offices and imagine the world outside. A single siren might cut through the air, under the distant crashing of a waterfall. Everything smells of pine and the dampness that follows each rainfall.

On this day, like so many others, the Glade is defined by absence. Empty desks at work, empty chairs at home, empty tables in diners. Some of the missing are at the hospital just outside of town. They suffered injuries in the great quake, but they'll be back to the grind before long. The others are never coming back.

Swoop down from your bird's eye view, down into the center of town, and peer into the window of the Hanscomb house. Vera Hanscomb stands at the kitchen table in a faded apron, trying to dole out oatmeal to a pair of whining children. Her hair falls loose in sweaty strands across her forehead. There are two empty chairs at her table. One for a grown man, another for a small infant. Neither will sit there anymore. In a matter of months Vera has gone from a bustling housewife to a single mother of two.

She sits through a breakfast of complaints and arguments, then excuses herself to wash the dishes. The suds are hot and they scald her hands as she works. She stares out the window at the pale morning sun and waits for the children to leave for the school bus. Then she dries her hands on a dishrag and heads upstairs.

Her house survived the quake unscathed, but there is one room on the second floor that might as well be quarantined; nobody dares to go inside. Some days Vera can't help herself though. Today is one of those days. She opens the door, slips inside, and closes it quietly behind her, as if afraid to wake whoever sleeps here. But no one sleeps here anymore.

There is a rickety wooden crib in the corner, surrounded by blocks and toys and an assortment of stuffed animals that Vera can't bring herself to pack away. She approaches the crib and rocks it gently. There is still a small dent in the blankets, as if as ghostly child lies there, asleep and dreaming.

Vera doesn't speak, or sing, or do anything but rock the crib. She wishes she had never hit that poor old man with her car. Her life, already hard enough, has been nothing but misery since then. She closes her eyes and kisses the headboard and wishes to go back to before everything changed. In that regard, she is not alone.

Enough. Let's leave her some privacy. Turn away from her window and continue down the streets of town, past the collapsed remains of Vivian Tracy's house, past the shuttered repair shop of the late Mike Schneider, past a cottage on the forest's edge where a forgotten woman used to live. There is life on these streets, yes, but everywhere you go, there are also vacancies. Little holes in the bustle that you feel more than you see.

The rebuilding has begun in earnest, and in many places life has returned to the normalcy of before the quake. In others it struggles to regain its standing. Families have been displaced; homes have been reduced to a few standing walls and a pile of rubble. Many find refuge with friends and family in town. Others leave town entirely. Pacific Glade is home, but it is a home in ruins, and for many it now holds scars and painful memories. The loyal will stay. But when winter comes, the Glade will be smaller than it's ever been.

For now, the air is cool with the crisp wind of a North Pacific summer. Follow the breeze along those winding roads until you reach the edge of Locklear Cemetery. There is a slow procession moving through the gravestones today: two rows of mourners, clad in black, carrying a pair of coffins. One is empty. The other is barely weighted down by the small body inside it.

Ruth Hannigan stands at the edge of the pit as the coffin bearers lower each casket into the ground. She rests her hand on her son Stephen's shoulder. Neither of them moves as the preacher recites the eulogy and describes what wonderful lives the deceased had lived. There are tears and sniffles from the crowd, but Ruth's eyes are dry. They have been dry since the day of the quake.

When the ceremony is over and the gravediggers have started filling in the holes, Stephen comes forward and places a small object in the dirt around Rory's headstone. It's a collectible action figure, a character from the games they used to enjoy. A drop of water splats on the figure's colored uniform from above. Stephen wipes his eyes and leaves the toy beside his brother's grave.

The crowd of mourners has dispersed, wandering back to their cars. Olivia Marconi leaves the cluster and approaches Ruth at the graveside. The sheriff has dressed her best for this somber occasion: crisp blue uniform, neatly pressed, with a distinctive curved-brim hat. She tips this hat at Ruth as she grows near.

"How are you doing?" the sheriff asks quietly.

Ruth twists the wedding ring on her finger, says nothing for a good minute.

"I'm alive," she says at last. "Which is more than I can say for them."

"He was a hero, you know," Marconi says. "He was the one who saved us all in the end. Things would have been much, much worse if he hadn't done what he did."

Ruth tries to smile, but it comes out as a grimace. "I know. I know. And I'm grateful that Stephen and I are still here. It's just…" She lets her hand fall. "You worry. As a wife, and a mother, you worry about your family's safety. And I know I'm not to blame for any of this, but I keep thinking… if only I could have done something… if only I could have protected them…"

"It was out of your control," Marconi reassures her. "It was out of everyone's control."

Ruth shivers. "I keep waiting for *him* to show up. Like he's going to stride in and tell us everything's okay, that he's got Mark hidden under that enormous coat of his. But I haven't seen him since the quake."

Marconi says nothing. She glances around the cemetery, as if Ruth's words are an invocation and this cloaked figure will magically appear among the tombstones. But no figure does. There are only the retreating backs of the mourners as they disappear back into the misty morning.

"Take as long as you need," Marconi says. "Janine's preparing lunch at the house when you get back. Chopped salad with raspberry dressing."

"I won't be long," Ruth says. Her voice is distant. She doesn't look at the sheriff as Marconi walks away; she doesn't look at Stephen when he mutters that he's going back to sit in the car. She only nods and tugs at the sleeves of her black dress and stares down at Rory's small casket, at her husband's empty grave.

Rain plunks on her skin, first one drop, then another. Then the clouds open up and begin to pour. She clutches her arms and shivers, but doesn't seek shelter from the storm. The ground turns to muck beneath her feet and the gravediggers abandon their project for the day, grumbling under their breath. Ruth stands alone above a pair of rain-soaked coffins.

She has held in her pain for so, so long. But there is no

one around, and streams of water are already running down her face, and she can't escape how much this moment feels like the last goodbye. So her veneer breaks. And under this cold summer rain, damp and alone, Ruth Hannigan finally lets herself cry.

*****

Let's linger in this place for a just a bit longer. The road is a-rumble with passing cars and bicycles, but Locklear Cemetery has its own sort of quiet, as if the wind itself knows to whisper here. The hours pass and the graves remain silent and solid. A bird nesting in the shadows of the mausoleum emerges to grab worms after the fresh rainfall.

Look: the clouds are parting, and the setting sun is visible, resting on the crest of Mount Palmer in that curious way it has. It casts a long shadow. Look closer, and you'll see a single figure walking through that shadow, striding down the path between the gravestones. She leaves the path and approaches a pair of graves, swollen with freshly turned earth. A lighter clicks in the dark, and the flame illuminates the face of Olivia Marconi.

The sheriff had curbed her urge to smoke for almost a year, but the quake had brought that craving back in full force, and she'd finally swapped her chewing gum for a pack of cigarettes. She touches the flame to her cigarette tip and takes a long drag. Then she blows a thin cloud of smoke toward the gravestones.

"I don't care what happened at the end," she says. "You were a damn good cop, Hannigan."

The smoke swirls and grows, takes on a light purple tinge, and Marconi realizes that most of it is coming from behind her. She turns to see an impossibly tall figure in a trench coat and gray fedora. The smoke billows from the softly burning cigar clenched between his teeth.

"Inspector," Marconi says.

The Inspector tips his hat toward her. "I came to pay my respects."

He steps up to join her by the side of the grave. Neither

speaks for a very long time. Then Marconi makes a small noise, almost like a sigh. She plucks the cigarette from her mouth and stares into the burning tip.

"You can't... I don't know. Bring him back to life?" She peers at the Inspector through the setting sunlight. "Do you have that kind of mojo?"

"If there was a body, maybe," he says. "But it would just be a walking shell. No memories, no thoughts, no motivations. It wouldn't be the Mark you knew." He looks off toward the mountains. "This way is better."

Marconi places the cigarette between her lips, her teeth gnawing on the end. "This isn't over, is it?"

"No," the Inspector says. "Mark closed the larger rift, but reality is still thin in Pacific Glade, and more entities will get through. And that's not even taking CAPRA into account. I doubt it died with Valentina Koeppel. These sorts of corporations always have someone higher pulling the strings, and they're not going to stop just because of one setback."

Marconi blows out another funnel of smoke. "So we've got all the eldritch monsters in the multiverse on one side, and a shadowy government organization on the other." She lets out a forced laugh. "Sounds like a real fucking walk in the park."

"It won't be easy," the Inspector says, staring down at the bumps in the soil. "You've seen where this road can end up. I know I may be asking too much, but... will you fight with me, Sheriff?"

Marconi lowers her cigarette and taps some ash onto the grass. "Of course I will."

If only they could see what we do: this unusual pair, two dots of defiant brightness among the darkness of the dead. The sun frames them from behind in brilliant orange. In a short while they will leave this place, back to the bustle of town, but for now they stand in the quiet and mourn their fallen friend.

A bright blue bird flutters down and rests on the top of

Mark's headstone. It tilts its head and studies the strange duo. Then the smoke drifts toward it, and it flies off with a chirp, wings fluttering as it disappears into the orange sky.

* * * * *

Here's how it is: despite the absence, despite the empty chairs, Pacific Glade is still brimming with life. It is a place that glistens with invisible connections, those threads that connect person to person in the web of community. Teenagers sneak out of their houses for secret trysts with their sweethearts; neighbors share gossip with each other at the supermarket; drivers turn up the radio and listen to Joe and Alan croon their dirty jokes. The threads stretch and sparkle across town. Everything - everybody - is connected, and on some level, they know this. Gladers look out for their own, after all.

See for yourself. On the edge of town, in that yawning dusk, Nico Sanchez pulls up to Abigail Shannon's house and helps her hobble down the front steps. Despite the bulky cast on her leg - and against her doctor's orders - Abigail has already returned to work at the station, spending her whole day working the front desk. She doesn't mind. The night shift tends to be on the quiet side, and besides, she spends most of it chatting with Nico. They're on a first name basis now, and their conversation is easy, natural. She likes him. Maybe not on a workplace romance level, but enough to be friends. And sometimes friendship is perfect.

Their cruiser passes Marconi's on the way to work, and they wave through the steam-frosted windows. The setting sun glares in such a way that they miss the shadowy figure in the passenger seat. Slip out of that crack in the window, why don't you, and follow Marconi home. The radio is on and nature sounds burble through the car's ancient speakers. She likes the white noise. It soothes her, like a warm bath, or a cigarette after a twelve-hour shift. Her passenger sits silently beside her and stares out at the twilit streets.

Janine is already setting the table when Marconi opens

the front door. Ruth and Stephen, the last of the Hannigans, emerge from upstairs and take their places at the table. This house has become their makeshift residence during the month following the quake. And even though it's not quite the same, even though the bathroom soap is all wrong and there are too many empty beds, they are welcome here. They have a home. In the aftermath of a crisis like theirs, sometimes that's all you can ask for.

Marconi places her keys on the hook, then fishes her wedding ring out of the dish on the counter. She slips it on her finger and gives Janine a kiss. Marconi's wife beams, frizz bouncing around her flushed cheeks.

"I brought a friend," Marconi says. "I hope that's okay."

There is no objection from anyone in the kitchen, so she approaches the front door and lets her visitor in. The Inspector ducks through the doorway and rises to his full seven feet, casting a thin shadow across the tiles. He looks sheepish - out of his element for once. But Ruth invites him to take a seat, and Janine doles out a handful of green beans, and Marconi smiles. She hangs up her coat and joins her family at the table.

Somewhere in the midst of all this, that stubborn sun finally sinks below the mountains. Night brings a closing of doors, as the Jeeps pull into driveways and the mothers tuck their children under the covers. A few stragglers wander through the darkness to the Hanging Rock, now rebuilt, and proceed to get spectacularly drunk. Otherwise the night belongs to the chattering of unknown animals, the rustle of the pines, the ever-present rush of distant water. Follow the river, no matter the direction, and eventually you'll spill back out into Lake Lucid. Water skimmers dart across lily pads, fish swim in slow circles under the surface, wind whistles by and sends ripples through the reflection of the moon. Now look up. Up past the trees, up past the lurking mountains, up to the circle of bright whiteness hovering in the night sky. It isn't hard to imagine the moon as a wide, gleaming eye in the face of some massive being –

an eye staring down at the town, at the forest, at the Neverglades, and marveling at the strange wonders of this quiet little world.

*****

Last year, my good friend Mark Hannigan gave up his own life to save the lives of his friends, family, and neighbors – indeed, the entire world as he knew it. Mark was perhaps the bravest and humblest man I ever met. He knew every case could be his last, and yet he never wavered, pressing on with that selfless, headstrong attitude I eventually came to admire. Even in that last moment, as I watched him ascend into the rift, he didn't hesitate. He was a fighter to the very end.

It's been a year since he left us, and I confess, I wasn't handling the anniversary well. I kept wondering if Olivia had been right. If it would be better to bring Mark back: empty, blank, utterly hollowed out, but alive. I knew it would devastate his family. I knew it would open old wounds and set them bleeding afresh. But I was in pain. I was wounded too. And in my pain, I made a hasty decision. I opened the rift and began searching for my lost partner.

I'll spare you the details of the journey. "I am large, I contain multitudes," as one of your eminent poets once said; but even in my vastness, I couldn't find a trace of Mark in all that empty space. The explosion had vaporized his body. If there was anything left of him to find, it was atoms on the breeze, molecular specks too small to reassemble. My long search ended in vain, with me returning, head in hands, to the rift between our worlds.

That was where I found it. The parasitic being who calls itself the Ender, who feeds on humans beyond the veil, who snuffs out light and brings death in the world next door. And suddenly I was overwhelmed with a thought: that if the Ender had taken Mark in his death throes, a spark of my friend might still exist. Not his entire essence, no; I could never be so lucky. But a spark.

To make a long story short, I managed to extract what

remained of Mark from within the Ender (it's a stubborn beast, but at the end of the day, it knows who it obeys). It looked like a tiny sphere of pulsing light, dripping with black tendrils, and when I gripped it, I could hear his *voice*. I could see flashes of his memories, glistening and vibrant. And I knew – this little orb couldn't bring his body back to life. But it could keep my friend alive, in the way only the truest of words can.

I held that orb, and I recorded his story, word for word, exactly as his voice described to me. These are the stories I've shared with you. You never knew Mark Hannigan, but I hope that through his words, you understand what a remarkable man he was. He wouldn't have wanted me to call him a hero. Maybe he would have found the title "corny"; maybe it would have just embarrassed him. But you've read his tale now. You can decide for yourself.

There isn't much left of Mark. Taking him from the Ender was like unplugging a machine from a socket, and now he's running out of charge. The orb is smaller than it's ever been. Shreds of light tear from it every so often and disappear. I know that eventually even this much will be gone. From here on, he lives through these words, and through all of you reading here. Whatever you do – don't forget him. Don't let that spark go out.

I think he's earned that much.

- *The Inspector*

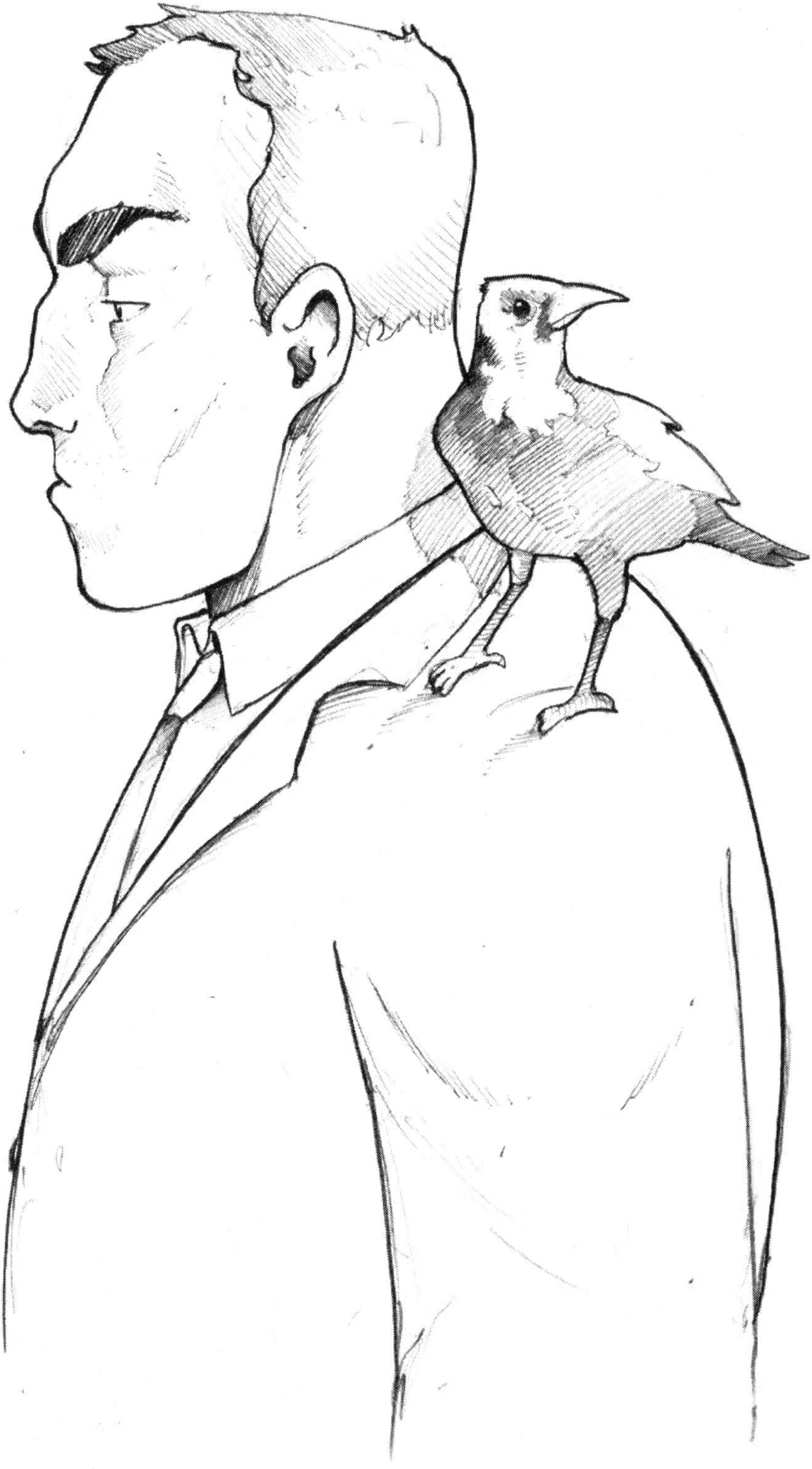

ACKNOWLEDGEMENTS

It takes a village to raise a child, as they say, and the world of the Neverglades would never have grown into what it is today without a whole community of readers, writers, listeners, and mentors. I owe an immense thanks to a number of people for helping this story come into being.

To Richard Ring and the staff of the Watkinson Library at Trinity College, for giving me the resources and financial support I needed to realize the early stages of this project. I set out to write a series of stories inspired by Sherlock Holmes and Edgar Allan Poe; what I found was a world entirely of my own. The Watkinson Fellowship provided me with the door I needed to get there.

To Sara Rivera and all the participants in her Science Fiction & Fantasy workshop at Grub Street. They saw the early stages of this collection and gave me tons of valuable feedback that shaped it into the book you're reading now. If you ever get the chance to take a class with this fantastic organization, please do so; I've never been surrounded by so many talented and genuinely helpful writers.

To the ever-supportive community of NoSleep, for providing a home for these stories. It still blows my mind that anyone can post their original horror fiction to a potential audience of over 13 million people. I was lucky that *The Neverglades* got the warm reception it did, and the reader response was truly humbling. I just wanted to share some stories with the world. You all convinced me that they were stories worth sharing.

To Lance Buckley, for creating such an eye-catching cover for this collection. Despite the old adage, we do judge a book by its cover, and this one oozes such an eerie, noir atmosphere that captures the Neverglades to a T. I couldn't have asked for a better first impression.

To Chris Bodily, for taking the characters in my brain

and bringing them to glorious life on the page. They look so much like I imagined that it's almost like you reached right in there and plucked them out, fully formed. No one else could have captured them quite the way you did, and I can't thank you enough for that.

To MrCreepyPasta, for giving these characters a voice, and for sharing the Neverglades with an audience I never could have dreamed of. At the time of me writing this, his narration of "Lost Time" has over *sixty-five thousand* views. We've come a long way since the Neverglades was a half-dreamed story I shared with only a few close friends.

And speaking of close friends: I would never have gotten to this point today without feedback and constant support of my writing group. Curtis Sarkin, Marla Krauss, Ben Pannell, Alla Hoffman, Alex Cottrill, Andy Cahill, Von Beckford, Shawnna Thomas – you guys are the best, and I'm grateful every day for having you in my life.

ABOUT THE AUTHOR

DAVID FARROW is the author of the Neverglades series and the Inspector Investigations on r/NoSleep, where he writes under the username -TheInspector-. When he isn't writing, you can find him infiltrating enemy headquarters or fighting off giant squids. He lives in Massachusetts.

Printed in Great Britain
by Amazon